D0821874

DREAMS OF THE N'DOROBO

DREAMS OF THE N'DOROBO

A Gape Turpin Adventure-Mystery

GARY GABELHOUSE

THE LYONS PRESS
Guilford, Connecticut
An imprint of The Globe Pequot Press

The Lyons Press is an imprint of The Globe Pequot Press.

10 9 8 7 6 5 4 3 2 1

Printed in the United States of America.

Text designed by Kirsten Livingston

ISBN 1-59228-066-8

Library of Congress Cataloging-in-Publication Data is available on file.

This work is dedicated to Cindy and Malindi, who
shared me with the wild places of this earth.

ACKNOWLEDGMENTS

A special thanks is given to the real UDT frogman, named within this work as Jimmy McCann, who, regrettably, must remain nameless. His technical assistance was important, and his service to our country over the decades has earned my deep respect.

Also, thanks goes to my friend and *first-pass* editor, Tom Frye. Without Tom's help early on, the finished work would be a dull shadow of its current form. Thanks also goes to my editor, George Donahue, who appreciated the character of my writing and allowed the *rough pearl* to be just that.

Finally, thanks go to Bill Erickson, who hauled my sorry butt down that hill and who has supported the writing of this novel and all of my efforts, literary and otherwise, ever since.

Gary Gabelhouse—2003

DREAMS OF THE N'DOROBO

PROLOGUE

NORTH LIKI RIVER, MT. KENYA, 1953

JIMMY WATCHED THROUGH A LATTICE OF BAMBOO AND NETTLES as the Mau Mau Oath Giver broke the bones of the tethered goat. The goat dumbly bleated at the snapping of each foreleg, and the Oath Giver, dressed in the green hides of colobus monkeys, mumbled the Kikuyu oath. The initiates sat wide-eyed, apparently stricken as the ceremony unfolded around the weak fire and the arbor of ki apple thorns.

Jimmy knew no Kikuyu and only *kidogo* (a little) Swahili. Regardless of not understanding the mumbo-jumbo of the Kyuke, it was obvious to him that this was, indeed, some very bad juju. The Oath Giver, using a small, sharp knife, cut the eyes out of the dying goat's skull and skewered them on the ki apple thorns of the arbor. The mumbling continued as the Oath Giver disemboweled the goat and placed the stomach matter into the fold of a wide, waxy-green leaf. Cutting the goat's throat, he drained some of the blood into the leaf. His words elicited a moan from the initiates. One of the dark acolytes uttered a keening wail as his eyes rolled back in his head. The Oath Giver directed the group to pass under the eyeball-adorned arbor and then passed the bowl-like leaf and its hellish sacrament to each initiate, who, in turn, shared in the communion.

Jimmy had remained perfectly still for over two hours and was more disturbed by what he saw than he was by the rash of insect bites and nettle welts he wore as a testament to his long crawl and silent vigil. *This wog needs killed in a hard way,* thought Jimmy.

Soft dripping sounds were the only evidence of the night's rain, which had turned into a cold mist. An occasional rivulet would careen down Jimmy's forehead, into his eyes. He absent-mindedly watched the oathing ceremony. He laid his chin on his forearm and quietly inhaled the smell of the forest floor. It reminded him of his mother's herb garden back in Ottumwa, Iowa: pungent, earthy, and green. Far off, he heard the bark of a zebra and wondered what beasties were prowling nearby, including him in the forest's food chain. Jimmy felt a long way from Iowa—there was a big difference between hunting quail in the plum thickets of his home state and hunting men in the cold, thin air of Kenya's White Highlands. He was sure the rest of the team was in position. He figured it to be about midnight, and time to break up this ghouls' tea party.

Jimmy brought his Winchester Model 12 up to sight on the Oath Giver's crotch. *This will be a eunuch experience for this wog fucker,* thought Jimmy, silently chuckling. The hollow thunk of the Model 12 was drowned out as the deep-throated rattle of the Thompson 45s and the explosion of Tree's Browning automatic rifle kicked in.

The oathing initiates were rendered into screaming, bleeding stick figures against the low light of the fire. The eye-adorned arbor was blown apart and its structure scattered, like an offering, over the carcass of the goat. Miraculously, the Oath Giver had eluded Jimmy's shotgun blast and was running down a game trail with amazing agility for a man as old as he seemed.

Springing up like a cat, Jimmy ran after the Oath Giver, his legs tingling and weak from his long forest vigil. The Oath Giver, likely a Mau Mau lieutenant, was as a shadow among shadows as he plunged deeper into the bamboo. The game trail entered a meadow-like island in the forest, and Jimmy saw the Mau Mau skitter into the huge moss-covered cavity of a camphor tree. Jimmy instantly stopped his pursuit and dropped on his belly, carefully listening and watching. For certain, the Oath Giver was hiding in the cave of the tree. Jimmy crawled slowly to the base of the camphor tree. Holding his breath to listen, all he could hear was the dripping forest and the coursing of blood in his ears. Nothing else. He crabbed forward into the bole of the tree. Surprisingly, the ground inside felt like packed dirt and was totally dry. Jimmy's skin prickled—he must be within a few feet of the Mau Mau. Unsure who was predator and who was prey in this deadly game of silence, Jimmy again held his breath and listened. Again there was nothing, just a roar of silence. Jimmy opened his mouth and flared his nostrils; tasting the air like a wine taster, swirling the air over his palate, he detected the smell of kerex stove fuel, as well as the musty, stale scent of old human sweat. His hand touched a smooth wooden object on the dirt floor of this arboreal cave. It was an old wooden spoon, probably used for making *ndizi* and *ugale*.

The sound started as a purr and slowly evolved into a throaty, gurgling growl. Then more silence before Jimmy heard, just a few feet away, a deep *umph-umph* grunting sound. Pointing his shotgun in the direction of the noise, Jimmy slowly fished for and found his Zippo lighter. Slowly, he moved the lighter under his belly to muffle the click of its opening. Now, with the lighter open and held ready in his left hand, he placed the barrel of the shotgun on his left forearm, and his finger found the trigger.

Focusing totally into the darkness of the bower on the source of the noise, Jimmy flicked the lighter. At first it looked like a man dressed in a leopard skin, but the face was all wrong:

angular shadows played across bared white teeth and yellow eyes not really human, changing in a kaleidoscope of shadows. As Jimmy's finger tightened on the trigger, the leopard curled its lips and let loose a low growl, its devil eyes burning with an almost human hatred.

Instinctively, Jimmy pulled the trigger, then quickly pumped another shell into the chamber and fired again as he rolled onto his belly. It was dark again in the tree cave and deathly still. Searching along the line of his roll, Jimmy found his lighter and quickly flicked the flint. The shadows of the tree cave were empty. Spying an old used candle sitting atop a Blue Boy butter can a few feet away, he lit it, and the room in the tree trunk was cleansed of its darkness.

Jimmy found his flashlight and thrust its beam into all the recesses of the tree cave, ready to shoot from the hip, his finger playing light on the shotgun's trigger. The tree was clearly a hideout where a handful of Mau Mau could sleep warm, curled together on the packed, dry floor. There was no sign of man or leopard. Jimmy heard the bushbuck call of the tracker. All was secure.

Jimmy stood in the dripping bower of the camphor tree, with its moss-covered trunk like the beard of a wise old man. He mused on how the old Mau Mau could have escaped him and what he had really shot at in the tree cave. He had heard of the nearly impossible feats ascribed to leopards, but couldn't believe one could survive a point-blank blast of a shotgun. The forest seemed to be holding its breath as Jimmy turned back toward the ambush site. He was startled when he heard a tree hyrax scream in the indigo of the forest night. Jimmy slowly and very carefully walked back to the campsite-turned-abattoir. Despite the wall of vegetation between him and the killing field, Jimmy could smell the rancid mix of fire, smoke, feces, and blood, which of late was the unique smell of the White Highlands.

1

NAIROBI, KENYA, 2005

THE 747 HOVERED OVER THE MIST LIKE A LANNER IN SEARCH of prey. The red African sun was mottled by spirals of mist as the Dutch KLM flight touched down at Jomo Kenyatta International Airport outside Nairobi. Gabe Turpin peered out the window, seeing the lorries, like giant beetles, trundle along A-116. He smiled to himself as he looked at nothing in particular. He was back. He had worn his mountaineering boots and his parka on the plane to avoid the excess-weight fee so rigorously adhered to unless you flew first class. Gabe's six-foot-four-inch frame was nearly spring-loaded into his seat like a jack-in-the-box. There had been barely enough room for his feet under the seat in front of him. His left foot had fallen asleep somewhere over Cairo. He had that hollow feeling behind his eyes and a bad case of cotton mouth, even though he had brushed his teeth in the smelly closet that was the plane's bathroom no more than an hour before. Not wanting to spend any more time in that cramped closet than necessary, he only briefly assessed himself in the mirror. The light coating of grease made his thinning hair look even sparser. Gabe's coat was always shiny after hanging in the air for a day. He sighed, remembering the days of tight dark curls in the absence of character.

The plane shuddered as it touched down. The taxi to the terminal was quiet yet heavy with the expectations of three hundred passengers. Walking on stiff, wobbly legs, Gabe took his place in the customs line. It always seemed to Gabe as though the customs agents imagined, for their own entertainment, an improbable story line about why Gabe was really in Kenya. When they were unable to shake him up and make him confess his guilt, they stamped his passport with decorum and a knowing smile on their faces.

"What is the nature of your visit?" said a tall, good-looking agent. He wasn't a Kikuyu, most probably a Luo. There it was—that smile. Gabe decided this guy's name was Smilin' Jack.

Gabe answered, "I'm here on an anthropological expedition to Mt. Kenya. The research is sponsored by The Explorers Club and the Babson Foundation for Ethological Studies."

Dropping *The Explorers Club* name was important because Richard Leakey, who had been in charge of the Kenyan government's administrative branch and the son of the famous Louis Leakey of Olduvai Gorge fame, was a fellow of The Explorers Club. The Explorers Club, with its Upper East Side Manhattan five-story brownstone building a half block off Park Avenue, was one of Gabe Turpin's favorite haunts in the great city of New York.

Here was a last vestige of the old Elizabethan men's clubs, although women, such as Sally Ride, were members now. Gabe was convinced The Explorers Club was nothing more nor less than a sophisticated forum to perpetuate the manly tradition of getting dirty, sleeping on the ground in strange climes and places, and pursuing adventures that were the stuff of dreams for adolescent boys and tomboys alike. Explaining more of the great mystery through scientific method, and having a hell of a good time doing it, especially under adverse conditions, was what The Explorers Club was all about. It was also a refuge from New York City's manic pace. There, one could sit quietly in a leather wingback chair, between a narwhal horn and a mounted Cape buffalo head, reading a book or scientific journal or perusing ancient maps while sipping a drink. The Explorers Club was also a refuge from the oppressive heat and cold of Manhattan's concrete canyons, with their ever-present smell of garbage and human urine. The Club was not so much a financial sponsor of Gabe's expedition as it was ceremoniously supportive. Gabe carried The Explorers Club flag in his rucksack for that photo op that would invariably result in a display in the Club's lobby and, perhaps, in its Rolex-sponsored magazine.

The Paul and Edith Babson Foundation for Ethological Studies was one of Gabe's regular funding sources. In the earlier years of his field studies, Paul and Edith Babson were wonderful philanthropists whom Gabe actually enjoyed being with. He quickly learned that both Paul and Edith were living out their unfulfilled dreams vicariously through the exploits and adventures of those like Gabe, who didn't have the common sense to know they'd grown up to be adults. Gabe began to regularly write and talk with the Babsons, even when he didn't need their money. Edith was the best audience. She would hang on every word, eyes wide as she seemed to actually see the Cape buffalo charging down the narrow bamboo game trail.

Gabe kept in close touch with the Babsons and was truly saddened at the news of Paul's death some three years before. Edith, old and wonderfully wrinkled, maintained her joy in philanthropy and anthropological field studies. When Edith received Gabe's proposal to study the elusive N'dorobo tribe of Kenya and to demystify some of the dark legends of magic and witchcraft about this lost tribe, she sent a bank draft for fifty thousand dollars the same day. Gabe would get Edith some unique native artifact, or "banger," as he called them. It would mean a lot to her. She never considered such things to be trifles or hollow gestures.

⬥⬥⬥⬥

Smilin' Jack's eyes followed Gabe's every move, yet he maintained that knowing smile as Gabe gathered up his rucksack and walked onto the escalators down into the concrete pit that was the airport's baggage claim area. The sting and hurt of—again—leaving his wife, Cindy, and his daughter, Malindi, had subsided to a dull ache. His long relationship with Cindy was framed by separation anxiety. For a month before an expedition, his dread would grow. He knew so well that long walk to the plane and the hole it made in his heart every time. One expedition was so long it nearly killed his spirit. On this trip, he found the only way he could deal with such a prolonged absence was to set a specific date when he could first think about even *thinking* about being back home. There were four very abstract and desperate stages to this process: 1) not even thinking about Cindy and home; 2) first thinking about *thinking* about Cindy and going home; 3) thinking about Cindy and going home; 4) going home to Cindy.

Malindi was named after a town north of Mombassa on the coast of Kenya. During one of his first field expeditions, Gabe took R and R in Malindi. The town was magic—a Hemingway Africa, with calls to worship floating in the hot air, which shimmered and distorted the Arab dhows bobbing about their business offshore. Drinking tea poured from an ancient brass urn by a Sikh and sitting among squalling children and goats, Gabe vowed that if he were to ever marry and have a daughter, he would name her Malindi. Years later, he did, and he did.

As thirsty as he was, Gabe avoided the drinking fountain. A few years before, he had drunk deeply from this particular fountain and had shit his pants in the taxi no more than twenty minutes later. That first night in bed, thinking he had to break wind, Gabe realized too late that it was not a fart, but fecal material honking right-of-way. The sheets had cost him two dollars. The maid asked if Gabe wanted to keep the soiled sheets, since he had paid for them. For three days he had had the mamba trots. He would wait to buy something to drink at the hotel.

Gabe gathered his luggage—a rucksack, a huge Lowe Alpine Expedition pack, and a large canvas duffel. With wooden legs and a head full of cotton, he walked out of the airline terminal . . . into Africa.

Diesel was the smell of Africa—diesel exhaust mixed with the smoke of wood fires and the country smell of hay to make a perfume that was Kenya. In the city center it was different, with the country hay replaced by the smell of rotting fruit and human urine. These smells of Africa were like old friends. Gabe breathed in deeply, smiling to himself. He was back in the cradle of mankind. He was back in the belly of the beast that was Africa. He was back where the beast was alive and well.

The taxi drivers circled like reef sharks waiting to find their next dinner.

"Begoni shillingi Hotel Tropic?" Gabe asked the nearest driver the fare to the hotel.

He had to carefully filter the driver's Swahili, and wished he had asked in English, for the driver was babbling on as though Gabe actually understood him.

"Kidogo Swahili" (a little Swahili), said Gabe.

"Five dollars," replied the driver in broken English.

"How many shillings?" continued Gabe, knowing the man could double his money by changing the American greenbacks on the black market.

"Two hundred shillings."

"Sow-sow. M'zuri," Gabe said in agreement with the fare.

Gabe normally stayed at the Fairview Hotel, which was adjacent to Uhuru Park and kind of out of the city center. He had tried a number of hotels during his stays in Kenya. The New Stanley, wherein mingled a few road-weary expats who could afford the menu, had a highly mediocre cuisine and gave off an air of desperate commerce. The stories of trust babies set loose in this belly of the beast were written in the stress lines on their faces, framed by unclean, dusty hair. They projected the kind of spiritual fatigue that comes from too much reality.

The legendary Norfolk, where adventurers used to shoot lions from the front porch and down their gin and pinks at ten in the morning, was good only for dining and drinking. The small, expensive rooms were beyond Gabe's grant budgets. However, one could wile away the hours sitting on the porch nursing a White Cap beer and watching the pretty Kikuyu college girls, and later dine on a steak sandwich and fries for a reasonable sum.

One time, as a misplaced favor for his friend Ted, Gabe procured the twenty-four-hour services of two Kikuyu maidens for twenty dollars and a box of scented soap. Ted, who had gained a steady girlfriend stateside just prior to their expedition, disappeared when Gabe closed the deal. Gabe found his friend hiding in the bushes beside the birdcage in the open-air plaza area of the hotel, long after the Kikuyu maidens had lost interest in their john and left for some dive on River Road.

The Fairview supposedly was full this evening, but would have a nice room for him the next day. He would schlep his gear to the Fairview the next day to settle in properly. He told the driver to go to the Jeevanjee Gardens in the city center. Next to this park was the Hotel Tropic, the cheap hotel where he'd spend the night. He could reorganize his gear in the park without much interference from the roving bands of money changers and scam artists.

A small radio taped to the taxi dash was playing Mama M'Binga's latest hit. The song had that tinny, repetitive rhythm that sometimes overpowered Mama M'Binga's singing—rendering it something not quite recognizable as music. The music from the radio was accompanied by the squeaking of the taxi, as they went down the road on shocks that had lost all absorbing qualities. The taxi entered the roundabouts with determination to not give way—even to the large lorries that threatened to crush it. Sitting in the threadbare Peugeot, bouncing up and down, teeth rattling, diesel fumes coating his body, accompanied by the wails of Mama M'Binga, Gabe had come back to his spiritual home.

Let off at the Jeevanjee Gardens, Gabe methodically set his gear down on the ground, which was a rusty red color and littered with jacaranda leaves. His first foray onto Mt. Kenya would require three weeks' food and one change of clothing on his back, supplemented by parkas and cold-weather gear. Much of the clothing and supplies lying on the ground would not be needed until his second trip in. This gear he stashed in his giant duffel. The gear for the upcoming trek in was organized and distributed throughout the Lowe Expedition pack.

"Are you American?" asked a soft voice behind Gabe.

"Yes, I'm American," replied Gabe.

"Good. You can possibly help us?" said a young, light-skinned man, most likely an Ethiopian, definitely not a Kikuyu or even a Kenyan. He was flanked by two other, smiling youths—all with stained and rumpled clothing they had most likely lived in for some weeks or months. Some of their shoes had laces. Their eyes were filmed with red, and their teeth were snaggled and rotten.

These youth were the hyenas of the city center. Gabe knew these roving bands of scam artists tended not to be violent, but still did not trust them. He thought they had the potential to blow and commit acts of hideous violence beyond the belief of most humans. Gabe had spent much time with Ricki, a young Kikuyu who was as affable and pleasant as one would want. However, Gabe realized, after sharing a tent with him for a month on a field expedition, that Ricki's brain was a writhing mass of snakes. The highly suppressive Kikuyu culture bottled up the sexual tensions of the tribe's young men. Ricki was a time bomb of repressed sexual violence and depravity. Through this experience, Gabe understood the terror of being a colonial during the Mau Mau revolt, hearing the sweet, soft voice of a trusted employee tell you how your penis would be cut off and placed in your dead wife's vagina, tamped in with a broom handle.

"How could I help you?" asked Gabe with a neutral stare at the Ethiopian.

"Our parents were imprisoned and killed during the Mau Mau, and I have been trying to support my brothers since then. I have a chance of a job loading food goods, but must place a deposit on the hand truck. Might you loan us twenty dollars for our deposit? I will be able to pay you back twenty-five dollars from my first day's pay."

Gabe knew this was bullshit. For one thing, if their parents had been killed in the Mau Mau, which was in the early fifties, their kids—these scam artists in front of him now—would be at least fifty-five years old. The oldest one was maybe twenty-two. The other thing, there was no hand truck job in Kenya that paid more than a couple of dollars a day. Gabe had found such work in Mombassa years before, when he'd had less than two dollars in his pocket and a plane ticket not good for another month. This was, indeed, bullshit.

"If you don't take off right now, I'm going to scream 'thief' at the top of my lungs. You have until the count of three."

Gabe began to count, and got to "two" as the trio of slicksters disappeared like smoke dissipating into the jacarandas of the park.

Gabe continued his gear sorting, and, satisfied with his job, lugged the pack and duffel to the Hotel Tropic across the street.

The Hotel Tropic was a dive. Gabe threaded through the street vendors selling corn grilled on small charcoal stoves. The front desk of the hotel was just that—an old wooden desk, upon which was kept a huge ledger. The old Kikuyu methodically wrote Gabe's name and passport number in the ledger, never bothering to look at Gabe directly. The makeshift lobby smelled of foods fried in lard or some other animal fat. Navigating the narrow stairs was difficult with his packs and duffel. The room, on the second floor and offering a view of the scenic City Park, had one small metal-frame bed and a single lightbulb that hung from the center of the ceiling. The toilet had no water in the bowl or reservoir, and the faucet had too much water and dripped incessantly, leaving a nasty-looking stain in the sink.

Gabe opened the torn drapes and looked out onto the park. He could feel the heartbeat of the city. Horns were wailing, and *matatu* touts drummed up passengers for the out-country taxis—usually a Suzuki pickup with a box into which were crammed twenty or more travelers. The country buses would loom some time after one heard their approach and would disappear in clouds of diesel smoke, some passengers precariously hanging on to the door frame. Sunbirds, with their iridescent green heads, flitted through the trees of the park, apparently moving in time to the tinny third-world music that played from every street corner.

Gabe was beginning to slow down. He was dog-tired and needed to eat something, regardless of the quiet nausea that always claimed him after twenty-four hours of hanging in the air. He threw his gear on the bed, checked the wallet that his daughter called a purse, slung it over his head, and tucked it safely down the front of his shirt. Years before, while in Otavalo,

Ecuador, trying to relate the celestial angles of Incan architecture with those of the Great Pyramids, Gabe had his wallet stolen by Colombian bandits. His purse was the answer to such problems.

He pulled off his Lowe Alpspitz mountaineering boots—he referred to them as his iron maidens—and slipped into his Nike Lava Domes. Generally, if Gabe was going to a market he would clip a pair of old running shoes to the outside of his rucksack adjusted at a casual angle that would generate the most attention. Sometimes, Gabe would bring a half dozen pairs to be used as trade goods. Invariably, the eyes of every huckster in the market would shift to those shoes. After much protest, he would trade his shoes for bangers and souvenirs. He would then walk away with his handicraft and clip another pair on his pack and continue his trading mission.

Gabe wasn't interested in trading or shopping for bangers now. He needed to find some *chakula m'zuri* (good food) and cut through his thirst with a White Cap, *baridi sana*—very cold. He clomped down the stairs, past the old Kikuyu who appeared to be sleeping in his chair, and headed for the verandah of the Norfolk Hotel and an early dinner.

2

NAIROBI, KENYA, 2005

As he walked down Kimathi Street toward the police station and the university, he saw the beggar wrapped like a dervish in soiled, greasy clothes, sitting beside the bowl, no energy for any movement or activity. Gabe remembered how he and his daughter, then eight years old, had seen a leper outside the city market. The leper was wrapped in loose, dark, gauzy shrouds, with most of its face ravaged away by the bacillus. Malindi had chosen to identify the beggar as a woman, although there was no way to really tell.

"Will she get better, Daddy?"

"No," Gabe replied. "She'll never get better."

Malindi had seemed to accept that without much emotion. This type of experience, Gabe knew, forged a moral person from a child much more efficiently than an upscale Montessori school.

The sun was low in the west by five thirty. Here on the equator you always had a balance of twelve hours day and twelve hours night, no matter what the time of year. Some unnamable bird made pleasant sounds as Gabe made his way toward the Norfolk. Finding many of the tables empty, he took a prime place closest to the railing of the verandah. Almost immediately, the well-appointed server was asking him for his drink order.

"White Cap. *Baridi sana,*" said Gabe.

Gabe had grown to appreciate Kenya's cheaper beer—White Cap—the Hamm's beer of Kenya. Tusker Premium was the *pombe* of choice among the jet-set crowd who spent their time and a bloody fortune at Keekorok Lodge in the Mara, floating in hot-air balloons and lounging around the pool like hippos at M'Zima Springs. Gabe preferred a White Cap, and sitting on the fender of his Suzuki just out from Fig Tree Camp.

Gabe nursed his White Cap and mused at how it had come to this—how he was here, chasing ghosts and legends on Mt. Kenya and not being a real person with a real job. He supposed it was his father who started it. His parents married early in life, quashing a life of adventure as a merchant marine for his father. For as long as Gabe could remember, his mother referred to his father as a "Roamin' Russian." Gabe's father loved to travel, but finances strictly limited travel to the family cabin in Minnesota or camping near home.

His dad had always said, "Invest in experiences. They can never take 'em away from you."

Gabe's mother always helped her sons pursue wholesome hobbies and spurred Gabe's inherent love of rock and fossil collecting, buying him every *Zim's Golden* book on the subject. Gabe's Grandma Mitzner gave him his first books about Africa. Gabe would pore over those texts for hours in the bitter-cold afternoons of Nebraska's winters.

Mrs. Weir, a teacher in the gifted students program at Gabe's elementary school, helped things along. Knowing of Gabe's fossil, rock, and artifact hunting expeditions on the huge piles of sand and gravel behind his grandpa's house on Y Street, she encouraged him to read *Archaeology* and *History in the Dead Sea Scrolls.* Gabe lived the adventures of Heinrich Schliemann, helping the author find the lost city of Troy. He wrapped himself in the wonder of expeditions to the tombs of King Tut and hung on every word and detail—with a special interest in the curse of King Tut.

Then his brother had brought home H. Rider Haggard's *King Solomon's Mines*. That tore it. The images in the book were so vivid that Gabe would often dream he was both Quartermain and Sir Henry, he liked and identified with both characters so much. The terrible witch-doctoress, Gagool, filled Gabe with a frightening fascination, kind of like the terrifying thrill he got as he broke into the haunted house on Sheldon Street and went into the room where the Widow Martin had chopped up her grandkids with a garden hoe.

He shared with his friend Chester Harris his fantasy of exploring tombs and cutting through jungles to find adventure and danger in far-off places. He wasn't sure, but it seemed as though there would still be some lost tribes or civilizations that needed finding when Gabe got old enough to sniff them out. He was impatient to have at it, but was stuck in the reality glue of being a ten-year-old.

Gabe's brother, during one of their rock and fossil hunting trips to the gravel pile, did find a flint arrowhead. Gabe found a fossil shark's tooth that same day. If they had been adults they would have been drunk for a week. Gabe remembered that when things were bad he needed only to think about the great treasures they had found that day and he would recover from his malaise. That had been a banner expedition—to the exotic deserts of sand and gravel at Ready Mix Concrete, behind Grandpa's house.

The *combi* buses, full of rich people dressed like Jungle Jim, began to arrive and drop off their safari clients to soak in the luxury of the Norfolk. These were the nouveaux riches. The old money chartered a plane from Keekorok or Amboseli to Nairobi, forgoing the washboard roads out of Narok and the terror of passing lorries on the road up the escarpment of the Great Rift Valley.

Gabe ordered another White Cap with his steak sandwich and Kenyan chips—french fries cooked in lard with sweet, runny ketchup. He watched as Kenyan college students bustled about, walking in the dusk or leaning on the handles of gigantic old bikes, quietly talking with each other.

Gabe's beer and sandwich arrived about the same time the open-air bar began to come alive with music and laughter that spoke of great release. The air at the bar had a mixture of the two most dangerous chemicals in the world—alcohol and testosterone. Gabe coated his chips with the runny, sweet ketchup, sure that all the grease would someday clog his arteries tighter than a duck's ass.

Gabe thought about the expedition as he stared into the night, full of flying bugs and the omnipresent smell of diesel. It was on his second climb of Mt. Kenya, back in the seventies, that he first encountered the reputed magic, or juju, of the N'dorobo.

He had caught a taxi to Wilson Airport, where the Mountain Club of Kenya met every month. Waiting in the warm afternoon sun for the club members to show up, Gabe watched a stream of white families, escaping Uganda's latest upheaval, arriving in Kenya in private planes. Families who had forgone their very life in Uganda walked on wooden legs with empty eyes to prearranged benefactors—a network of desperation. The faces of fathers holding the hands of young daughters were grimly set. The contacts and benefactors had, to the individual, that look of distrust in their own providence—for it could happen here next month. After all, this was Africa.

Shaking himself from his doldrums, Gabe spotted Vince, an American expat with whom he'd spent much time on Kenya's mountains and in the bush.

"Pombe, m'zuri sana—baridi sana sahib?" Vince offered Gabe a good, cold beer with a colonial greeting.

Behind Vince was an odd assortment of Kenyan citizenry that shared one passion—climbing Mt. Kenya. Dougal was a particularly wiry, hard-core climber who felt at home as much on the steep rock at Hell's Gate as he did doing a severe alpine ascent of the Northey Glacier, carting a forty-pound pack up the vertical ice. Gabe, Vince, and he had entered into a discussion of Gabe's upcoming climb on Mt. Kenya.

"What route are you going to use going in? Sirimon River?" asked Dougal.

"No, I thought the Chogoria route. I haven't taken the time to go in from that way before and I hear it's pretty wild," said Gabe.

The Chogoria Track was on the less known north side of the mountain and supposedly had fallen into disrepair—all but disappearing in places. It wound its way through the bamboo of the lower slopes and up into the forests of camphor, hyacinth, and Saint-John's-wort, depositing the climber onto the moor at about eleven thousand feet.

"Better watch out for the mist people," said Dougal. "That's where that lost tribe of N'dorobo are said to offer sacrifices to old N'gai, the god of Mt. Kenya, who lives up on top. Better make sure they don't include your tender parts in their sacrifice."

"I haven't heard of any lost N'dorobo on the mountain," said Gabe.

With a wink to Vince, he added, "But I'm sure that story plays well with your prettier clients and keeps you warm in your bag, mate."

"No, I'm not bullshittin' ya. You should take care on the Chogoria. Last year, I found two Brits, who were Lake District supermen, walking around dazed and all fucked up. They kept bawling and babbling about how this crazy wog fucker dressed up in monkey skins just appeared from out of a camphor tree and strangled both of their porters. Then he cut off their dicks and scooped out their eyes with a spoon. It seemed he just ignored the Brits. Drained the porters' blood—bled 'em like you would a goddamned gazelle. Kept chanting and mixing blood and hair with leaves he'd take from his pouch. I would guess the Brits passed out when they saw the crazy fucker drink the mixture, muttering and chanting. They said they didn't pass out, but did claim the wog just disappeared."

"You mean got up and ran away?" asked Vince.

"No. He just disappeared. Sitting on his haunches one second, gone the next."

"That's absolute bullshit, Dougal," said Gabe. "That didn't happen. I've known those Lake District wonders to be heavy into the shit. After they get bored with their pints, they drop a tab or two and it's Katie-bar-the-door. That wasn't mumbo-jumbo juju on the Chogoria, that was a bad acid trip."

"Think what you will, mate. But do take care," said Dougal. "Those blokes saw more than tracers and psychedelics. They saw some bad shit. Maybe it wasn't what they said, but it was something pretty fuckin' weird. Take care, Gabe. Get to the moor quick and fuck the acclimatization in the forest."

Afterward, Gabe had difficulty finding transport from Nanyuki on the north side and had chosen to go in from the south side, past McKinder's Camp, up beside Oblong Tarn and Two Tarn Lake, and to the north side of the mountain, forgoing the Chogoria Track. His trek in had been uneventful and absent of crazed N'dorobo shamans.

The verandah of the Norfolk was becoming more active, as was the nearby open-air bar. Gabe paid his chit and walked out into the air, which was full of the smell of wood and charcoal fires, as thick as the smell of roasting chestnuts on the streets of New York around Christmastime. In the hotel, he walked along, exhausted, and heard what sounded like doves cooing in the park. He walked past the old Kikuyu at the front desk and nodded. The old man just stared at Gabe, protected by that veil that lowers over an African, sealing him off from the world. Gabe walked up the stairs and flopped down on the bed. The springs creaked at every shift of his body as he sought a comfortable position. The bar at the foot of the bed hit Gabe about mid-shin. Gabe assumed a modified fetal position and found a restless sleep.

He watched the banana knife pointed at his eyes circle and circle. His focus was only on the knife. Ralph Chang Bazaan didn't exist at this point. Only the knife. The sounds within the semicircle of the Bazaans and the Vampires, all shouting for their champions and taunting their enemy, was heard as if passing through thick cotton. With sweat in his eyes, the acid taste of fear in his throat, and without looking down, Gabe Turpin took off one of his boots and stuck his hand in it. The moment of commitment was about to come. Both Bazaan and Gabe knew it.

Gabe Turpin was the Vampires' designated fighter. Because he was younger than some of the Vampires, he was not the gang's leader. He just fought their battles and therefore enjoyed an unusual freedom from much of the gang's protocol and pecking order. Bazaan, on the other hand, was both the leader of his gang of ethnic mongrels and their fighter. The gangs of the neighborhood, with unusual wisdom, had organized the fighting system, since too much criminal talent was wasted in an all-out gang fight.

Tradition was that a circle of gang members surrounded the two fighters. It was sacrosanct that there be no interference from the fight fans, even if one's fighter was rendered unconscious. The fight continued uninterrupted until the winning fighter was done, regardless of the condition of his opponent. For this reason, Gabe didn't want to get knocked out or pass out. He had seen Bazaan fight before. He remembered how Bazaan placed the leg of one unconscious fighter's knee up on the railroad tracks and stomped down on it. Methodically, Bazaan then placed each limb on the tracks with the joint up and broke knees and elbows with his stomps. No, Gabe didn't plan on going down.

Now Gabe was concerned that Bazaan had produced the knife, a mild breach of etiquette. Most fighters prided themselves on their pure fighting talent and endurance and rarely, if ever, used an extension or augmentation of fists or feet. But Bazaan could pull a knife if he wanted—there were no rules binding him. Rules were for the spectators, not for the fighters.

Gabe aimed his punch at the knife. It worked to a degree, as Bazaan's knife hand deflected off the boot before Gabe's other hand could come into play. The knife sliced along and up Gabe's left arm, cutting shirt and skin. Gabe only noticed the sharp, not altogether painful sting as his right hand grabbed the meaty part of Bazaan's knife hand. He threw the boot off his left hand and grabbed Bazaan's knife hand with it, putting his thumbs in position on the back of Bazaan's knife hand. He pushed Bazaan's hand, bringing it up and pivoting, and continued pushing Bazaan's hand and arm down to the ground. He drove the left side of Bazaan's face into the concrete, using his arm as a lever. The knife clattered free.

Gabe had purchased Bruce Tegner's Complete Book of Self-Defense *at Gold's department store a month or two before. He practiced this arcane art in the garage, on Davey Lucas, so his parents wouldn't see what was going on. Davey didn't much like the practice sessions, but complied all the same. Davey was always a bubble off and not too smart. He seemed to have gotten dumber after he sneaked up behind Gabe during an intergang squabble and hit him in the back of his head with a croquet mallet. Gabe, on the verge of being knocked out, grabbed a two-by-four off the garage floor and returned the favor. Davey's parents didn't take him to the doctor, perhaps explaining his advancing stupidity.*

Gabe kicked Bazaan in the face three times, and then went to work stomping on his floating-rib area. Bazaan didn't scream or cry out, but instead let out little huffing noises as the kicks landed. Gabe couldn't tell if Bazaan was really out because the blood on his face masked any facial vital signs. Gabe kicked Bazaan in the throat for good measure and heard the deep swallowing sound that always resulted from this technique.

Gabe went down, slamming his left knee into Bazaan's ribs, grabbed a bunch of the thick, coarse Chinese-Mexican hair, and pulled Bazaan's head back. He seemed to be out. Gabe got up, looked at Bazaan's toadies, and methodically spread their leader's legs. He took about two steps back and launched himself forward, viciously stomping down on Bazaan's crotch. Bazaan twitched only slightly, but all the spectators grunted to themselves. Gabe assessed the cut on his arm with casual concern and realized it would not require stitches.

He looked toward his fans and said, "That karate shit really works. Let's go get a 3-V Cola."

Gabe jerked nearly awake in the darkness of his hotel room. Rolling his head side to side on the sweat-soaked pillow, he moaned as the roaches skittled back and forth across the walls. Some with wings glided and landed atop Gabe's pack and duffel. During this most lonely hour of the night, the room was full of old horrors and heavy air.

The Vampires ambled down Holdrege Street on their way to Lincoln's Grocery. They assessed the street and alleys for any signs of an ambush. They were dangerously close to Sheridan territory. The Sheridans were Native Americans who seemed to be still mad about Wounded Knee and they executed their own versions of Little Big Horn, dominating the area north of Holdrege. Lincoln's Grocery Store was a converted house that sold a little bit of everything, but most important, it had 3-V Cola, the only sixteen-ounce bottle of pop available. Lincoln's was owned by an odd couple. Mrs. Lincoln still wore World War II nylons, with the dark seam down the back, inside sensible shoes. Her white hair was always in a bun. She helped her husband, who was hideously scarred. It had taken

Gabe years before he could even look at Mr. Lincoln. Everyone said somebody threw acid on his face when he was a kid. The result of this never-talked-about tragedy was a face that was a puddle of waxy flesh.

The Vampires took their 3-Vs out on the porch, into the heat of the afternoon. They did not smell the poverty, as did those who lived in the southern part of town. "Poor" has a distinctive smell of not enough baths, fried food, and sour milk. The smell hangs in the air like gauze sheets. The Vampires had been a part of that smell their entire lives and had no way to contrast it against anything else, so to them the smell did not exist. Gabe licked his thumb and rubbed the dried blood off the cut on his left arm. It didn't really hurt much. He'd had much worse.

"Let's go over to my house and mess around," said Chester Harris, a wavy-haired kid whose parents were Bible thumpers and would have just shit if they knew what things their only son was up to. They were poor as church mice and just as trapped. Mrs. Harris always wore the same dress. She had that look of quiet desperation shared by most of the women of the neighborhood. She knew she should have more in her life, but was clueless as to how it had come to this. Her Bible and her prayers buoyed her above an otherwise empty life.

Gabe and Chester walked in through the broken screen door. Chester quietly talked with his mom. Then he was beaming.

"We're gonna have round steak tonight," said Chester, projecting a prideful, yet thankful, demeanor.

Meat was a rarity in the neighborhood. The usual fare was Velveeta Cheese and noodles or some generic casserole or fry cakes and molasses. Chester was going to have meat tonight.

"Want some milk?" Chester asked Gabe, offering him the Tupperware pitcher of watery powdered milk that was stretched as thin as Mrs. Harris's neck.

"Naw. Milk and 3-V don't go good together," said Gabe.

Mike Renner pounded on the back door. Mike was a real loser and a Vampire wannabe. His father was a terror for the kids of the neighborhood. He was always taking kids out into his shed and threatening to make them drink poison. Rumor had it that Mr. Renner had been in prison for trying to kill his wife with a hammer. One time Mike, Chester, and Gabe had been dragged into the shed by Mr. Renner. He produced a big ball-peen hammer and started talking crazy. Gabe kicked the man in the nuts and ran, with Chester in tow. Mike stayed in the shed. They didn't see Mike for about a week afterward. His right eye was still nearly swollen shut when they saw him again, and there was a moist cut in the corner of his mouth that was having a hard time healing. His dad was the ruination of Mike. Mike was spoiled fruit, damaged goods, with no spirit left to prop him up. Mike was a loser.

Mike had a worried look on his face.

"Have you seen my dad?" he asked Gabe and Chester.

"No, why? What's wrong?"

"I don't know," said Mike. "He's taken off and mom says she doesn't have any money left to buy food. I hope he comes back soon."

"Don't worry about it. He'll be back," said Chester.

The three went over to Mike's house and around back to the alley, and found themselves rummaging through the remains in a burning barrel when they first smelled it. The smell was kind of sweet, but it burned the back of Gabe's throat. It got stronger as the trio went over to the storm-cellar door.

"What is that smell?" asked Chester.

"Dead rat or cat," said Gabe.

The boys opened the creaking door of the storm cellar and threw it back. It made a loud banging noise. Cautiously, they moved down the rotten wood that served as stairs. The smell was so strong now that Gabe's eyes began to water.

"What's that over there by the stove?" asked Chester.

Gabe peered through the half dark and began to sense something very bad was about to happen.

"Get back!" Gabe cried too late, as Mike walked up to the heap on the floor.

Gabe would never forget Mike's scream. It opened a pit that was not human. Chester just fell down in a fetal position. It was as though he was physically knocked down by the scream.

At first it was hard to say who it was, since there were just shreds of flesh where a head used to be, and a shotgun lying at an angle across the body. The first scream was bad. The second scream was unbelievable, as Mike and Gabe, at the same time, saw the unmistakable four-fingered hand of Mike's dad. The scream went on and on.

⟡⟡⟡

The scream woke Gabe. This was not your ordinary scream. This was the groaning scream of a grown man. This kind of scream involves the stomach and tears the guts with deep sobs. Gabe realized the scream was his own. He jerked violently in bed and sat up, not sure whether he had actually screamed or just dreamed the scream. The roaches were busy on the walls and floor of the hotel room. The water was still dripping in the sink.

3

NAIROBI, KENYA, 2005

RALPH CHANG BAZAAN SAT IN THE NEW FLORIDA NIGHTCLUB on Market Street evaluating the Nairobi whores. For five dollars in U.S. greenbacks, Bazaan knew he could choose the prettiest of the bunch and defile her in any way he wished. Once, while doing his wet work in the Sudan, Bazaan had flown to Mombassa for a brief respite and had bought a teenage whore from her keeper for two hundred dollars. He had taken her back to the Kilifi Hotel and violated her every body orifice. Bazaan had climaxed with deep, shuddering thrusts at the moment the whore gave up her life to his strong hands around her throat. The last, weak spurts of his semen entered the corpse.

Drinking a Pimm's Cup, poured into a proper copper mug, Bazaan smiled at a pretty Kikuyu girl, probably not much older than would be one of his younger daughters—about fifteen or sixteen.

"Ni nataka tomba moto, m'zuri sana! Begoni shillingi?" (I want a very good, hot fuck. How much?), Bazaan asked the girl with a laugh.

"You are not a nice man," replied the girl. "But I could make you nice for enough money. Are you staying at the Hilton?"

"No, I'm staying at the Norfolk."

"Will you buy me dinner and then breakfast at the Norfolk, or will you just buy me some *ndizi* and porridge at a *duka?*" asked the girl, trying to close the deal and quantify the scope of the job. A good American or European customer could, for an evening's pleasure, keep her for a month, as long as the john was not aware of the bleak economics of life in Kenya.

"I'm hungry and I hope you are, too," said Bazaan as his arms herded her into the darkness of the disco room.

Tom Jones was singing "What's New Pussycat?" as Bazaan and the whore picked their way to a corner booth amid the wildly dressed bureaucrats dancing with Travolta-mimicking movement, their cow-like women barely moving at all. Bazaan ordered another Pimm's, a White Cap for the whore, and some chips. He absently stroked the whore's breasts, staring at the broken glitter ball as the dim light filtered through the smoke of cheap Kenyan cigarettes sold in onesies and twosies in the nearby market.

Bazaan was tired and not really up for any sexual gymnastics with this Nubian bimbo. The whore was not unattractive, but Bazaan felt every year of his half century and just wanted a convenient release. He sipped his Pimm's as the whore gulped her beer and devoured the ketchup-drenched chips like the desperate slut she was. Bazaan ordered another beer for the whore and some of the spicy *Samosas* he loved so well. *Samosas* were the hamburgers of Africa. Sometimes they were made with meat, sometimes with just potatoes and peas wrapped up in a unique dough and fried in fat. He munched on the meat *Samosa*—goat meat, he figured—as he nursed his drink.

Bazaan took out a five-dollar greenback and stuffed it between the whore's breasts. Then, slowly, he cupped the back of her head with his left hand and firmly directed it to nuzzle in his lap. The whore was proficient at her trade. Bazaan slumped back and enjoyed the oral ministrations as Pink Floyd sang "Money."

Yeah, thought Bazaan, *money, it's a hit. Don't give me that goody-goody bullshit.* He was always clear as to his mission in life and the coin of its trade. He killed people for money. He killed lots of people for lots of money. Greed and the need to kill were as a separate being that possessed Bazaan's soul and fought to stay alive.

Yes, Bazaan had found his calling that day on Phon Pot Road in Bangkok, where he got his first job from a Frenchman with more money than courage. He remembered the nervous frog, Jean Luc, as they sat in a dingy bar and watched a pretty Thai dancer smoke a cigarette with her vagina. The uterine contractions of the dancer were evidenced when her mons would tilt—kind of a pelvic nod—and puffs of smoke would issue out of her love tunnel. Bazaan sat there equally absorbed in watching the human hookah and the ferret-like movements of Jean Luc.

With one hundred thousand dollars down and an additional two large after a successful mission, Bazaan sauntered down the street and, later that evening, along with five other faceless foreigners, violated a drugged Thai girl. The girl's life was then auctioned to the highest bidder. Bazaan, with his newfound wealth, easily won the bid. However, he unwittingly became the star in a snuff film that night, as a camera noiselessly rolled in an adjacent room. Although the shadowed and dimly lit room made it difficult to see details of Bazaan's face, it offered enough light to evidence the gush of arterial blood that spurted in a stream from the girl's neck. Bazaan bucked violently, assaulting the girl from behind, and added his spurts of semen to mix with the blood. Her life flowed out on the floor and ended as Bazaan's penis went flaccid.

Within one week, Bazaan had taken out an entire opium operation of hill tribesmen in the Golden Triangle. The hill folks were under the leadership of a Hong Kong filmmaker who found running the poppy through I Corps and Air America was better than making martial arts movies. Bazaan had killed thirty-five people that week. Yes, he understood his insanity and he believed a mercenary was nothing more than a paid psychopath. The crazier the merc, the higher his pay.

Money and the pleasure of killing were the only elements of Bazaan's life. He held in disdain those who espoused political tripe that was supposed to justify their horrors. *Money, it's a hit. Don't give me any of that goody-goody bullshit.*

Bazaan absently cleaned his penis with the whore's cheap cotton dress, got up, tossed down his drink and one last *Samosa,* and walked out of the nightclub. On Market Street he walked east toward Kenyatta Avenue and listened to the quiet voices of street people and the occasional sound of tinny African pop music coming from some darkened corner or room. He could hear the lorries growling through the roundabouts on Uhuru Highway and smell the smoke of charcoal fires issuing from the shanty-towns toward the river.

Bazaan's sensory reflection was interrupted by that rush and tingle of alertness that had saved his life so many times before. Suddenly, Bazaan's calm was replaced with caution honed to a sharp edge. He saw the tall American walking down Kenyatta Avenue, and his caution deepened. There was something about the American that shouted danger to Bazaan.

He was certain this American was not on the flight from Nice to Amsterdam's Schipol Airport. Nor was he on the Dutch KLM flight through Athens, on to Nairobi. Yet there was something that bothered Bazaan about this man. Bazaan stood in the shadows of a jacaranda and watched the man as he walked south. Bazaan was sure he was American. His shoes—Nike Lava Domes—loudly announced his nationality. Only Americans wore

Nike or New Balance. Bazaan wore the cheap *Bata* shoes of Africa when not in the field—keeping his nationality unknown. Few could accurately place his mix of Chinese and Mexican blood, which was further obscured by his local *kikoy* shirts and *Bata* sneakers.

The man turned east by the Jeevanjee Gardens and disappeared from sight. Bazaan shrugged off his unease, feeling this case of nerves was most likely due to jet lag and general fatigue. He walked north on Kenyatta to the Norfolk and found an empty table on the verandah.

As Bazaan waited for his order of Pimm's and curry, he noticed a piece of paper on the floor of the verandah next to his chair. He bent over, picked it up, and absentmindedly scanned the shorthand-like notes scrawled in pencil on Babson Foundation stationery. Bazaan's neck hairs rose and a rush of blood flooded to his brain, leaving him short of breath as he read the words written on the stationery:

N'dorobo / Dream Walkers?
N'dorobo / Skin Changers?
N'dorobo / Astral projection?
N'dorobo / Voodoo link?

With no logical link, Bazaan just knew—was certain—the tall American walking down Kenyatta Avenue had written these words. Bazaan had little appetite for his curry now. He rotated his Pimm's Cup again and again with his left hand as he processed the data. How could this stranger—this American—be aware of Bazaan's mission in Kenya?

Bazaan had first heard about the N'dorobo assassin from an old Underwater Demolition Team (UDT) bluewater diver and ex-mercenary named Jimmy, who lived with a pacemaker in his chest, oxygen tubes up his nose, and a Bombay martini in his hand. Just at the end of the Korean War, the shooters and looters of UDT-21 were basically out of a job—cooling their heels, itching to blow something up or shoot bad guys. President Eisenhower saw a job custom-made for these UDT rogues and brigands. Outfitting several teams with state-of-the-art weaponry and ordnance, as well as a new image that begot respect within all branches of the military, the president sent these SEAL ancestors to East Africa to very quietly get very involved in supporting Mother England in Kenya's Mau Mau revolt. Jimmy was one of UDT-21, sent to the slopes of Mt. Kenya to ferret out Mau Mau groups loosely associated with General Dedan Kimathi.

4

UDT-21 COVERT MISSION, MT. KENYA, 1953

FOR WEEKS, JIMMY SLEPT IN THE BOWERS OF CAMPHOR TREES and ran the game trails through thick bamboo, executing search and destroy missions with a handful of frogmen led by a colonial named Seamus and his N'dorobo tracker, Sendeo.

After the first week of carnage, bad things began happening to the platoon. The first death had occurred during the night as the platoon was sleeping in their bivvies, a thin trail of smoke from a quickly extinguished cook fire the only evidence of their presence. Jimmy had gotten up in the gray and misty predawn to relieve himself. His wool fatigues were damp and uncomfortably cool as the wet folds of cloth touched his skin. The forest was dead silent except for the dripping of water onto the vegetation of the lush forest floor. Without thinking, he had rolled out of his bivvy bag and grabbed his Winchester Model 12 in one motion. In the dense forest and bamboo, Jimmy much preferred a shotgun to the Stern 9mm or the ineffective Thompson submachine gun. He walked down the game trail about ten yards into the stand of bamboo and pissed on the ground, then focused the stream on a big beetle lumbering through the duff. Walking back to the campfire, Jimmy nodded at Seamus, who was readying the morning tea. Seamus poked the fire until he saw the glowing embers and placed on them some of the dry grass and wood shavings he kept in a waterproof bag. He blew on the embers until the flames caught hold, rewarding his efforts with quiet crackling. Seamus poured a handful of tea leaves, a handful of sugar, and a handful of powdered milk into a pail of water, mixed everything with his Kabar knife, and set the pail beside the fire. He carefully placed small twigs and then larger sticks on the fire until the flames were steady and stable. Then he placed the pail of tea on a grate of stones to boil.

Jimmy, looking for the rations bag, stepped over a sleeping frogman who called himself Tree. Jimmy slipped on the wet ground and landed on Tree's sleeping form. Jimmy cursed to himself and fully expected to have to defend himself from an instinctive counterattack by Tree. However, no attack came, nor did Tree even wake up. Jimmy looked at his right forearm and saw it was soaked with blood—then he saw the black pool of blood around Tree on which ants and other forest insects were busily dining.

Standing up, Jimmy took the toe of his boot and nudged the bivouac sack that fully enclosed Tree. He then noticed a long slit in the bivouac bag from which welled some sort of brownish, vile-smelling fluid. Kicking the flaps of the tear back, Jimmy felt the bile rise in his throat as he saw what was left of Tree.

His eyes were just bloody, empty sockets, and his rib cage had been opened with the care of a butcher not wishing to ruin prime cuts of meat. It was pretty obvious that some of Tree's innards were missing—most noticeably his heart and stomach—rolls of intestine and some other sack-like organs were the lonely inhabitants of the body cavity. Jimmy rolled back the head and looked into Tree's open mouth to see that his tongue was also gone. Upon closer inspection, the final indignity revealed itself—both penis and scrotum had been removed, with surgical precision.

Seamus's N'dorobo, Sendeo, looked at Tree's remains and muffled a wail. Jimmy looked at the tracker to see that he had rolled his eyeballs back in his head and was rocking on his haunches like an autistic child.

"*Thahu,*" said the N'dorobo in a keening whisper. "*Thahu m'baya-sana.*"

"What the fuck's *thahu* mean?" asked Jimmy, wiping his sleeve on the wet grass, trying to remove Tree's blood.

"A bloody bad curse," answered Seamus, who was still staring at Tree's corpse.

"I've seen this before," Seamus went on. "The Mau Mau Oath Givers take parts of a human body and use them to perform an oath-giving ceremony, just as they do with goats and livestock. They generally stick the eyeballs on the thorns of a bush that forms a kind of arbor and ceremony area like the one we blew the shit out of last week. They mix bits of the victims' blood and organs and have the initiates take part in the communion. They get the Mau Mau initiates to take an oath of loyalty and servitude to the cause. If they go back on their oath, the oath acts as a *thahu,* or curse, and kills them."

"Why'd they take his dick and balls?" asked Fastball, another UDT shooter who had been standing guard since four in the morning.

Seamus replied, shaking his head slowly, "That's for real important oaths where they want no possibility of defection, no matter what we do to the wogs. They generally impale the penis and scrotum on a green stick and roast it over a fire. Then, the female initiates are impaled on it and the males sometimes get buggered with it or have to put the organ in their mouth. I'll tell you, that really seals the oath for sure."

Jimmy knew that a large percentage of Mau Mau murders and defilements of European colonials were done by women enlisted into the Mau Mau. He had often wondered about what would make an otherwise docile Kikuyu *mama* or dutiful *bibi* kill the white children she had watched and coddled since infancy. Now he understood why a peaceful Kyuke woman could become a murdering demon from hell. *Yep,* Jimmy thought, *a toasted prick up the cooz would probably tweak about any woman, Kikuyu or otherwise.*

Jimmy threw the ripped bivvy over Tree's corpse and turned to Fastball. "How in hell did some puss-nutted cock-breath come in past you and do this? Did you hear anything?"

"No. In fact it's been kind of spooky quiet. When I first came on at four, the mist rolled in quick and thick. If I had heard anything, I couldn't have seen 'em. But then, just as quick, it rolls out and I did hear a tree hyrax wail, just once. I about shit myself because he was right over my head. After that, though, it's been as silent as a debutante's fart."

Sendeo methodically packed his small kit and walked away from camp, looking into the last remnants of mountain mist. Looking up in the direction of Nelion and Batian, the main peaks of the mountain, he spat and made a cutting motion with his hand, hoping N'gai had heard his prayer of safety. Later he would strangle a goat in sacrifice to the god who lived on top of the mountain. Now all he could bind his prayer with was his own saliva.

The other members of UDT-21 dug a shallow grave and buried what was left of Tree. They saddled up and moved through the green, cool forest, without noise. Jimmy and Fastball had found a promising site in their recon the day before—a cave with a blind entrance and a bunch of thatched lean-tos. The cooking fires were still warm to the touch. The Mau Mau group must have been out hunting for colonial prey at the same time UDT-21 was hunting for the Mau Maus. Today UDT-21 would carefully move to within two klicks of the target and, at about zero one hundred hours, position themselves around the sleeping camp and wait for first light.

Jimmy was a sniper and could send a round of his Weatherby 470 up the nostril of his choice at two hundred yards. He did not just carry this rifle, but cradled it like a baby. He would position himself on a tree limb and, starting at first light, methodically pick off the unfortunate Mau Mau, with Danny, Fastball, and Seamus forming a killing field for those Jimmy flushed with his sniper fire. Their Thompson submachine gun and shotgun fire would cut to ribbons the panicked and confused Mau Mau, who would probably still be bleary-eyed from too much *pombe.* Tree had carried the heavy BAR that was used to blow apart huts and hideouts—and everything within. With Tree taking his dirt nap, his wet work would now be done by Puffy, a Nebraska linebacker kicked off the team and out of school for beating up ten frat rats at a homecoming party. Puffy liked this work and, due to his iron-pumping routines, could work the BAR as if it were a kid's rubber-band gun. Sendeo refused to carry a gun and hoped for the opportunity of close work with his broadsword-like *kisu* and his spear, with its willow-leaf-shaped head.

UDT-21 picked its way up the game trails that were claustrophobic, green tunnels through the bamboo. Several times in the day the patrol would stop as they heard a large animal crashing through the vegetation, not knowing whether the creature was running away from them—or at them. Jimmy took what they called the martyr position on point. *Hell,* Jimmy thought, *I could plug a buff square between the eyes and kill him dead, and his momentum is still gonna kill me.*

The tunnels through the bamboo suddenly opened onto a small, grassy meadow ringed with giant hyacinth trees and Saint-John's-wort. A stream fed from the snowfields above trickled over the basalt boulders as sunbirds flitted overhead, their bright plumage an iridescent green glitter thrown into the sunlight.

The spoor of forest elephants, like small bales of hay, littered the meadow. Jimmy, on point, was the only one to see the colobus monkey sailing in the canopy above the clearing—a vivid black-and-white kite suspended in the air for a moment. The colobus were the trapeze artists of this jungle. Dressed as vividly as circus aerialists, their black-and-white-striped capes would seem to flutter in the breeze as they sailed from limb to vine with unique grace.

The light was dim, and Jimmy saw clouds creeping up the valley. He imagined that about two klicks away the Mau Mau women would begin to kindle their cook fires and prepare the *ndizi* or *ugale* and porridge. That would be the Mau Mau's last meal, for tonight Jimmy and UDT-21 would be in place to ply their lethal trade at first light.

Jimmy, Seamus, and the rest of UDT-21 silently ate their pemmican rations and washed the fruit and fat down with water. Sendeo squatted on his haunches a short distance from the group eating nothing, having retreated behind the blank stare only Africans can summon at will. Sendeo absently stared at the blade of his *kisu* and stroked it with a soft piece of rock he had found earlier that day along a streambed. The old N'dorobo squatted there beside a stand of bamboo, the hood of his anorak shadowing his face, looking for all the world like a melancholy grim reaper.

"Saddle up, cock-breaths," said Jimmy. "Time to do the hokey-pokey and spread ourselves around. That's what it's all about."

Like all high-altitude climbers, the group moved slowly—first, two steps and one breath. Hours later they were taking one step and breathing in and out slowly, quietly, twice. Night had fallen. The old N'dorobo signaled Seamus with only a light touch on his shoulder, then the rest of UDT-21 froze in the darkness as they heard the bushbuck call made by Sendeo. Their bodies were singing with bites and wounds from crawling through nettles and thick undergrowth the last half klick. They could smell a herd of Cape buffalo nearby, their cattle-like odor mixing with the rumble of the buffs' growling stomachs and flatulence, and a spattering sound as one old bull relieved himself not twenty yards away.

As they slowly moved forward, they saw one, two, then three cook fires, their low flames making dark silhouettes of those moving around the cook pots in the small amphitheater of a clearing. Closer, they could smell the porridge and hear the quiet singsong voices of the Mau Mau. Jimmy found a perch in a camphor tree that overlooked the clearing. The rest of the group melted noiselessly into the forest's undergrowth. Jimmy began to settle in and, once he was as comfortable as one can be under such conditions, focused, with his sniperscope, on the Mau Mau below him.

Most of the Mau Mau wore an odd mix of military clothing and green animal hides. It was a dark and somehow unhealthy dichotomy. The Mau Mau, mostly farmworkers or house servants for white colonials, had turned away from Western trappings and touchstones and had found their own way—perverting their native Kikuyu traditions to become something quite different. A horrific hybrid of cultures, the Mau Mau triggered a quick wave of revulsion in Jimmy as he watched the macabre drama unfold backlit by the cook fires.

Jimmy watched alertly as all the Mau Mau ceased their humming talk and an old man walked slowly out of the cave in the rocky escarpment behind the small clearing. This was certainly not one of the Kikuyu Mau Mau. This man looked like Sendeo, with the sharper, finer features of a Maasai or a Samburu.

Dressed in colobus skins and holding a beaded cane topped with a small animal skull, this man was clearly a shaman—possibly an old N'dorobo shaman at that. Jimmy wondered how such a man of power within the reclusive N'dorobo had come to keep company with these Kyukes. The shaman had a large gourd, a calabash, and an assortment of stoppered bamboo containers tied together with twine or hemp. He also had a grass-woven basket slung over his shoulder. Methodically, the shaman placed his possibles in front of him and squatted down, looking up and staring, it seemed, right at Jimmy, despite the hundred yards between them.

Jimmy involuntarily winced as the shaman's sharp, raptor-like stare appeared to focus directly on him, right back through the scope. As impossible as it was, Jimmy's neck hairs stood out and he had to forcefully suppress the roar of blood that coursed in his ears as the shaman continued his unblinking stare at Jimmy through the sniperscope.

Jimmy tightly closed his eyes and again opened them into the darkness of the forest. Without the scope, the shaman was not much more than a small, dark blob barely highlighted by the cook fire in front of him.

There was no way he could have seen me, thought Jimmy, taking solace in the layers of dark and vegetation between him and the object of his fear. He found himself sweating in the cool air of the forest night. Sweat fueled by fear always had a rubbery smell of body ketones, unlike the sweat that was come by honestly from hard work. Jimmy hoped the shaman couldn't smell his butyl aroma or hear his pounding heart.

Jimmy waited for some time before he could bring himself to look again through the sniperscope. Adjusting the scope, Jimmy saw the old man—a dark and methodical necromancer—busily measuring powders he poured from his bamboo beakers. The rest of the Mau Mau silently watched the shaman as he retrieved his basket from the shadows behind him. With great ceremony, he slowly waved the basket and its contents in a purposeful pattern and then held it over his head and directly toward the main summits, Nelion and Batian. He opened the basket, deftly reached in, and produced a small snake. He held it high in the air, its small gray body circling around the shaman's wrist.

Jimmy couldn't tell for sure, but it looked like the Hines viper, small, gray, and deadly poisonous. The shaman was pressing the jaws of the snake into what looked like a passion fruit. The Mau Mau let out a high-pitched hum of mixed surprise and reverence. The shaman gently placed the snake back into the basket and continued his arcane alchemy.

He took the fruit that had been injected with viper venom and added it to his mixture of powders in the calabash to form a thick paste he stirred with a bone. He spread the paste on a dark green leaf and quickly popped the whole thing in his mouth.

The shaman sat quietly, his gaze again leveled on Jimmy, who was still watching through his sniperscope. He mouthed silently, almost as though he were talking directly to Jimmy. Then the eyes of the shaman rolled back in his head, and his eyelids shuttered the bloodshot whites. The shaman began to shake and spasm and fell down on his back, nearly upsetting the basket with its deadly serpentine contents. His whole body became a rippling contraction of muscles.

The shaman frothed at the mouth and began to breathe with shallow, wheezing breaths. Then, suddenly, he lay still on the forest floor beside the cook fire. Jimmy could see no rising of chest or belly that would signal breathing. There was only the quiet of the Mau Mau facing the old man. All was silent in the forest.

Without warning, the wail of a tree hyrax caused both Jimmy and the Mau Mau to start. Then he heard a loud "What the fuck?" from Puffy out in the darkness of the team's killing field. Then, there were just screams in the night—terrible wails of torment and death all around him. Hearing the screams of pain, Jimmy knew his team was gone—dead. Wondering at his own survival, Jimmy willed himself to focus intensely on the scene in front of him. Through the sniperscope Jimmy could see that no one had moved. The old shaman lay there as though dead, the Mau Mau silently looking with downcast eyes at the embers of the cook fires. One last scream echoed in the forest, and Jimmy heard the grunt of a Cape buffalo.

As Jimmy gripped his 470, he peered through the scope at the shaman. Still there was no breathing movement from the old man. Safe in the camphor tree, Jimmy figured he'd make sure the old wog was dead and take him out with a shot to his exposed temple. Holding his breath and slowly squeezing the trigger, the crosshairs of the Weatherby steady on target, Jimmy suddenly felt his head pulled back by an unseen hand and cold steel cutting and stinging his exposed throat. Instinctively, and from his squatting position in the bower of the tree, he propelled himself backwards and head-butted, immediately burying his head in the armpit of his attacker, protecting his vital throat and its arteries. He clawed for testicles and again violently bucked his head back as he pivoted to face his attacker, who was kneeling on his narrow perch.

Jimmy's mind began to fall to pieces as he saw the colobus skins of the shaman in the weak light of a crescent moon. The old man was holding a *kisu* dripping crimson, as rivulets of his mates' blood ran down the shaman's arms. Impossibly, the old man lying by the cook fire a hundred yards away a second ago had just tried to cut Jimmy's throat!

The shaman smiled and licked the blood on the *kisu* and, wide-eyed, formed a circle with his mouth, uttered

"Wwoooooo," and started to laugh—the noise sounding incredibly like a hyena nosing around camp.

He came at Jimmy, his long knife sweeping the air in ceremonious arcs, completely absent of fear, oblivious and obviously impervious to Jimmy's arsenal of weaponry. Jimmy found himself staring at the arcs of the *kisu* as though mesmerized. In the presence of this impossible nightmare, his brain and his training had left him completely. Jimmy then reacted in the most primal of ways—he made a break for it.

He threw himself out of the bower and tucked and rolled onto the forest floor. Without pause, he ran away from the tree, the shaman, and the Mau Mau camp, keeping his body center low. Nettles slapped his eyes. He jammed fingers against rocks and trees as he continued his primate-like run, his heart pounding and his body covered in fear-sweat. As his training began to reassert itself, he took stock of his direction and slowed down to a fast-paced walk that finally turned into the deliberate, slow, stealthy pace of a UDT point man. He considered going back to see if any of his team were still alive and wounded. But considering what he had just experienced, self-preservation held sway and Jimmy continued to . . . run for his life. He could begin to see the shrouds of cloud and fog as it filtered against the trees in the gray light of predawn. He rubbed his stubbled neck with its newly acquired cut. It stung painfully, yet would probably not even require stitches. Just as the light was starting to claim the forest, Jimmy stopped and quickly sank to the ground as he heard the wailing cry of the tree hyrax. Then, all was quiet but for the gurgling sound of an unseen stream and the pounding of Jimmy's heart as he blankly stared at the moss draping a camphor tree like a funeral shroud.

5

MT. KENYA, 1953

JIMMY FORMED A PLAN TO FIND THE SIRIMON RIVER, WHICH was one ridge over if he wasn't mistaken, and then ran down the Sirimon track to the military base set up in the farmland outside Nanyuki. With the heavy-barreled Weatherby slung over his shoulder and his Winchester Model 12 shotgun on the ready, Jimmy skulked down the game trails, pausing on a regular basis to assess his surroundings and to listen for any sounds of pursuit.

Filling his canteen at a small stream, he heard a bushbuck bark and wondered if it was really a bushbuck or whether it could possibly be Sendeo. Had Sendeo escaped the shaman as he had? The bark issued from a tangle of bamboo and undergrowth. Jimmy spoke quietly, "Sendeo, is that you?"

"*N'dio Bwana* Jimmy," said Sendeo in his very quiet voice as he walked forward out of the bamboo, his body center focused down. "Seamus is gone. Now I must go to the east, back to my people. You are very lucky to be alive, but must never come back, for the *thahu* is for you. The *thahu* will certainly kill you if you come back to Kerrinyaga," he added, referring to the mountain's native name.

"Going east is going right back in the direction of that camp," said Jimmy. "Don't give that old spook a second chance to split you."

"No. He will not kill me. I am not a part of the *thahu.* I do not fear the old man as you do, *Bwana* Jimmy. His *thahu* has no power over me. So I must go."

"How can you be sure he won't decide to kill you in return for losing me?" asked Jimmy.

"Because that old man is Terrari, my oldest brother," Sendeo said, with some embarrassment. "I must go now. The Sirimon Track is just over the ridge. Once on the track, run as swift as the gazelle and you should come by no harm. *Kwaheri rafiki* Jimmy." (Good-bye, my friend Jimmy.)

Sendeo melted into the bamboo and was gone. Jimmy, still holding his open canteen in his right hand, squatted on his haunches. The stream gurgled around his boots. Jimmy drank long, refilled his canteen, and quickly took account of a large ridgeline tree by which to navigate. Jimmy found the Sirimon track that ran along the river. The track was a trail that, lower down the mountain, would gradually turn into a mountain road, passable in a Jeep or truck. Then the track intersected farm roads outside Nanyuki.

Jimmy began a steady jogging pace down the track. It felt safer to be in the open of the cleared track—running away from the close, dark horrors of the night before. As he ran, Jimmy felt both anger and shame thinking about his team, all dead and offered as fodder for the carnivores of the forest. The sun was starting to burn through the mist and clouds, and Jimmy began to sweat. Rivulets of sweat mixed with the tears in his eyes. Soon, the full equatorial sun was beating down on him as he steadily ran down the cut through the mountain forest.

He came around a bend in the track and surprised a herd of Cape buffalo. Grunting and dipping their heads as they began to run away, their heavy bosses some four feet wide, the buffs galloped away with huge, nodding movements of their heads. Jimmy began to smell the charcoal fires of small farms and heard the distant sound of a vehicle grinding through its gears. It was getting closer, and Jimmy took cover just off the track. Bucking and swaying through the muddy ruts of the track, a British troop transport made its way like a drunken dung beetle up the track toward Jimmy.

Jimmy studied the situation with intense focus, wanting to be sure that all was as it should be. He didn't want to stick his dick in a bad hole at this stage of the game. Once sure of his safety, he slowly walked onto the track twenty yards in front of the slip-sliding transport. The truck lurched to a halt and idled. Its diesel smell, combined with the smoke of rural cook fires, mimicked the outskirts of Nairobi.

"What the fuck is some puss-nutted cock-breath like you doing strolling about the countryside on this Sunday afternoon?" shouted the passenger in the cab of the truck.

Out stepped the biggest frogman in the Teams—Charles Ulysus Farley. In UDT training, his brother tadpoles would call him Chuck and then guffaw as they roared, "Just call him Chuck U. Farley." Charlie, as he preferred to be called, was always chewing on a cigar, preferring to eat it rather than sully its properties by setting it on fire. At over six and a half feet tall and 275 pounds, Charlie was an imposing figure and one hell of a soldier, but his size diluted others' perceptions of his real intelligence.

Trying to muster his UDT bravado, Jimmy barked out, "I'm just looking for *mi flor de marinero,* Chuck. Are you my little sailor flower? Or are you just Chuck U. Farley?"

Jimmy tried to guffaw, but the laugh was lodged between a spasm of involuntary swallows—the kind of nervous reaction induced by extreme stress or fear.

Charlie walked over to Jimmy and placed a hand on his shoulder. "What the fuck is goin' on, Jimmy? You look like you saw yourself one bad motherfuckin' spook. Where's the rest of your team? Where's Fastball and Puffy?"

Jimmy looked down at his feet and quietly answered, "Man, they're all gone. I gotta get the fuck off this hill. Ain't nobody gonna believe the shit that went down here. Pack your ass back down to Ops in Nanyuki and let me get some sleep on the way down. Get your ass off this hill, Charlie."

Jimmy pointed his chin up toward the main peaks and added, "The big bad wolf is waitin' up there."

As it was, Charlie had to drop off a team of British commandos to shoot and loot the lower slopes on the north side of the Sirimon River. He knew he would not get much farther up the track in the transport than he was now.

"Okay, Jimmy, let me off-load my Limies and I'll take you back to Ops."

Jimmy, looking down at the mud of the track, said, "Charlie, don't let these Brits go up there. Just take 'em back down with me."

"Can't do that Jimmy. Orders. Born to serve."

Jimmy lay on his back, his eyes wide open, looking at the canvas-covered frame of the transport swaying back and forth as the truck crawled down the track. Every time he closed his eyes he would see the N'dorobo shaman staring at him with the sharp obsidian eyes of a raptor. He puzzled over the notion of an N'dorobo shaman aiding and abetting Mau Mau. The N'dorobo tribe was really not so much a tribe as it was a label put on a number of small groups that had migrated down the Nile and then come east into what is now the White Highlands of Mt. Kenya and the Aberdare Mountains. The term *N'dorobo,* coined by the Maasai, meant "poor people" and was applied to the emigrants because they had no cattle—the currency of the Maasai and their northern cousins, the Samburu. Basically, the N'dorobo were gatherers of honey and defined their lives by beehive hunting and honey gathering. The N'dorobo also ate the meat of wild animals on a regular basis, since they had no cattle to sustain them. As well, they would often trade their honey with the Maasai and Samburu for cattle products, such as milk and blood.

The N'dorobo were a people wrapped in myth and magic. On occasion, an N'dorobo would walk out of the forest and into colonial East African culture. Those few who associated with the whites had their own undefined reasons for doing so and rarely mixed with the Kikuyu or Luo workers on the farms. They were excellent trackers and seemed to know how animals thought—they could predict the behaviors of their prey with uncanny accuracy. For this reason, the rare N'dorobo willing to cooperate with the rebels was used to track and hunt the human prey of the Mau Mau.

It was whispered around Kikuyu cook fires that the N'dorobo were indeed skin changers who could become snakes or buffalos and disappear into the forest, to reappear almost instantly some distance away. There was no record of war between the N'dorobo and any other tribes in East Africa. The Maasai *morani*—fierce warriors themselves—had a saying about the N'dorobo: "One cannot fight the morning mist. One cannot fight the dark of evening. So, how would one war with the N'dorobo?"

Jimmy made it back to Ops outside Nanyuki and then on to Nairobi. In his sitrep (situation report) with naval intelligence officers, he relayed the story exactly as it had happened. Then, exhausted and on the verge of a physical and mental breakdown, Jimmy took R and R in Mombassa. There, in the heat of the coastal sun, he languished and tried to treat his nightmares with frequent doses of gin—about three fingers per dose was prescribed. On Twiga Beach, just outside Mombassa, Jimmy had rented a beach *banda,* a small, thatched hut with a bed draped in a shroud of mosquito netting, an old wooden chair, and a small table for preparing food. Jimmy sat in the chair outside the *banda* and watched the waves shimmer in the setting sun. Several dhows, with their shark-fin sails, were setting out for the evening fishing. The waves seemed to flatten in the failing light, and the sea became a sheet of slate as night claimed the coast.

Jimmy sipped his gin, then opened his throat and gulped the last of the drink down. There he quietly sat, with a stupid smile on his face in the wake of the alcohol that burned its way down his throat. Jimmy continued to smile in the dark, having found that warm, gentle haven created by a half dozen strong drinks. Some months later, Jimmy mustered out of the Teams and found follow-on work in the Sudan and Chad—popping wogs for fun and profit.

The pencil-dick paper pushers at naval intelligence didn't believe much of what Jimmy told them about the shaman incident until the reports began coming in from upcountry. One colonial militia leader after another was slashed to death, despite the extensive security in place. Most of the corpses were found in a bed of blood and viscera, the locks on the doors and windows still secure, and none of the household, including guard dogs, apparently aware of any intrusion.

Around the cook fires of the farms, workers began to whisper of the Dream Walkers. The Dream Walkers were said to walk in the dreams of their victims, steal into their houses or compounds, and, at will, slash them to death with a *kisu*. They would then walk the trail made by the victims' souls and escape undetected.

The Dream Walker assassinations then began to be directed at Kikuyu moderates and colonial sympathizers. Military intelligence, working with operatives from the CIA, investigated fifty-seven Dream Walker assassinations before it issued a situation report to both the secretary of state's office and the office of the Joint Chiefs of Staff:

> "Upon the investigation of fifty-seven military and civilian assassinations, we can draw no solid conclusions as to the perpetrator or his/her method of securing entrance into areas, most of which were considered to be secure. Anecdotal evidence of local tribal superstition is also inconclusive and does nothing to offer hard evidence as to the assassin(s)' method of breaching building and military security.
>
> "All assassinations appeared to be ceremonial in nature, accomplished with a large bladed weapon. In all cases, the eyeballs of the victims were missing, apparently taken with a smaller bladed instrument. In addition, major body organs and genitalia were often missing.
>
> "Ancillary Information: A detachment of UDT-21 was apparently killed as it set up its S & D op on the south side of the Sirimon River on 07-28-53. One team member escaped and was debriefed. The surviving team member gave statements consistent with local tribal superstitions. Such corroboration warrants further investigation.
>
> "Current Recommendations: Short of assigning guards to any and all colonials and/or local colonial

> sympathizers, we can recommend no means by which to offer security to these individuals. No military or security recommendations can be made at this time."

Unofficially, the translation of the sitrep issued by the spooks in MI and the CIA could be read as, "These assassins are bad juju and we're fucked. And we'll be goat-fucked if we can't figure out a way to unfuck ourselves."

In the ensuing years of the Mau Mau revolt, hundreds of colonials and colonial sympathizers were assassinated by what was commonly referred to as the Dream Walkers.

Finally, bested by the Mau Mau and their Russian backers, Mother England handed its colony over to Jomo Kenyatta and his political machine. Kenyatta, an Oxford-educated Kikuyu imprisoned by the colonial authorities, was said to have been the mastermind of the Mau Mau revolt, directing General Dedan Kimathi and others from his jail cell. The oathing ceremonies and the use of the colonials' body parts in those ceremonies were also alleged to be creations of Kenyatta. Some said that, because of his postgraduate education in cultural anthropology, Kenyatta knew which psychocultural buttons to push in order to elicit unwavering allegiance and enable common Kikuyu to commit the most heinous and inhuman acts.

The Russian Bear had much interest in Kenya, with its strategically valuable port in the Indian Ocean. And Kenya needed all the rubles it could garner, as it crawled the path of nationalism. Such was the basis for the chummy relationship that soon grew between the KGB and leaders of what were now referred to as the Freedom Fighters. The Russian intelligence machine soon caught wind of the ultimate assassins called Dream Walkers. Having no problem recognizing paranormal applications to military and intelligence operations, the

Russians investigated the Dream Walkers in an open-minded, utilitarian manner.

Years after the Mau Mau revolt and Kenyatta's rise to Kenya's presidency, Bazaan ran into Jimmy at an arms show in Bangkok. Jimmy was getting blind drunk on the Bombay martinis so graciously offered by their host. Jimmy spilled his guts to Bazaan about N'dorobo Dream Walkers as Bazaan drank water with a twist of lime and made a tight grimace to acknowledge the fictitious bite of alcohol. Stone-cold sober, Bazaan kept mental notes of Jimmy's babbling, cataloging each bit of detail.

The second time Bazaan heard about the Dream Walkers was from an ex-KGB colonel named Ivan Vlastig, who had turned to protecting Medellín drug lords after the breakup of the Soviet Republic. What he learned about the Dream Walkers from the Russian ex-agent indeed corroborated what Jimmy had said a few years earlier.

The Dream Walker assassins became an obsession with Bazaan, for he took his trade very seriously. Also, he was eclectic, and felt compelled to add to his killing proficiency anything that would work. So he did not rule out the wild stories about Dream Walker assassins as irrelevant to his growth as a killer of men. Quite the contrary, he was wide open to anything that would get him safely within the killing range of a target.

Bazaan had pursued the trail of the Dream Walker assassins for years and was convinced they were still active and living in the forests of Mt. Kenya.

Bazaan threw down his Pimm's, paid his chit, and slowly walked off the Norfolk's verandah through the lobby and into the internal courtyard of the hotel. Smelling the sweet scent of flowers in the dark of night, he walked to his room, kicked off his *Batas*, stripped off his *kikoy* shirt, pants, and semen-stained boxers, and collapsed on the bed naked.

He threw the crumpled note from the Babson Foundation on the valet at the foot of his bed as he got up to wash his penis and pubic hair. He desperately needed to shut off his brain and get some sleep. Popping a tablet of Halcion and firing up a tightly wrapped joint made with local ganja, his thoughts were carried away on the smoke of the cannabis. As he sat up in bed, Bazaan's head slowly nodded forward and he collapsed into a prone position. The small butt of the joint, sitting like an offering in the ashtray, sounded one final pop as the ignited seed issued a fanfare to the darkness of a dreamless sleep.

6

NEW YORK AND KENYA, 1980

GABE TURPIN HAD HEARD OF THE N'DOROBO SHAMAN OF Mt. Kenya in his early days of climbing in East Africa. The Brits, on climbing holidays, would often report they saw an old man dressed in skins and wearing sandals scampering about the rocks or snow at over fifteen thousand feet, usually well after midnight. It appeared that the shaman did not particularly like the Brits and would often respond with slights and insults when questioned or pursued by the climbers. Always, the old shaman was said to disappear, melting behind a large rock outcropping or ice column. He was just not there when pursued by the climbers, curious as to how an ill-clothed old man could climb so high over technical ground without the aid of any modern climbing equipment. Stranger yet, the old shaman was never seen on the mountain during the day, nor was he seen much lower than fifteen thousand feet. Some of the kitchen staff at the Naro Moro River Lodge noticed the old man never left his small hut outside of Naro Moro much before nightfall and was always back at his cook fire in the morning light. Local Kenyan climbers, such as Vince Fayad and Mt. Kenya pioneer Iain Allan, tried to put the pieces together: the shaman's high-altitude sightings, coupled with his domestic routine, would require him to travel thirty kilometers in, up a few thousand feet of steep rock and ice, and be back within a twelve-hour period, a feat that was deemed impossible for one dressed in skins and sandals and whose age was easily over seventy years.

Gabe remembered the first time he had seen the N'dorobo shaman, back in 1980. Gabe and his climbing companion, Bill, were waiting in the JFK terminal as all passengers on Pan Am Flight 833 to Nairobi were called to gather at the gate. There, a State Department official blandly read a statement that all but emergency and diplomatic travel to Kenya was canceled, due to a coup d'état in progress. Gabe and Bill considered their attempt of Mt. Kenya's North Face an emergency.

Three hours later, they were the only Americans on the flight, stretching across the empty seats and dozing among the handful of anxious Kenyan politicos. Nervous men sweat and smell uniquely of fear. This aroma lay like a blanket over the plane. Tight, desperate laughter accompanied the nervous belching of the politicos who faced losing their newfound Western luxuries—the products of graft and corruption.

Gabe mused on their fates as he observed the fidgety Kikuyu sitting across the aisle in the standard uniform: a bad sports jacket, a stained tie, and white socks in cheap brown loafers. The man fidgeted and made much of scraping his plastic dinner plate clean with his small airline knife. Again and again, the man scraped the side of his plate, removing the imaginary gravy—his bloodshot eyes betraying his fear. If it went the wrong way when the plane touched down, this diplomat would likely kiss a rebel's panga blade—bullets probably being in short supply.

If he was really a catch for the rebels, perhaps they would necklace him as a public show. Necklacing was a creative and horrible execution endemic to Africa. The executioners would tie the victim's hands behind his back and place over his head and shoulders a tire filled with gasoline. They would touch off the gas, and the combination of flame and burning rubber made for a screaming human candle running with death's desperation, only to fall squirming on the dusty ground, twitching and screaming in a puddle of urine and feces. Gabe had seen a necklacing once in Uganda. He hoped never to see another.

They landed after the sundown curfew at Jomo Kenyatta International Airport. The stress and instability was reflected on all of the faces in the airport. Gabe and Bill had been passed through customs almost as an afterthought, since rebels had held the airport no more than a few hours before. Job focus was nonexistent among the Kenyan customs staff. The politicos were ushered by friendlies into vehicles and left in the night like bats on the fly.

Gabe and Bill had reserved cheap accommodations at a hostel outside Nairobi. With no means to get there, Gabe began to schmooze an army officer. A half hour later, Gabe and Bill were being driven to the hostel in a loyalist troop transport full of soldiers with big guns and bare feet. With the engine of the transport still running, Gabe could hear gunfire and see the fires burning in Nairobi, a few miles to the northwest of the hostel. Once there, Gabe pounded on the door of the hostel, which seemed to have lost power—not one light could be seen in the building.

"*Tahfadali, tahfadali*" (Please, please), said Gabe fervently.

The hostel's door opened an inch and an oily Indian voice said tersely, "No rooms!"

The army officer assured Gabe and Bill he knew of a good hotel in city center. He would take them there.

The transport ground through its gears and executed a slalom run through debris and overturned barrels set on fire by rebel factions across the street from the Jeevanjee Gardens.

"There is the hotel," said the officer, pointing across the littered street at a small sign that was in need of new paint and, hence, could only whisper its name: Hotel Tropic.

Gabe and Bill shouldered their packs and cautiously peered outside the transport, looking for snipers or rebels bent on taking some target practice. Clomping across the street at a sprint, in mountaineering boots, Gabe reached the door of the hotel and threw it open. Looking like a great blue giant, Gabe filled the doorway with his body, his pack riding high over his head. He was breathing fast, more from fear than exertion. The noise of his entry disturbed the sleep of the night manager/bell man/maid/owner of the Hotel Tropic. Without a word, the old Kikuyu pushed a greasy, ancient register across the table toward Gabe. Bill slipped into the hotel's multipurpose, dingy front room and said in a sarcastic manner, "Great."

Sleep eluded both, so they watched the troop movements out the grimy window of their single room. Bill and Gabe were rooting for the loyalists and were heartened to see so much heavy equipment and so many troops moving in to secure the city center. The room's roaches appeared indifferent.

Upon waking, the city seemed to barely remember the bad dream of the attempted coup. The streets were as quiet as a graveyard in the steel predawn. Cautiously, shop owners and public servants poked their heads out of windows and doors to assess the mood of the city. The mood was deemed by most as benign. Buses started to run, shop owners opened their *dukas*, the jobless riffraff wandered about and collected around small grills covered with corn and popping kernels. Another day had come to Nairobi.

Gabe and Bill went to the British consulate. Gabe had met Iain Allan a couple of years before through Iain's business partner, Vince Fayad, who was also an old climbing partner of Gabe's. Iain's wife, Jill, worked at the consulate.

"I'm surprised to see you, Gabe," said Jill, as the two Americans entered the office area after being announced by the consulate's rod-stiff receptionist and its security chief. "Are you here to climb?"

"Yeah, that is if we can make it to Naro Moro. What's the story? Is there transport?"

"You won't get to Naro Moro for at least a week. The rebelling faction was the air force, and Nanyuki is where their main base is. There's nothing moving in that area until the government troops clean up the rebels who have retreated into the farmland and forests around Mt. Kenya. The only traffic is lorries moving in food for the area and the government troops. Other than that, there's no private or public transportation that can get you from Nairobi to Naro Moro and the park."

Frowning, Gabe asked, "Is there anything you can do? To lose a week would cut out our R and R trip to the Mara after the mountain. I really was looking forward to Fig Tree Camp, martinis, and sneaking into the pool at Keekorok to ogle the birds. Can you help us out, Jill?"

"Sorry, Gabe. I'm stuck here as much as you boys are. You could always try to stow away on a food truck," Jill said with a laugh. "Wouldn't be the first time for you to try something a little irregular, now would it?"

"Good idea," Gabe mumbled. His mind was working as he issued a preoccupied good-bye to Jill, who had a wary look on her face, tinged with a slight smile.

"They're serving the grilled trout at the Naro Moro River Lodge tonight. I hope you enjoy it."

"I'll tell you about it when we're back," said Gabe over his shoulder as he and Bill walked out of the consulate.

⋄⋄⋄

The dried fish smelled bad, but the greasy tarp with its unspeakable stains smelled worse. The exhaust filtered through the rotting bed of the truck to make Gabe's and Bill's eyes water and their noses run buckets of snot. They had paid the driver one hundred shillings for berth on his fish truck, which was going to Nyere—via Naro Moro. They were instructed to nestle into the dried fish and pull the tarp over their heads so as to avoid being spotted by soldiers on the road and at checkpoints. The dried fish were like ten thousand scabs that stank and attracted the ubiquitous flies of Kenya. It was a solid four hours to Naro Moro, given the checkpoints.

The throaty exhaust of the fish truck rumbled as the driver geared down. The truck stopped, and Gabe heard the driver's door open and a crunch of footsteps around the bed of the truck. A soft tap-tap-tap on the tarp was accompanied by an equally soft voice saying, "*Jambo sahib,* we are here. No one is on the road. *Pese-pese sahib.*" The driver urged Gabe and Bill to be quick about it.

Gabe and Bill unfolded themselves, gingerly stepped through the fish, threw their packs onto the dusty side of the road, and sprang off the back of the truck. The Naro Moro River Lodge was a little over a mile away. A small wooden sign beckoned visitors traveling the A-116. Off to their right, a mantle of clouds sat on Mt. Kenya's summits, hiding the snaggled peaks. The sun was hot on their necks as they hefted their gear down the dusty road. The smell of cook fires mixed with the scent of flowers and foliage.

Upon entering the grounds of the Naro Moro River Lodge, one stepped into the colonial Africa of the fifties. A trout stream ran through the property, which was covered in fragrant trees and lush foliage. The main building had the wonderful stone architecture so typical of Kenya's colonial period. The lodge's receptionist registered little surprise in seeing the two Americans amble in through the foyer after parking their huge packs outside on the steps. They signed in, no questions asked, and were given the keys to their cabin. Europeans trapped by the coup were still sipping chai and sitting around tables placed on the lawn. The morning sun was warming the air, and the humming of insects soon mingled with the coos of doves and the soothing sound of water running over rocks in the nearby stream.

By the time Gabe and Bill had bathed the fish scales and scent off their bodies and stored and given a cursory sort to their gear, it was lunchtime. The promise of a bit-early White Cap called the two to the lawn tables. They sipped the strong beer and ordered cheese and tomato sandwiches with chips—and two more White Caps. The Maasai waiter served the sandwiches, and Gabe saw he had tucked his distended earlobes over the tops of his ears like a Westerner would button the collar of an oxford shirt: neat, tidy, and businesslike. The Maasai made small holes through the earlobes of the young boys and girls of the tribe and over time placed larger and larger wooden plugs into the holes, stretching the earlobes dramatically. Gabe found that Maasai *morani* (warriors) coveted 35mm film canisters, into which they would place their small possibles and then store the container in the earlobe hole. The waiter, with his four-inch pierced earlobes, well appointed in a starched white shirt and waistcoat, provided a sharp cultural contrast quite common in the young nations of the continent.

Gabe and Bill planned to do the North Face Direct route on Mt. Kenya. In order to do this, however, the best approach was from the Sirimon Gate up from Nanyuki. As it was, that approach was problematic because the rebelling faction of the Kenyan military—the air force—had its main base just outside

Nanyuki. Normally, one could charter a four-wheel-drive Suzuki to drive up to the Sirimon Gate entrance to Mt. Kenya National Park and be off-loaded—no fuss, no muss. However, due to the coup d'état, the Naro Moro River Lodge had canceled all such transport to the mountain.

Gabe talked with Cerril, the mountain's store manager at the lodge, seeking his advice on how to get to the mountain's base.

Cerril mused for a minute and said, "I'll ask Muneje if he'll take you. He has an old truck that may make it. But I bet he'll beg off. Those rebels will be pretty desperate at this point, all scattered about the countryside up Nanyuki way. Muneje isn't particularly brave, and he needs that truck to keep his wives in babies and porridge. Won't want to press his luck with rebels on the run. Anyway, I'll ask him to stop by your cabin and give you a shout."

Gabe and Bill wandered back to their cabin, taking the time to study the shadows of trout hanging silent in a pool nestled into the crook of the stream under a jacaranda. The apparent peacefulness of the grounds belied Gabe's concern and worry. To have gotten this far and be turned back for lack of a way to drive thirty kilometers would be a bitter end to a long-planned adventure. *Sure,* he thought, *we could wait for a few days.* But in Africa a few days was longer than just a few days, and even short delays have a way of turning into epics.

On the porch of the cabin, Bill was filling the stove with kerex fuel from a red aluminum bottle as Gabe daubed more Sno-Seal onto his Lowa boots. Gabe looked up as a man dressed in a tattered sports coat and grease-stained khaki pants addressed them politely in the quiet voice of an African.

"Mr. Cerril says you wish to be taken to Nanyuki."

"Not exactly," said Gabe. "We want someone to take us up to the Sirimon Gate to the park. We don't want to go to town. We want to go climb the mountain."

"That will be very difficult," the man responded. "I have been told that many men have fled Nanyuki and are hiding in the forests around the mountain. They will be cold and very hungry. They will kill us for our clothing and food. It would be very foolish to drive to the Sirimon Gate. There will be many bad men waiting for such foolish people."

Gabe pleaded his case. "We must go to the park. We have spent much money to get here and do our *shauri.* I do not think men on foot could succeed in stopping your truck. I think it is a good risk. We will pay you well for your service. Would you drive us for eight hundred shillings?"

Eight hundred shillings was equal to fifty U.S. dollars. Gabe had offered the man the equivalent of a half year's wage for a two-hour truck ride.

"*Hapanna* (no). It is too little for such dangerous work. Pay me two thousand shillings and I will drive you. You must pay my wife before we leave."

Gabe said to Bill, "This guy isn't planning on coming back, that's why we have to pay his wife. And if he's not coming back, neither will we. This guy is either way too spooky, way too clever, or knows this to be a fool's mission. What do you think?"

"Are there any other ways to get to the north side of the mountain and not go close to Nanyuki?" asked Bill.

"Well," said Gabe, "we could go in from the south and to the met station. But then we'd have to go up and over the west arm of the peak and drop down into Kami Tarn and high camp from the south. I haven't a clue about the route—haven't been on that side of the mountain."

Trying to form another option, Gabe asked Muneje, "How much to take us to the met station?" Gabe was referring to the meteorological station perched in the forest on the south side of the mountain.

"One thousand shillings—and you must pay my wife before we leave."

"Well," said Gabe, "since the met station is only half as much, I'd say we have a fifty-fifty chance of making it there alive. Whatcha say? Wanna go for it?"

"Yeah. Let's go for it," Bill said as he fished out five purple hundred-shilling notes and handed them to Gabe. "Here's my contribution to the widow's trust."

Gabe and Bill quickly off-loaded their packs from Muneje's truck. The ride up through the ruts of the track had loosened Gabe's bowels considerably, and he couldn't wait to be left alone with TP and the bamboo. They had not encountered any rebels on their short trip from the Naro Moro River Lodge. Forgoing all caution of acclimatization, Gabe and Bill struck out from the met station and trekked up the track through the dense forest of the mountain.

"We need to get high quick," said Gabe. "I figure if we can make it to about twelve thousand feet we'll be clear of any *bandidos.*"

As it was, they tucked camp away a half mile from the track, knowing that hungry men don't have much energy to pursue the opportunity of a full belly. Hidden high in the heather and heath, Gabe and Bill made their first camp at over eleven thousand feet, in the middle of the Vertical Bog. They had to forgo the luxury of a cook fire and ate dried pemmican in the gloom and mist of a Mt. Kenya evening. Clouds and wet vapors soon enveloped their hideout of a camp. The clouds were like cold, freezing cotton balls as they assembled in the dark. There was no noise—only a smell of wet air—as they pulled their polyester bags snugly over their heads and slept dreamlessly, exhausted after the ground covered and the mental cost of the day.

7

MT. KENYA, 1980

After a good night's sleep, Gabe and Bill pushed on to over thirteen thousand feet among a stand of giant senecios, and, for the first time, they felt safe from any rebels with bad intent. Here they made camp, and the next day hiked up the arm of the peak to well over fourteen thousand feet for acclimatization. The day after they pushed past McKinder's Camp, a veritable hotel of shelters that were unusually empty and had a ghost town feel. With only a cursory inspection of the empty huts, Gabe and Bill pushed north of the camp, losing and gaining thousands of feet of altitude, and finally dropped into the high camp of Kami Tarn, high on the mountain's north side. There, they off-loaded their gear into the climbers' cabin and fixed a quick supper of chicken-soup base, curry, and rice with raisins and peanuts as garnish.

Exhausted, Gabe and Bill cleaned up their evening dishes. It was now quite dark, and Gabe heard a clanking and clunking movement coming from the col that ushered out of the scree from Oblong Tarn to the south. Shadows that were men doggedly walked toward camp. A porters' party had been sent on as a vanguard to make nice the camp for the touristos who would follow. Gabe and Bill watched the porters, wondering at their poor clothing and equipment. The porters, dressed in a collage of torn rain gear and old Wellington-style boots, off-loaded their goods and quickly coaxed a fire from the trunk of a giant senecio. A pail of water and milk was placed on the smoky fire and handfuls of tea were thrown into the brew, along with copious quantities of sugar.

Gabe and Bill took advantage of the fire and, along with the porters, stared at the orange and yellow ribbons of flame, contemplating the primal image. Gabe mused that watching fires was a form of ancient entertainment that encompassed all of humankind. The fire popped and crackled as steam issued from the brewing chai. Finally, the chai was ladled out with an enamel cup, making soft clunking and gurgling sounds that soothed. Gabe and Bill gratefully received the steaming offerings with two hands.

Wordlessly, they sipped their chai around the cook fire at fifteen thousand feet. It was dark as indigo now. Kami Tarn, although only ten yards away, was only a rumor in the dark of the Kenyan night. The small cook fire barely illuminated the dark faces of the porters. Most were shrouded in anoraks, castoffs from previous clients.

There was no cue as, very quietly, one of the porters began to hum a tribal tune. The voices of Kenya were soothing even in the common, everyday life of Nairobi's city center. Here, the humming-turned-singing was hypnotic. Gabe and Bill listened, finished their chai, and silently took their leave to go to the hut earmarked for climbers. The porters found poorer quarters in a crude, dirty A-frame perched an appropriate distance away from the climbers' hut.

In the musty dark of the hut, Gabe and Bill fluffed their bags and climbed in. Both were dog-tired and getting cold. The soothing songs of the porters continued, and Gabe found himself smiling in the dark of the hut. The relaxed, soothing state of mind that provided almost a physical tickle gently ushered Gabe into a floating sleep.

The rats screamed in the rafters, and their brief but intense confrontation resulted in one of the rats falling onto Gabe's sleeping bag with a plop. It scampered off and rejoined the fray. Rats were screaming everywhere under the roof of the hut. Another rat was thrown from the ring and landed on Bill's face, which elicited quite a scream in its own right. The screams of fighting rats were issued against the background sound of rat feet, with their sharp little claws crisscrossing the nylon of the sleeping bags.

Unable to sleep in this nightmare, Gabe and Bill hurriedly sought escape into the cold of the alpine night. Their breath hung in clouds around their heads. The stars shone off the Northey Glacier, and Gabe could hear the hum of total silence.

"Fuck that," said Bill. "Cold or not, I'm not sleeping in that fucking zoo."

Bill hunkered down in some scree beside the tarn and zipped his bag shut, his nose peeking out of the opening like a snorkel. Gabe walked around the boulders by the camp and answered nature's call. Steam issued up from his pool of urine as though he'd pissed acid that burned the ground. He studied the urinary phenomenon. It was good he was pissing—a sign he was amply hydrated. Bored with the steaming piss, Gabe studied the basalt boulders that were like gardens of lichen and petrified bracts.

He heard the clatter of rocks, probably a rock hyrax. Then he heard the unmistakable cadence of human feet crunching toward him through the frozen scree. In the weak light reflected off the glaciers and snowfields, Gabe saw a wild figure scampering among the boulders. Wishing to remain unnoticed, Gabe shrank into the deep darkness of the boulder. About ten yards away, the figure stopped and stood there, like a macabre scarecrow. Animal skins on the scarecrow flagged gently in the breeze, which issued like updrafts over the snowfields. Gabe studied the figure and stared dumbfounded at the feet of the night visitor. Gnarled, bare feet wrapped in cheap sandals made of used tires flexed themselves in a crusty patch of ice. To Gabe, this was clearly an ill-clothed old man, probably in need of help.

Stepping from behind the boulder, Gabe greeted the old man, *"Jambo m'zee."*

Gabe's salutation offered a polite recognition of the visitor as a wise man. *"Habari?"* (How are you?) Gabe continued to address the scarecrow dressed in monkey skin and sandals. "Do you need help?"

"Did I need your help to get here?" replied the scarecrow in a sarcastic tone. "What have you come so far to find here, *mzungu?"* The scarecrow referred to Gabe in a derogatory Swahili slang term for white man.

The strange old man continued in a taunting tone, "This mountain whispers your death, *mzungu.* Can you not hear it whisper to you even now? All you will find here is your death."

With continued civility, Gabe asked, "Would you like me to brew some chai, *m'zee?* I'll get the stove started."

Gabe turned toward camp and fished in his Gore-Tex parka for matches. Hearing no footsteps behind him, he turned to the scarecrow, but saw only a patch of ice against the gray scree.

Then faintly, almost as if he were saying it silently to himself, Gabe heard the old man say, "N'gai whispers your death, *mzungu.* When you hear the death whisper, you will know a bit of my craft. You must die and walk in your own dreams first, *mzungu.* Then your dreams will be as the N'dorobo." The old man's laughter echoed off the igneous walls and was engulfed by the silence of the mountain.

Gabe stared at the towering buttresses above him as the vapor-filled air glistened like fairy dust. The clacking echoes of falling rock issued from a nearby couloir as a rogue wind blew down on the camp. Gabe heard the cry of a hyrax issue from the blackness of the mountain's North Face. He felt a trickle of fear-sweat run down his neck, despite the icy breath of the mountain. Gabe was deeply troubled by this surrealistic encounter as he made his way back to camp.

Rethinking his plan to tell Bill of his encounter, Gabe snuggled into his bag and silently stared at the stars. At this altitude, the stars were to Gabe like permanent points of fire, since the thin air offered no purchase for distortion. Gabe stared at the sky until the stars disappeared in concentric order and left a cone of darkness as the focus. *Perhaps it was only a dream,* Gabe thought. But then, he posed to himself, *What is a dream, and what is real?*

Lost in the cosmic conundrum, Gabe fell into a troubled sleep. He moaned in his sleep, haunted with dreams of old black men dressed in rags—as obsidian gnomes played with gray vipers.

Gabe had set his alarm for two a.m. as they would pick their way up from the tarn and find the start of the North Face Direct route on Mt. Kenya. The route's starting point was marked with a circled cross chiseled into the rock face, about an hour's stiff hike up from the tarn. The route would take them up some two thousand feet of vertical face and deposit them just below the Amphitheater—with Firmin's Tower, the crux of the climb, looming overhead. Gabe planned on a bivouac just below the tower. Then they would climb the remaining five hundred feet in the morning light and descend back to Kami Tarn by nightfall. Such were Gabe's plans.

Within a half hour, Gabe had shit himself. Where or how he contracted the bug, Gabe knew not. That was okay; some years before he had climbed on Mt. Kenya for a week with his own shit frozen into his shorts. They found the route's mark, and Gabe led the first pitch in the gray of early morning, his fingers and hands frozen as he gripped the basalt of the mountain. Gabe's body remembered the drill—move and breathe, move and breathe. At over fifteen thousand feet, every expenditure of energy took its toll.

Gabe, having run out over a hundred feet of rope, set up the first belay. He reeled in the rope as Bill progressed up the face. Gabe focused on the few remaining stars and the shadow of the face as he belayed his friend up. He knew the first pitches of climbs were always a bitch. Now he could slip into his mode of upward movement. *That is the only way to climb a mountain so big,* thought Gabe. *One rope-length at a time.*

Gabe led the next pitch and the next, and found himself on very difficult ground, much harder than the climbing guide had rated the climb. He realized he was off-route. In the darkening gloom of an equatorial afternoon, Gabe desperately moved over the rock faces to his right, hoping to find the route of the North Face Direct. Now he must, again, find the route and press on to the base of the Amphitheater.

Gabe was traversing narrow ledges less than two inches wide and ice covered. It was dark, desperate work. Sensing the route to the North Face Direct was lower and to the right as one faced the rock wall, Gabe set up a rappel site and set up three anchors into the rock. Not knowing if the rope had reached a ledge of safety, Gabe backed off the wall and descended into the pit of darkness. Coming to a two-foot ledge about thirty feet down in his rappel, Gabe called up to Bill and went off belay. Every thirty feet was insurance in this dark, blind rappel.

Bill followed Gabe down to the ledge. Gabe, wanting to re-rig the rappel, found the rope somehow stuck in the blackness of the rock face above him. Without protection, Gabe climbed up without even being able to see the rock wall, feeling his way up the face until he found the rope looped around a chicken-head—

a rock outcropping. Gabe freed the rope and climbed down to the narrow ledge, a half mile of air beneath his heels as he backed down in the darkness.

Gabe did one more rappel down and found ground he had been on before. Instinctively, he knew he was back on the North Face Direct route, with its couloir just below the Amphitheater and Firmin's Tower. Here, Gabe and Bill set up anchors and roped into the wall for an uncomfortable bivouac. Bill was quite sick and had taken to silence—very unusual in one who would, Gabe often said, argue with a possum.

The rockfall woke Gabe, and he saw the blue sparks of rock hitting rock a few inches from his face. He could hear the whining, ricochet sound of rocks-turned-bullets as they came down the face, ejected from the freezing ice fields hundreds of feet above. A rock careened off his temple and knocked him unconscious for a moment. Shaking his head as he had in his Golden Gloves boxing days after receiving a good tag, Gabe found himself slumping in his bivouac. Bill was shitting bricks.

"Are you okay? Gabe, are you okay?" he heard Bill saying.

Shaking the stars out of his head, Gabe uttered a simple, "This is bullshit."

Gabe listened and watched as the rocks hit near his head, any one a fatality if a few more inches his way. He shook from his fear—shook uncontrollably in the cold of the Mt. Kenya night.

After an hour of such continual fear—imagining his death dozens of times—Gabe grew hungry and found an Energy Bar in his pack. Feeling he would gain one more plane of protection from the rock missiles if he hunkered down below a rock buttress to his right, Gabe clipped himself into a new position, munched his Energy Bar, and retreated into a kind of spiritual invisibility. Eventually, the fear exhausted him and he found a fitful sleep.

Upon waking, Gabe felt with horror that he might be insane. He didn't know where he was, who was with him, or even who he was. He was reduced to a primal organism trying to survive. Gabe tried to focus his eyes. A ledge of rock. In a cocoon of nylon. Clipped in, leaning on a pack.

Surrealism. Nonreality. It was audible. Gabe—now nothing more than a mass of cell tissue in the nightmare world—understood some words made by his friend Bill. *Okay? God, I'm not even here,* thought Gabe. He could feel his life flowing out. The death whisper was persistent. There was nothing but confusion and despair. He was dead. They were dead. This was just the noise before they succumbed. The ultimate pissing in the wind.

Lacing boots with sausage-like, leaden fingers on feet seemingly miles away. Everything was seen through inverted binoculars. Barely enough balance to sit upright—the death whisper was everywhere. The promise of rest and an exit from this nightmare world of inability. The death whisper was everywhere about them.

Gabe crawled off the ledge and, with ultimate absurdity, started the first rappel down. He was a functional animal. Going down, a reptilian brain using the crutch of judgment and experience in order to survive. A world beyond articulation. Beyond recognition.

Check your rappel system three times and don't let go of the rope, the inner voice tells him. It chants this like a mantra of survival. *Three times. Don't let go.*

Blending, fluid, in and out of consciousness, reality. Consciousness flooded back when Gabe's head slammed into the wall, the mantra not allowing him to let go of the rope. A dumb animal with primordial focus, he continued down. Continued down in order to . . . live. The death whisper was everywhere around him—in him. He, a cow-like, drooling organism trying to not die, trying to not drown in the blood flooding his lungs, trying to not let his head explode from the interstitial pressure of the edema. Gabe tried to think only about . . . what had to be done next.

In a narrow chimney, two feet of the double rope left in his right hand. Heels dangling free. Drowning in his own fluids. Brain and eyes bursting. Gabe stopped his descent. *What now?* he thought. The death whisper was everywhere now. It whispered, *Let go!*

Feeling like a three-year-old caught in dangerous surf, Gabe struggled to think. He dangled at the abyss, drooling blood fluid, and stared at the rock with unfocused eyes. Then, he saw the rusty piton. He tied off on it and, unable to think or talk, waited for the other thing above him to descend to face the futility.

The other thing showed fear, exasperation, and more fear. Gabe retied a sling on the piton's shaft, making room to thread the rope through the eye of the piton. Crazy, irrational, but, at the time, as good as anything. Clipped into the rope looped through the loose, rusty piton, Gabe started to rappel off, only to be riveted by the eyes of his friend.

Summoning all remaining conscious resources, Gabe uttered the ultimate black humor statement. "We aren't going to make it anyway," he said with a shrug as he rapped off, not caring, not even looking at the piton as he descended.

Gabe blacked out and came to again, dangling a few feet over a large terrace. He let go of the rope, which burned ugly welts as it ran over his palm. He crashed down, lying in a heap, moaning and dying. The death whisper was now in line with Gabe's racked, rasp-like breathing.

Then Gabe started to crawl. Unable to stand due to the edema pressure on his brain centers, he scuttled down the boulder field with movements like those of the deformed beggars in Nairobi. Between boulders, sliding down short walls, attempting to stand and falling on stiff arms, Gabe coughed and spat blood and tissue. He crawled for what seemed . . . days.

Gabe smelled the base camp at Kami Tarn before he could see it. The soft, metal sounds of pots placed on rocks, the rustle of nylon, and the smell of kerex stove fuel greeted his arrival.

And then Gabe saw another thing dressed in blue, asking him, "Are you okay?"

The thing was a doctor from a British team of climbers. The decrease in altitude made Gabe's beast mind relent somewhat.

Gabe replied, "I have pulmonary edema. I have to get down. You can hear my lungs from there, can't you?"

"Can you continue?" asked the doctor.

Such a typically Brit thing to say, thought Gabe. Without answering, he crawled to his backpack and gear, stashed what seemed years before, and off-loaded most of the gear onto the doc and Bill, who had struggled in behind. Gabe leaned against a huge basalt boulder and got between the two. Legs of rubber, spitting blood, dehydrated and exhausted, Gabe, in the best British hard-man tradition, continued down.

In such a fashion, the trio began to descend the mountain. The British team had a radio, and contact was made with the park office. Park director Phil Snyder, an expat, contacted Jonah, and a makeshift African rescue team was formed. The rescue team began to go up the track from the Sirimon River, hoping to intercept Gabe's party as they went down via Shipton's Caves.

The trio slowly descended and, at Shipton's Caves, at about thirteen thousand feet, Gabe needed to rest. Despite the drop in altitude, Gabe's breathing was erratic, and he continued to hack up blood and tissue from his lungs.

Darkness was all around. Still drooling blood spittle—white exhaustion—no percentage in trying anymore. Needing to crap,

Gabe hung on to the two bodies and evacuated his bowels. Bill wiped his ass somewhat clean. For someone with Gabe's sacred pact with self-reliance, this signaled that all was lost. As a baby, Gabe had to be tied into a rocking chair with a tea towel and rocked to sleep. He would not succumb to the ministrations of others, his own mother included. And now he couldn't wipe his own ass. All was lost.

Then the mother of all nightmares began for Gabe. He was positioned in his sleeping bag and tucked into his bivouac sack. His breathing continued to be erratic and difficult. The doctor injected Gabe with morphine to relax his breathing center, at which time Gabe proceeded to die. No heartbeat and no breathing. The doctor tried CPR, to no avail.

Crying, Bill yelled at Gabe, "Don't you die on me you son of a bitch!"

Bill realized he must go back and tell Cindy, with her infant daughter, that Gabe had died. Knowing Gabe would want everyone to know how he went out, Bill grabbed his camera and took a photo of Gabe's cyanotic body held in the embrace of the bivouac sack. Tawny elephant grass and basalt boulders full of lichen framed the funeral pyre.

As he lay still and dead in the grass on Mt. Kenya, Gabe's life—his reality—shifted. He was . . .

In a sea of green—waves like water in benzene, of perfect proportion—no surface chop, no whitecaps—fluid, green, gigantic waves. And floating. Warm. Safe. Huge waves worlds high—safe—no fearful relativity. No uncomfortable sense of perspective. Green waves worlds high—galaxies high—huge—floating—safe—secure.

Then, a restrictive tunnel—not so much freedom. Yet not so much restrictive as . . . focused. A wave turned in on itself—a huge, subprimal force refined and focused . . . inwardly.

From the perspective of ten feet overhead, Gabe dispassionately saw passing French climbers looking at a body, blue-faced and calm, in a bivouac sack, hands instinctively in the crotch area, perhaps the last act of searching for an umbilical cord lost a lifetime ago. There were shrugs, the marshaled acknowledgment of a really bad deal. Knowing that to empathize was an invitation to weakness and inability, the Frenchmen moved on and up the mountain.

The essence of Gabe's life was like water in a sea anchor, the anchor permeable, allowing the flow of water within and without, yet separating and manifesting the shape of a life. Humanity and relativity of being, like the sea anchor, were held fast by the body, mind, and . . . reality. The essence wanted to merge with the ocean that also gave it form.

Then, the anchors were severed—the mind, the body, the relativity of being were gone. Reality collapsed. Floating, floating away on slow manta wings, reality disappeared—gone—no form.

Then, choice—a speck of dust in the focused eye of the godhead. Choice—not a thing, but a manifestation of the stardust of being. Choice. And choice was real—the only thing real.

Faced with the impossible task of, again, living—giving form where none existed—Gabe dreamed himself . . . back to life—dreamed his world . . . back to . . . reality.

As an artist, his dreams were brushstrokes on a huge, empty canvas. Gabe dreamed back his reality.

And then, having resisted and gained release from the force of peace, the force of calm—the force of death—he reentered the maelstrom. He was, again, in the storm of morphine nightmares and hallucinations.

Gabe's wife's grandfather, an old Wyoming rancher, perched like a vulture at his feet and said, "Aw hell, you're dead. Goddammit, just give it up."

Then, in a necrotic metamorphosis, the old man decayed in front of him—still talking. His talk degraded to jabbering and then into primal animal squeals and screeches. Finally, a skull screaming, demon-like. To follow were other nightmares—too awful for Gabe to ever recount—involving loved ones and himself.

Then, there was the image of a black man in an anorak who stood silently at the foot of Gabe's bed in a hospital. Gabe heard religious singing—the songs of God from the Bible school days of his youth. Gabe was angry—he had died and left a daughter without a father—a wife without a husband—the breaking of personal commitments.

Gabe began to regain consciousness and saw the source of the religious singing—the polished, obsidian faces of African nuns.

A wrinkled French mother superior standing beside Gabe's hospital bed said in thickly accented English, "We pray for you. We sing for you."

Gabe closed his throbbing eyes and tried to hook on to some form of reality. He lay there in bed for days and continued to hear the words of the old shaman dressed in monkey skins offered days and years before, "*N'gai whispers your death,* mzungu. *When you hear the death whisper, you will know a bit of my craft.*"

Gabe recovered in the mission hospital outside Nyeri. However, this experience unhooked him from what most experience in their day-to-day lives as reality. Gabe had simply . . . dreamed himself alive—re-created his entire life. For decades to follow, Gabe remained fearful for the resiliency of his dream. He expected to wake from his dreaming at any time to find himself below Firmin's Tower . . . swallowed by death.

8

KENYA, 2005

GABE WOKE TO THE COOING OF DOVES IN THE PARK OUTSIDE the Hotel Tropic. Red-eyed and with a roaring jet-lag headache, he decided he needed to get out of Nairobi and on to Naro Moro *pese-pese* (quickly). Avoiding the bathroom of his hotel room, Gabe walked downstairs past the old man who maintained his catatonic vigil over his greasy, dog-eared guest book. Gabe walked past the market and visited the public latrine that was not much better than the facilities in his hotel. He then ambled to the New Stanley and dove into the breakfast buffet, taking his repast alfresco—away from the clanging, banging, and loud talk of the dining room with its green jungle motif. Eating mango and melon with toast, sweet butter, and marmalade, Gabe washed down the food with a cup of strong coffee heavily diluted with milk. He thoughtfully savored each bite of a passion fruit's dark flesh as he mused about his plans to study the reputed witchcraft and paranormal activities of a band of N'dorobo supposedly living secretly on the northern slopes of Mt. Kenya.

For the past year, local farmers had reported to the DC (district commissioner) their loss of goats and livestock, which allegedly were being used in witchcraft ceremonies by a band of wild men living in the dark forests of Mt. Kenya. One family outside Nanyuki even claimed their infant boy had been abducted by unseen perpetrators and sacrificed in some arcane ritual. The body of the boy was later found along a track on the north side of Mt. Kenya, but the police said the forest's scavengers had rendered any forensics inconclusive. For all they knew, the boy could have been taken by a leopard and then partially devoured before the cat was spooked off the kill.

Jonah N'tembe was a park ranger who often walked the forests and moors of Mt. Kenya, to aid those in trouble after a bad storm, the sick, the injured—or just if he felt something amiss on his mountain. En route to McKinder's Camp, where a climber had been reported to be seriously ill with altitude sickness, he reported seeing a camp of N'dorobo off the Chogoria Track. Curious as to the business of these forest people, Jonah had gone back to the site of the N'dorobo camp only to find a forest devoid of any sign of habitation. All signs of the campsite were gone, even for the sharp-eyed ranger. The N'dorobo had melted and disappeared like the morning mist in the hot equatorial sun. Thinking such a thing was unusual, Jonah reported the incident to the DC.

Porters carrying loads to McKinder's Camp also had reported seeing forest people dressed in skins watching them from the edge of the forest as they ascended what was called the Vertical Bog on Mt. Kenya.

In correspondence to the DC and the curator of anthropology for the Nairobi Museum, Gabe had learned that, indeed, there might be a remnant band of N'dorobo living in the forests of the northern slopes of Mt. Kenya. In a phone conversation with fellow Explorers Club member and past head of Kenyan government services, Richard Leakey, Gabe had learned of the tales of the N'dorobo Dream Walkers of the Emergency, as the Mau Mau revolt was now referred to by ex-colonials. Leakey had been initiated as a Kikuyu tribesman and, hence, knew much about the histories and cultural practices of Kenyan tribes. Leakey reported to Gabe that a number of the N'dorobo incidents appeared to be again taking the shape of the Dream Walker assassinations of the Emergency.

In confidence, Leakey also told Gabe of hearing whispers from upcountry about a resurgence of oathing ceremonies in the area around Nanyuki and Nyeri. It appeared that KARU, the Kenya African Restoration Union, a splinter group from the powerful Kenyan political party KANU (Kenya African National Union), was staging rallies and making bad talk against Kenya's new president, Mathew Odinga.

It seemed that KARU members were, for the most part, from the Kalidan tribes of Kenya—a conglomeration of small, splintered tribes accounting for less than ten percent of the nation's population. The N'dorobo were a Kalidan tribe, as were the Meru and the Kipsigi. These small, politically weak tribes were dominated by the Kikuyu, the largest and most powerful tribe in Kenya. Government legislation was about to be passed that would effectively disenfranchise the Kalidan tribes and force them from their lands around Mt. Kenya. Clearly, the Kikuyu saw the rich farmland—good for growing tea, coffee, and pyrethrum—as prizes to be distributed among its brethren.

Some KARU bosses were said to be organizing assassination cells and borrowing the Mau Mau oathing ceremonies as a means to ensure security and loyalty to the cause. Also, Abraham Okande, the head of security for KARU, was said to have ties with many unsavory parties, such as the Jihad Martyrs Brotherhood—a spin-off of the Al Qaeda organization, which funded the embassy bombing in Nairobi five years before. Leakey felt the weird juju reported on and around Mt. Kenya was not so much an anthropological concern as it was a threat to the young nation's security and stability.

Pledging the help and support of his offices, Leakey asked Gabe about the doings of The Explorers Club, and was particularly interested in the exotic fare of the last annual dinner, always held at the Waldorf in New York. Then Leakey signed off and Gabe looked at his notepad, trying to unravel the myth, magic, and political realities of this Gordian knot.

Gabe's research work and intelligence gathering had evidenced a consistent pattern of invisible N'dorobo assassins, entire N'dorobo villages that would appear and disappear like rain-forest brigadoons, and an undercurrent of an age-old tribal secret held by the N'dorobo. The secret hinted at ceremony and sacraments that gave the ability to be a Skin Changer, or even disappear and traverse large distances—a sort of jungle astral projection. Gabe's academic interests were in the ceremony and sacraments that supposedly resulted in such fantastic abilities. Simply, Gabe found cultural magic to be intensely interesting, offering an intriguing proposition for one's own growth and evolution.

Gabe's plan to study the N'dorobo was simple: taking a page out of the book of animal behavior field studies. He would simply make camp in an area rich with sign, and wait. As Jane Goodall did with chimpanzees and Joy Adamson did with lions, Gabe would do with the N'dorobo. After all, the N'dorobo were as much of the forests as the *bongo* or the buffalo.

Gabe walked back from the New Stanley. Feeling the itch to get on with it, he went back to the Hotel Tropic and signed out. Not wanting to hump his gear to the Fairview and then, again, to Naro Moro, Gabe checked his duffel with the old man at the Hotel Tropic. He canceled his reservations at the Fairview and tottered on down toward River Road in search of transport to Naro Moro, his giant pack listing back and forth beneath his strides.

Forgoing the *matatus,* Gabe found a Peugeot taxi that would take him directly to the Naro Moro River Lodge and charge him the equivalent of fifteen dollars. He placed his Lowe Expedition pack in the backseat behind the driver and unfolded himself beside it, behind the British shotgun seat on the left. Gabe saw the dash of the taxi decorated in gold lace with tassels shaking back and forth, activated by the potholes of the Kenyan freeway. It seemed as if Mama M'Binga was omnipresent, as the tinny radio issued her wails of emotion. Gabe vacantly stared out at the culture of urban Africa.

They soon were in upcountry Kenya, where the asphalt roads were bordered by the red lines of footpaths, the red soil of Kenya exposed by millions of bare feet. Here, rural Kenyans commuted between their gathering of water or cutting of firewood and their mud-and-wattle homes. Gabe wondered at the depth of desperation represented by so much humanity with so little currency to support it. Shaking his head free of these cobwebs of despair, Gabe studied a text on the Mau Mau and its tidbits of perspective on the Dream Walker assassins. Gabe had retrieved a situation report filed by military intelligence and declassified under the Freedom of Information Act that included some interesting information on the purported mythology of the assassinations of colonial loyalists and military personnel, including a nightmarish account from a former UDT man named Jimmy.

Gabe read the hellish account and its impossible reporting.

Gabe wished he had taken enough time to track down this Jimmy, who was said to have experienced an actual assassination attempt of a mystical or supernatural nature.

Gabe wrote some notes in his journal and found himself, again, reflecting on the Kenyan countryside and its people. The Peugeot taxi raced by the cheap hotels of villages, harboring the traveling salesmen of a third-world country. The markets were a blur of color and slow-moving people.

Gabe caught his first glimpse of Mt. Kenya as the taxi rounded a corner and plied on toward the lodge. There, its summits cloaked in clouds, rose the gray-green base of Kerrinyaga, Mt. Kenya, the home of God—N'gai. The vegetation beside the road was thicker and lusher now. The taxi lurched onward as the radio blared what sounded to Gabe like Cajun accordion music. For so many years now, and so many times, Gabe had come up the A-2 Highway with Mt. Kenya as his goal. He saw little change.

The Peugeot slowed as Gabe saw the sign on the A-2 for the Naro Moro River Lodge.

"Go to the lodge. Don't stop here," directed Gabe, realizing he did not want to hoof the kilometer plus. Sure, the entry to the lodge on foot would be soft and gentle and offered some advantages, but he was ready to get on with his job.

The taxi plied on over the gravel-and-dirt road, gearing down as the parking lot came into view. Gabe hefted his pack out of the taxi, paid the driver, and strode deliberately to the lodge's front desk. He checked into his climber's cabin and deposited his pack in the front room of the rustic abode. Nearly two o'clock; they would still be serving lunch.

Gabe took a table on the lawn, and a familiar waiter with his earlobes looped over the top of his ears took his order. The White Cap beer came quickly. Gabe drained the brown bottle and ordered another to come with his sandwich. The roast beef sandwich with horseradish and chips quieted the rumblings of Gabe's stomach, and he finished off his repast with Kenyan AA coffee, Stilton cheese, and a passion fruit.

Gabe went back to the climber's cabin and began sorting gear and food. With obsessive-compulsive drive, Gabe sorted, stacked, and packed his gear according to when he would likely need it. He then turned to his food stores, purchased in the market and at an Indian not-so-super market. The afternoon clouds blunted the edge of the tropical sun. The lodge had been a haven for so many years now. For Gabe, sitting on the cabin's porch was like sitting with an old friend. Gabe smiled to himself as the insects hummed in the last warmth of the day. The clouds, heavy with rain, and the setting sun displayed an amazing performance of shadow-puppetry as Gabe sorted and packaged.

Gabe bagged the dried milk and placed the plastic package in the breakfast pile lying on the rough wooden floor of the cabin. He then methodically repackaged the instant soup bases and spices in another bag. The first tear came, unbidden, and dropped into the rolled oats. Gabe's vision clouded over as the tears streamed silently down his face. His stare was focused not on the packaged food, but rather, into another decade that was, for him, full of pain.

In 1974, during the peak of another killing drought in East Africa, Gabe and his expedition had come to the luxuriant Kenyan coast for R and R after a month on a field expedition up the Galana River. They had been in search of a tool-making site reported by one of Louis Leakey's student grunts, working the digs at Olduvai. For a month they dodged mambas, crocs, and hippos—never finding the treasure of chipped obsidian they looked for. After camp was made at Ras N'gomeni, the expedition members began to dispose of their rancid, wet stores, throwing the moldy bags of oats and maize meal in what looked like a public dump.

Soon, a throng of Kamba women and children appeared and began to create a vision of hell on earth. The eyes of the women grew feral as they fought one another for the bags of garbage. The dead eyes of their pot-bellied, stick-legged children reflected nothing at all. They fought with desperation—over garbage. A small kisu *was pulled by one of the women, and then another woman lay still, bleeding. A stick-figure boy squatted over his gutted mother and dumbly watched as her intestines, lying like rope on the dusty ground, still churned, pink, gray, and liquid.*

Gabe intervened and sent for the police. However, the desperate crowd still throbbed with intense violence.

Gabe cried out, "Hapanna! Hapanna! *(No! No!)* Nataka chakula? Sow-sow." *(Need food? Okay).*

Gabe's voice thundered over the crowd of women and children. He and his tent mate, Mitch, began to reclaim the garbage to repackage the spoiled food in hand-sized rations.

Gabe, looming over the crowd, formed a line with the women and tried to assure the mothers in his mzungu *Swahili that they would all receive some food. Gabe's mind became unhooked. He was sobbing without knowing it as he went about the business of repackaging the garbage. He watched himself as from a great distance—packaging garbage for the children of Africa.*

Mitch just silently sobbed and kept saying, "Oh my God. Oh my God."

He finally grew silent and, with his chin on his chest, bundled the garbage, not daring to look up.

Gabe could not shoulder the burden. He remembered seeing a stash of the expedition's miscellaneous expense money thrown carelessly in an open bag next to the topo maps in the Land Rover. He directed Mitch to finish the repackaging and cautiously went to the

Land Rover. He grabbed a big handful of the brown five-shilling notes and quickly stuffed them into his pocket.

Gabe and Mitch ceremoniously handed out one package of garbage to each of the women, who now stood docile and cow-like, eyes on the supply of plastic-wrapped filth. If a woman had a child, they were given five shillings, compliments of Gabe's theft. Gabe couldn't believe he was doing this. He knew the rancid food would cause diarrhea and further debilitate the women and children, who were already dehydrated and malnourished. The five shillings, in reality, were empty offerings, like shoveling shit against the tide. Most of the children would be dead within the month. Gabe had robbed from the rich to give to the dead.

Gabe watched the night claim the coast, the reflected light turning the sea a molten gold. His spirit was burned and dry from the day's horror. He sat in the thatched shelter of the Harambe Bar and nursed his banana beer, watching the leper dance in the deepening shadows. His was a mixture of guilt for stealing the money and uncut horror at what he had seen and been a part of. Mitch had simply walked off without saying a word after the rations of garbage had been doled out. The last Gabe saw of him, he had crawled into a fetal position inside the mosquito netting enclosure of their tent.

Somehow, some way, Gabe felt he must repay the theft. To have both theft and poisoning on his mind was too great a burden. In the morning, when they went to Mombassa, Gabe would find a job and replace the stolen funds.

In the shantytowns and in the huddled warrens of third-world countries, people just lie down where the reaper takes them, and die. Removal of the bodies requires human intervention. The presence of a dead body somehow makes itself known up and down the alleys of a shantytown, carried by the line of nonverbal communication within these pits of despair. Untouchable workers, having no other hope, are charged with removing the corpses and disposing of them in a purifying inferno. Such employment Gabe found in Mombassa.

Each man on the crew had a handcart made of rough wooden slats on a basic steel frame, with old lorry tires jury-rigged on a crude iron axle. On Gabe's cart, there was an iron yoke one could grasp for better purchase and leverage in wheeling around the necrotic cargo. The flatbed of the cart could accept two to three bodies across, depending on the size of the deceased, but three was the rule. Gabe, with his strong Western muscles, could haul up to nine bodies on his cart—three layers of three corpses across. Crunching, crunching, the cart was wheeled to the crematorium on the beach, just in view of a mosque.

The bodies of the dead were like husks—light and free of the gravity of life. Gabe would reverently and gently pick up these husks of recent humanity and carefully stack them on his cart. At first, the smell of bowels set free of this world assaulted Gabe's senses. Rarely could he stack the bodies without an unspeakable stain appearing on his forearms or chest. Gabe wore the feces, blood, pus, and urine like medals and epaulets on a ghoul's uniform. He learned that feces and urine are death's fanfare.

Gabe's epiphany of horror came one morning as the dhows were coming in from the evening's fishing for jack mackerel. Wheeling his cart, Gabe was aware only of the syncopation of tires on dirt in the giant shadow of predawn as he made his way to the shantytown. There, by the road, a man in a long white robe who sold shells to tourists by day silently pointed up a lane. Gabe doggedly pulled his cart up the lane as the lean-tos and housing took on a more desperate nature. Gabe plied his trade through the early morning.

The eyes of a disheveled woman dressed in cheap merikany *cloth demanded Gabe's attention. She pointed with her chin down a dark alley between rows of shacks made of tin and cardboard. Old newspapers scattered about the alleyway flagged in the coastal breeze, and Gabe could see dark, shapeless forms slowly going about their business. The dark wraiths sat around billycans in which burned meager cook fires that coaxed only a slight modicum of flavor from tired tea leaves. Gabe smelled feces and knew he had found work.*

There she was—a woman wrapped in brown, gauzy shrouds, lying still as death, for she was . . . dead. There, among the Blue Boy butter can and other litter, a Daily Nation *newspaper as a blanket and a cardboard as mattress, a woman had simply quit living. Gabe squatted and studied the crypt and the corpse.*

As he gathered up the shell of a body, a weight tumbled out of the folds of the shroud. Gabe looked down to see a caricature of a female infant lying laconic on the floor of the hut. Its nakedness revealed a swollen belly and puffy labia with stick-like legs and arms. The baby could not have weighed more than fifteen pounds.

It laboriously breathed, conserving its energy, not crying out as it tumbled to the floor. The infant's eyes shuttered closed and then slowly opened. Its eyes were rheumy and milky and somehow frog-like as they slowly opened and closed. Gabe's mind raced. Already seriously beyond things human, Gabe could not make choices as he was used to. Here, he had a dead mother and a near-dead infant in a country defined by death. He chose quite quickly.

He stacked the mother onto the corpse of a man whose fingers had been devoured by rats. He placed the docile daughter on the belly of the corpse. It snuggled into the cold flesh of its mother with no disruptive movement. With haste, Gabe wheeled his cart to the crematorium pit. There, he set aside the infant and mother, placing the corpses of three others like cordwood onto the kindling of the timbers soaked in kerex fuel. Gabe touched off the blaze and watched as the bodies contracted and shrank, their fingers and faces incinerated, shrinking rather than expanding, as did the Fourth of July snakes on the hot concrete of a Nebraska summer. He gently picked up the mother and placed her on the fire. The fire was really kindled now and consumed the corpse in an orange halo.

Then, Gabe picked up the infant girl and detected the shallow breathing as its belly billowed slowly, softly. The infant gave a lazy yawn and closed its eyes, as though tired of the world—tired of life. Held in his hands, the infant was beyond living, beyond understanding, in this world of death. Gabe placed the girl on the fire with its mother. It uttered only a slight mewing noise as the flames delivered it from life.

Gabe walked back to the shantytown, the wheels of his cart crunching on the dirt track, the iron yoke supporting his arms as he made his way back. He was done for the day—done forever. He collected his daily pay, got blinding drunk on pombe, *and woke in the dark of the night to the mewing noise of an infant being burned to death. Just as he would wake for decades to follow.*

Gabe finished repackaging food stores for his trip in search of the N'dorobo. He felt empty. His spirit was as thin as a rail.

Go nuts on your own time, Gabe had often offered as advice to his best friend, a psychologist with a penchant for going nuts on Gabe's time. Gabe went nuts on the porch of the climber's cabin, on his own time.

His eyes still wet and red, Gabe found a strange solace in individually packaging his toilet paper and matches in double bags. He sat on the porch of the cabin in the gathering dusk of a White Highlands evening. The sweet smell of a softwood fire in the lodge, the gurgling of the stream, the smell of diesel and charcoal from nearby huts helped bring Gabe out of his malaise. With a crooked smile, he reflected on the risks of packaging food.

From Naro Moro, Gabe got transport via a Land Rover from the lodge to the Mutindua market with its half dozen houses, and then on to the Forestry Department Station and the gate to Mt. Kenya National Park. He signed into the battered accountant's ledger that served as the government's formal park register and paid his fees to both the national park and the Meru County Council for track usage. Forgoing the good campsite at the station, Gabe and the driver forged on up the track past the Bairunyi Clearing on to the Chogoria Bandas at three thousand meters. There, he off-loaded his pack, paid his driver, and slowly plodded up the Nithi Gorge.

Gabe made camp in the dwindling light and quickly organized the camp in the camphor-and-bamboo forest. His Jansport tent, designed for four, provided luxurious accommodation. He methodically organized his gear to be available at a moment's notice. Such organization had served him well in many epics and crises of the past on both climbing and field expeditions.

With his MSR stove heating his pot of water, Gabe relaxed and let the forest take him in. The silence was total. No birds, no noise issued from the wall of green leaves and moss. The stove rumbled softly, and Gabe became aware of the sound of his own heart beating fast, his breathing seemingly just skimming, barely fulfilling his need for oxygen.

He focused on the forest canopy and spotted a black-and-white streak that suggested a colobus monkey in flight. He shifted his gaze toward the green tunnels of bamboo around camp and saw the yellowish green of a vervet monkey nosing toward his camp. Gabe waited in the gathering gloom as the clouds down below marched up the Nithi Valley and coated the camp in fog and vapors. He settled in for the long wait.

Every morning, Gabe would conduct a concentric-circle survey of his campsite. Using his Magellan GPS unit, Gabe trekked out and scoured the jungle for any sign of the elusive N'dorobo. He found only a billycan and a broken honey pot for his trouble. In a clearing, he found an old campfire made in the bowels of a camphor tree, but saw no recent evidence of habitation. Already a week into his first field staging, Gabe wondered what he was really doing with the Babsons' money.

9

KENYA, 2005

RALPH BAZAAN WOKE EARLY AND SURVEYED HIS ENVIRONMENT without opening his eyes. The Kikuyu whore's ministrations of the night before were a vague memory. How he had arrived where he was unfolded in his mind, and he relaxed. He had come awake hungry, and quickly pulled on his *Batas* after donning his *kikoy* shirt and khaki pants in the small room of the Norfolk. He found the breakfast buffet in full swing and savored every bite of omelet, fruit, and toast. He quickly chased down his breakfast with sweetened chai and purchased a *Daily Nation* from the lobby proprietor, as well as a cigar for his enjoyment during the late-afternoon cocktail hour.

His jaw clenched slightly as he saw the article on page three. It was, for him, a cue to act. Scanning down the page, Bazaan found the coded location of his dead-drop for instructions. Methodically going through the code of columns, words, pages, and lines, Bazaan learned his dead-drop was the Kumbu Kumbu shop in Nairobi's Intercontinental Hotel. The Kumbu Kumbu shop was an upscale handicraft shop that specialized in the wood carvings of the Kamba and Makonde. It was prearranged that he would ask if a consignment for Mr. Chen had come in, a Kamba Tree of Life carved in ebony. Mr. Chen was his cover while in Kenya—a buyer of handicrafts for Pier One Exports.

Bazaan walked across town, past the post office and its two dozen pay phones, on to the Intercontinental Hotel. The queues for the phones were thirty deep, shiftless young men and women making a phone call a social event. Regardless of whether the phones actually worked—or if they even knew how to use them—-it was *in* to be seen in Kenya using a phone, evidence of how modern one was. Bazaan walked through the continental-style lobby past the fresh flowers that filled every nook and cranny of the main floor with a sweet, spicy aroma.

He made his way through the hotel entrance to the Kumbu Kumbu shop. Upon entering the shop the smell shifted from lilies to wood and polish. Here, thousands of ebony carvings filled the upscale shop, which was laced with batik art and jewelry. The verdite pendants and silver or gold bracelets were crafted like those supposedly made from elephant hair and offered by the hucksters in the market.

Bazaan went to the desk, where a pretty Indian woman was working figures on her calculator. She was slender, with long black hair and malt-ball eyes. She seemed to wear a constant smirk.

"Do you have a consignment for Ralph Chen?" asked Bazaan. "It is a Kamba Tree of Life."

The Indian woman went to a stack of papers on the small desk, rifled through them quickly, snatched a stapled series of sheets, and, without speaking, went into an alcove off from the shop. She tottered back, carrying with both hands a Tree of Life—the African totem pole—this one nearly three feet tall. The black of the ebony contrasted with the streak of yellow at the base, as was common in ebony carvings. It was a work of incredible detail and nearly shouted its status as true art.

Bazaan studied the magnificent piece and said, "The price was confirmed at 750 U.S. Is that correct?"

"Yes, that is correct," said the brown beauty.

Bazaan regarded her heavy arm hair and mused that her nether region would also be heavily hairy. He had taken more than his share of northern Indian women while working as a mercenary among the Sikhs. He rather enjoyed the downy black hair on their upper thighs and their lush, dark, soft triangle of pubic hair.

"I need to ship it by post to the U.S. Can you expedite that here?"

The pretty clerk answered, "Of course. Shipping to America?"

"Yes. Here is the address," said Bazaan as he handed the woman a Pier One Imports business card.

"That will be $850 U.S. How do you wish to pay for this?"

Bazaan produced an American Express card in the name of Ralph Chen, and the clerk ran it through, but did not bother swiping the card.

"The lines are down today. Haven't been able to raise American Express all morning. Anyway, here is your receipt, Mr. Chen, and your chit for customs. Thank you for your business."

Bazaan thanked the woman and sauntered out the door. It was past eleven o'clock, and he went to the Hilton Hotel coffee shop and set his receipt and a tablet down on the table. Sipping strong coffee treated with milk and sugar, Bazaan decoded the receipt. The decryption indicated the meeting would be held today at one thirty p.m. at the African Heritage Restaurant.

Bazaan took a circuitous route to the greatest offering of traditional African cuisine in Nairobi—the African Heritage Restaurant. He idled in the restaurant's handicraft shop, established behind the restaurant proper. Here, an assortment of African handicrafts were on sale for at least fifty percent more than one could find in the markets. He studied the seventy-five-dollar Maasai spears and the hundred-dollar Maasai masks. He bought a cheap musical instrument made of hollowed wood with pieces of steel tabs instead of strings. He paid with a thousand-shilling note, which made the clerk have to raid the restaurant cash to make change.

Bazaan saw Kaleem and Hussaf take a seat and quickly approached their table, offering a silent greeting as the Middle Easterners offered a "hello" without enthusiasm. Kaleem was dressed in an ill-fitting suit that bound his paunchy body. He had hooded lizard eyes and a mouth that was perpetually turned down. Like a giant chameleon, Kaleem studied Bazaan, his dark brown eyes apparently half closed. Hussaf, in contrast, dressed in a suit tailored on Savoy Street and had a lithe, bird-like body with the sharp eyes of a raptor. His high cheekbones and ascetically thin face framed a visage that spoke volumes of his religious zeal, his insanity.

Hussaf, the more affable of the two Arabs, ordered for the three of them. They ate spicy okra and yams, *ndizi* and *ugale*. Chapatis were in endless supply. All three washed their dinner down with passion fruit juice, switching over to mango juice and coffee for desert. Hussaf was the first to talk business.

"We had only one chance for you to earn your money. Now we have two targets for which you'll earn more than three times as much," said Hussaf.

Bazaan, unprepared for any changes, offered no response. He had taken the job that surfaced on his secure Web site because it got him closer to the source of his obsession. The splinter cell whose predecessors had masterminded the U.S. embassy bombings in Nairobi and Tanzania and perpetrated the 9/11 nightmare had, for their own reasons, apparently formed a relationship with KARU. Through the cell, KARU was offering Bazaan one million dollars U.S. to terminate the new Kenyan president, Mathew Odinga. Wanting to get closer to the source of the Dream Walker assassins, Bazaan had eagerly accepted the job. He had cleared with his employers that he would arrive in Kenya several weeks early to pursue some holiday relaxation prior to the job.

"And who is the other target?" asked Bazaan.

Hussaf said softly, "I want to make this clear. The second target is most definitely a secondary target—gravy, as you Westerners would say. Your priority is to welcome Odinga to the hereafter. If possible, take the other target. If you succeed only with Odinga, you will receive the one million dollars U.S. we've agreed to. If you do take number two down as well, your compensation is three and a half million dollars."

"Who is the second target?" asked Bazaan.

Kaleem spoke with a sneer. "The vice president of the United States."

He belched after making the proclamation and mopped up some of the *ugale* gravy with a chapati.

All three men sipped their coffee silently as the waiter noisily removed their dishes. The restaurant was in full midday swing.

Bazaan wondered about the new scope to his job, not immune from thoughts of an additional two and a half million dollars. How had Baker, a replacement for an unhealthy elected VP, come to figure in his equation?

"Why the American vice president?" Bazaan asked simply.

Kaleem now took the tiller of the conversation.

"The vice president is an exclamation point. If we can take out both, what hope is left for KANU and its political hopefuls? This is a gift from Allah. We could never have hoped to demonstrate such strength with the assassination of the leader of a comical shit-load country. Now we can quell any thoughts of resistance by killing one so tightly protected and of such importance. Kill only Odinga and it could still be seen as a lucky fluke. Kill Baker, and the fluke becomes a deadly capability."

"Do you have an itinerary for VP Baker?" asked Bazaan.

"Yes. It seems the new Kenyan president is worth a brief audience at a breakfast, and then Baker and Odinga will jointly break ground on the new industrial park outside Westlands that is funded by the IMF. He will then fly to the Maasai Mara reserve and join Richard Leakey at the Keekorok Lodge. There, they will dedicate the new anti-poaching fleet of helicopters funded by the Safari Club International. He will stay one night at Keekorok and then fly out the following morning."

"Where is the vice president staying?" asked Bazaan.

"He will be staying one night at the presidential compound and one night at Keekorok. They have taken all cabins and facilities at Keekorok. Also, the entire Mara reserve will be inundated with security and soldiers. Trying to stage your job there may be a lot of squeeze for the juice, as you Americans would say."

Bazaan stayed focused and asked, "When is the vice president scheduled to arrive?"

Hussaf replied, "July twenty-eight at eight p.m. at Jomo Kenyatta Airport. He will depart Nairobi on July thirtieth at eight a.m., again from Jomo Kenyatta Airport—if you are unsuccessful."

Bazaan counted and realized he had over a month before the arrival of Baker. What with the planning process and the setting up of exfiltration, he had a full three weeks to focus on his research of the Dream Walker assassins.

He had, through channels of the old Russian GRU, obtained a tome of information on the Dream Walkers. The documents included names and the field evaluations of two dozen assassinations. Bazaan had consistently seen the name of an old shaman called Terrari surface, again and again, as a ringleader of the Mau Mau and an N'dorobo adept in such arcane abilities. It was reported that after the Kenyan *Uhuru*, or independence from Britain, Terrari had discreetly taken up a squatter's residence in a single-room hut northwest of the Naro Moro River Lodge on a co-op project farm on the Ewaso Ng'iro River.

Bazaan, using a webmail account, had e-mailed two of his old lieutenants who had thrown in with Ralph after many a commercial war together. He would need their help on this increasingly demanding job and wouldn't mind their company on his research trip to Naro Moro and Mt. Kenya. Jesus and Edgar Sanchez were brothers from the barrio in West LA. Escaping a judge's sentence for theft and assault, the Sanchez brothers were given an alternative to incarceration—joining the Marine Corps. Due to their physicality and deceptive intelligence, the brothers both mustered into Special Forces as Marine Recons. They thrived in the heavy machismo warrior environment. They became very proficient at their trade. During the early days of the ill-fated Ethiopian peacekeeping mission, the Sanchez brothers had infiltrated Mogadishu some days before the televised SEAL landing that was a comical military goat-fuck.

The Sanchez brothers operated out of a *banda* owned by a longtime local friendly who did odd jobs for America's alphabet-soup agencies. The trouble started the day before the SEAL landing. Drunk on banana beer, Edgar decided to dip his wick in the honey pot of a pretty Ethiopian housekeeper. Fighting with unusual ferocity for someone so small, the housekeeper produced a kitchen knife and tried to stab Edgar in the heart. Luckily for Edgar and unluckily for the housekeeper, the knife glanced off his crucifix and slid along his ribs, opening a nice, even cut. Edgar, without thinking, broke the woman's neck and released her body, which fell in a heap at his feet. Sobered by the act,

Edgar found Jesus dozing in the equatorial sun outside the *banda*. He simply took his brother by the arm, escorted him into the *banda,* pointed at the body, and shrugged his shoulders.

The brothers, without speaking, packed their gear, quickly hiked to a remote beach, and waited for night. Under the cover of dark, and disguised as best they could as local merchants, they hired a car to take them as far away from Mogadishu as possible. They were simply swallowed up by the Dark Continent and found a wild freedom for their efforts. They lived by their wits and nerve for months thereafter.

When attacked by *shifta* in southern Somalia, the Sanchez brothers succeeded in killing five of the bandits before the leader offered the brothers a job, rather than a panga's blade. They had found home in the belly of the beast that was modern Africa.

Bazaan had met the Sanchez brothers in a bar outside Lamu. Between beers and war stories, Bazaan discreetly slid a card to Jesus. The laminated card had only a phone number on it.

"If you ever need private work, give that number a call," said Bazaan.

"Yah mon, I'll keep this safe next to my fucking heart," replied Jesus.

Calls were subsequently made. Small wars in smaller countries were won by Bazaan and the Sanchez brothers. The trio popped a cap in the ass of many a big fish in a small pond. Regardless of the political or economic insignificance of their world, they plied their trade with deadly efficiency. It was only a matter of time before these farm-league mercs had a chance at the major leagues.

Now Bazaan and his regulars came to the attention of the Qaddafis and the Bin Ladens. They were at least commercially viable in the marketplace of international terrorism. They were now very wealthy thugs, murderers, solvers of problems, squelchers of hope. They were executive assassins.

⁂

Bazaan drained his coffee, placed the cup upside down on the saucer, and looked first at Kaleem, then at Hussaf. His gaze was steely and cold and forced the viper-eyed Kaleem to shift his eyes away, to his coffee and cigarette. Gathering his war face and the energy to give it power, Bazaan's eyes became dead and drew down on the dandy, Hussaf.

"I'll take your job, little sugar boy. But you'll be making it five million. All or nothing. I'll do both for the money as a package. If either one is undone, go back to fucking your fat English whores. I'll never bother you for a pence."

The zealot, Hussaf, and his toady saw only one thing in Bazaan's eyes—death. It was clear that whose death it was made little difference. Knowing KARU had placed their budget at seven million dollars, both wanted to close this deal and focus the death as far away from themselves as possible.

"Done," said Hussaf. As he slid an envelope wrapped in a *Daily Nation* newspaper across the table, he added, "Same arrangements as before. Here is the one hundred thousand U.S. for expenses. Good hunting, my friend, and be careful. We have grown to value your services."

Bazaan maintained his dead-eyed stare and lit his cigar. Without shifting his gaze from Hussaf, he exhaled a cloud of smoke in the face of the Arab.

"Quit tellin' me what to do, sugar boy."

Bazaan got up and took his newly purchased musical instrument and his newspaper with him. Plunking on the metal tabs of the harp, he turned to Hussaf and asked, "How much would they nick me for making it four bodies, sugar boy?"

Bazaan's glare was insanely cold now.

In a disembodied tone, Bazaan went on, "Don't ever change my plans again. You can ask me, but never tell me. If you ever do that again, by your sand-nigger's god, I'll slit your ball bag and string your fuckin' leg through it. Shalom, motherfucker."

Bazaan clenched his cigar in a grimace of a smile and disappeared into the diesel smoke and rabble of Nairobi, plunking a tuneless melody on his wood-and-tin harp.

Bazaan walked back through the afternoon chaos of Nairobi. The city seemed to have daily moods. The early dawn when, with no one watching, the city reverted to its primal beginnings—fields of tall grass and the shadows of lurking lions, circling vultures, and lanners steeping for the kill. Then, there was the lazy, hungover morning with the whole city fighting through the haze of too much *pombe* consumed in dank nightclubs with canvas walls and polished dirt floors. The early afternoon was a time to pay tribute to the bustle of modern-day Africa, a time of hope and a brief focus on the possibilities of tomorrow. In the late afternoon, the city had lost its momentum. Routines, most of despair, were a lockstep for the empty-eyed residents fighting to stay above the crypt that was night. Dark ghouls haunted the alleyways, which shimmered here and there, glowing with the dim light of kerosene lanterns. At night, with the city's eyes closed, people could retreat to the quiet release of sleep.

Bazaan walked up Harry Thuku Road, entered the Norfolk, and went directly to the gift shop. There, he purchased another cigar, vowing to save it for after dinner, then went directly to the bar. He ordered a gin and tonic from the Luo bartender and bit back the burn of cheap hooch as he took his first sip. Bazaan had sensed someone's presence. He tasted the air and casually looked down to study the shoes of the person who was approaching behind him. Bazaan had processed the data, but needed no more information when he heard the man speak.

"Hola chingazo. ¿Cómo se cuelga?" (Hello fucker. How's it hanging?)

"Está listo para tu boca, mi flor de marinero." (It's ready for your mouth, my flower sailor.)

Bazaan turned and embraced Jesus Sanchez and studied the bar at the same time. Jesus was a sinewy, muscular man in his prime. His small frame was literally packed with sharply defined muscles. Jesus's physicality was daunting and underscored the danger of the man. Bazaan, with a quick assessment, reconfirmed that he and Jesus were the only non-wogs in the place—even counting Indians.

"It is good to see you, *mi amigo*. Where is Edgar?"

"Trying to talk a college girl into sex, where else?" replied Jesus.

Bazaan ordered a second gin and tonic and an order of Kenyan chips. They clinked glasses and sipped their drinks. Bazaan offered the chips. Jesus squeezed a bunch together and dipped them in the runny sauce, slurping down the greasy logs. Bazaan studied him with care. The aura that surrounded him was the same as it had been in many of their previous wars. The man would never die in a war. He could die one-on-one or by himself, but never in a war. His spirit was strong.

Bazaan asked, "Jesus, are you fully equipped? How soon can you be ready to go upcountry?"

"Tomorrow," replied Jesus as he fished another load of chips into his maw.

Now it was Jesus' chance to study Bazaan. He smiled, munched his chips, and took a draw on his gin and tonic.

"You still chasin' the weird fuckin' juju?"

"I'm still interested in the Dream Walker assassins, if that's what you're asking."

Bazaan had shared his research into the Dream Walker assassins with the Sanchez brothers. They were definitely not interested and couldn't see the leverage. They would roll their eyes, but did humor Bazaan with his obsession.

"Everybody needs a hobby," said Jesus. The Dream Walker assassins were, for Bazaan, quickly becoming just that—a hobby. Such is the fruit of desire and no results.

Jesus continued to study Bazaan. Then he spoke in a quiet voice, "Bazaan, with modern laser technology and ballistics, you might as well be invisible. Why hell, man, you can take out a fucker at a half mile with a laser-painted bomblet. Why don't you just quit chasin' the voodoo shit and get better guns?"

"For some targets it's hard to get within a klick. So shut the fuck up, Jesus. I need you and your brother for a job next month. Wouldn't mind your sorry-ass company before then. In or out?"

"In," answered Jesus quickly.

"Okay, tomorrow we'll go to Naro Moro. There, on the road from Naro Moro to Lamuria, on the Ewaso Ng'iro River, we'll find and debrief a wog I've been looking for for quite some time—an old shaman called Terrari who is said to have been a Dream Walker assassin in the Mau Mau. He lives now on a squatters' plot on a co-op farm north and west of Naro Moro. We'll sweat his ass and make some headway toward this juju shit, as you call it."

Jesus finished off the plate of chips as Edgar walked into the bar, his arm around a cute Kenyan college girl.

"Hola feo. ¿Qué pasa?" said Edgar, his eyes mainly focused on the pert breasts of his Kikuyu maiden as he and Bazaan briefly embraced. Edgar was a slightly smaller version of his brother, Jesus. Edgar was slightly built, but had cordy muscles and an intense quickness about him. His face was noticeably thinner than Jesus'. His eyes moved constantly, like a predator's—always gleaming with a deadly intensity.

"And who might this be?" asked Bazaan, addressing the young lady Edgar wore on his arm.

"Oh, yeah. This is Shalita. She's studying international relations at the college and is looking for a little fieldwork—you know, a little hands-on work-study. I'm going to give her an oral exam, and if she passes, she is eligible for the Sanchez Foundation scholarship—you know—twenty bucks and a bottle of perfume."

Bazaan smiled and shook his head, turned to the bar, and ordered another round of drinks, including a gin and pink for Edgar's soft hook.

"Still chasin' spooks, Captain Ralph? Or are you here to do something of value?" asked Edgar as he nodded a thanks to Bazaan, who handed him and the woman their drinks. Edgar undraped his arm from his new girlfriend and held the drink in his left hand, careful to keep his right hand empty and unoccupied.

Bazaan responded evenly, "With your help and your obviously open mind, Edgar, I hope to do both. We have a real job next month—Alpha class. I thought you'd like to chase spooks with me for a few weeks before, get you good to go on the thing of value."

Bazaan's coding the job Alpha class indicated a seven-figure contract. Both Edgar and Jesus silently wondered at the target, or targets. Clearly, this was not going to be popping a cap in the ass of some jungle-bunny politico. Heavy money usually meant heavy lifting, even in the life of an assassin.

As Edgar pondered the possibilities, he drained his glass, put it down on the bar, and gathered the young woman to his side. He absently fondled the left breast of the college girl, who merely leaned into his shoulder offering him an affectionate giggle.

Jesus sipped his drink and studied his brother and the young, attractive woman. Clearly, an Alpha job took precedence over even the horniest of brothers with the prettiest of sluts. They needed to get down to business, and this distraction needed to be managed.

"Edgar, perhaps the young lady would like to accompany you and me to the restroom. You two can have your way with each other as I dissuade anyone from using the facilities. Then get rid of her and the three of us can have dinner together and focus on this—opportunity."

Edgar understood what his brother was trying to accomplish. He had to give it to Jesus, he was trying to minimize the distraction of this babe and manage the problem but still get him laid. *What a bro,* thought Edgar, for him to expedite the mediation of a problem and at the same time expedite his brother getting fucked.

"Sounds *bueno*. Let's go," answered Edgar as he led the Nubian bimbo through the growing crowd, Jesus running sweep. Shalita looked only mildly confused as they walked out into the courtyard of the Norfolk. Regardless of her confusion, she followed docile, with a hopeful smile on her pretty face.

No one was using the restroom, and Edgar and the woman strolled in, Jesus placing himself squarely in the doorway, and faced out. The woman was giggling as Edgar started caressing her upper thighs, cupping her firm buttocks with both hands. He scooped her up and placed her on the wide counter of sinks that ran the length of the room. When she saw Edgar lowering his head, she placed both hands on his head, directing him down between her thighs. The cheap cotton dress had ridden high over her thighs, exposing the dark triangle of wiry pubic hair.

Jesus smiled to himself as he heard the girl's giggling and, later, her moaning as Edgar pleasured himself, seemingly pleasuring the girl, as well. Jesus wiled away the next half hour thinking not of the sexual gymnastics going on in the restroom, but of Bazaan's Alpha job, which could make him a wealthy man.

"Damn! Shit!" Edgar cried as he uncoupled from the woman. He was afflicted with a charley horse as he stood up trying to straighten his leg and pound out the cramp.

"You okay in there?" asked Jesus, wondering about the shift from passionate outcries to those of pain.

"Yeah. Just all this squattin' servicing her and then coming standing up kinda put a tweak on my leg. I'm okay. Hey, bro, thanks for understanding. This was one hot little number here. Do you want a turn? I think she'd be up for it."

"No, Edgar. Let's go have dinner with Bazaan and figure out what this job is that's gonna make us rich."

The woman washed her face and pulled on her dress to straighten the wrinkles. She smirked at Edgar, who smiled back at her as he hiked up his pants and zipped his fly shut. He fished a twenty-dollar bill out of his pant pocket. On the black market the twenty dollars in greenbacks was equal to about eighty dollars in Kenyan shillings. He added a five spot, and the young woman actually clapped her hands and offered a thank-you to Edgar as she was quickly ushered out the door and sent on her way by Jesus.

The Sanchez brothers came back to find the Norfolk's bar in full swing.

Bazaan was sitting at a small table alone and beckoned the brothers over. "Let's go to the Mt. Kenya Safari Club for dinner. They've got the best coquilles St. Jacques known to man. Anyway, I don't want that Kikuyu princess to be sniffin' around. Best not to eat where one fucks."

The Sanchez brothers laughed and waited for Bazaan to pay the chit, and then they went, separately, out of the Norfolk and into the cool of the Kenyan evening, with its buzzing insects and cooing doves.

10

KENYA, 2005

EDGAR MADE HIS WAY PAST THE HILTON HOTEL AND WEAVED through the walls of people waiting for a bus at the terminal on Temple Street. Others were just waiting for the next minute of their life to play itself out. Some idly munched on snacks fished from grease-stained paper sacks, wearing the look that spoke of a lifetime of complacent drifting. Edgar found the alley-like street he was looking for and entered the small office of Universal Rentals LTD. After a brief conversation, a contract was produced by the short Indian owner, who was dressed in a gray, banker-striped shirt, with its obligatory grease stain, and clashing gray pants that looked as though they had been slept in. Edgar's credit card was swiped and almost immediately the transaction was authorized, and the receipt was noisily produced.

The Suzuki SUV was driven up to the office door and Edgar, contract in hand, got into the vehicle, cautiously threaded his way to Haile Selassie Avenue, and joined the traffic flow. He entered the roundabout that ushered him onto Uhuru Highway and exited onto Kenyatta Avenue across from the post office. He drove up toward First Ngong Avenue and pulled into the Fairview Hotel. Jesus was waiting for him with several large duffels of gear and clothing. With the gear lashed on the roof rack, the brothers drove down Kenyatta and turned north on Muindi

Mbingu Street, past the police station, and pulled up into the loading area outside the Norfolk. Bazaan was sitting on the verandah drinking his last sip of tea as the brothers pulled up.

Bazaan beckoned the bell captain and his assistants, and they began to load Bazaan's duffels into the back of the Suzuki. With only a raised chin as a greeting, the three got into the SUV and motored down University, over to the Uhuru Highway, and finally north on the A-2 toward Nyeri. They were staging from the house of the expat Californian Phil Snyder.

Snyder had come to Kenya in the early seventies to climb and had fallen in love with Mt. Kenya and the people of the poorly equipped Mt. Kenya National Park. He never went home. Full of charismatic energy, he had organized a relatively efficient and capable mountain rescue team on Mt. Kenya. Snyder was not only an avid climber, but also a passionate pilot and hang glider. He quickly came to the attention of the Kenyan bureaucrats as someone who could accomplish much with nothing, which was the only thing in large supply in Kenya. Promoted to director of Aberdare National Park, he combined his love of gliding with his hate of poachers and became an avenging angel of the Aberdare. Noiselessly, Snyder would glide out over the forest and find poachers going about their business. The image of this giant bat carrying a long, blond-haired *mzungu* usually terrified and froze the poachers in their tracks, and Snyder, baseball bat in hand, would beat the living hell out of the gangs. When the poachers began carrying guns, Snyder mounted shotguns from his glider and fearlessly floated down on the gangs, laying a path of lead shot to clear his landing. Snyder was bigger than life, and a *People* magazine article about him referred to him as "the lion of Kenya."

Snyder had mysteriously lost his job when Richard Leakey was shuffled off the Wildlife and Parks Department to a position that was a general manager of sorts for the entire Kenyan government. Snyder quietly went to Sudan and started up his own privately sponsored national park. Early in its development, *shifta* bandits and poachers raided Snyder's would-be national park. Snyder went missing. Eventually, he was presumed dead. In reality, he had escaped and hooked up with a onetime love interest with a title carried over from Kenya's colonial days. Lady Smithington (Kathrine or, as she preferred, Katy) had taken Snyder in and set him up in a white-stucco country house on the outskirts of Aberdare National Park. She asked nothing as to how he happened to be back in Kenya, and he maintained his silence on the matter, as well. Snyder was given a job managing the Ngobit Fishing Club under the alias of Mike Wilson. He had shaved his Fu Manchu mustache and cut his graying locks, keeping his hair close-cropped. He looked different, acted different, from the "lion of Kenya," but still had a penchant for flying. He made an airstrip at the fishing club off the B-5 Highway. Lady Smithington provided him with an old Cessna she acquired from a refugee who had flown it in from Rwanda and landed penniless at Wilson Airport outside Nairobi.

The Sanchez brothers, needing private air transport to Ethiopia for one of their military contracts, had been referred to Snyder, aka Wilson. They quickly formed a close friendship in addition to a reliable business relationship. The trio flew together, drank together, and enjoyed each other's company immensely. They would stage from Wilson's country house as Bazaan chased his ghosts on the slopes of Mt. Kenya.

Slowly grinding through the gears of the Suzuki, Edgar caught sight of Wilson's white house peeking through the leaves of the forest. It was late afternoon and it had begun to rain after they made their way north out of Nyeri. Edgar had shifted into four-wheel drive as the road to Wilson's house became a spiderweb of small rivers and rivulets. The Suzuki cruised into the cinder drive and announced its presence with loud crunching. Unexpectedly, a few Cape buffalo were grazing in the front yard, the rain running down their bosses, making them appear like polished obsidian.

Wilson appeared from the front door—an old, wooden door aged nearly black in sharp contrast to the white stucco of the walls. Wilson had on a yellow Helly Hansen slicker, its hood up, shadowing his toothy smile. He shouted at the buffalo, unafraid, making shooing motions with his hands. The buffs lumbered off into the dense foliage surrounding the house, one depositing a large, wet turd before rounding a jacaranda.

"Jambo sahibs, habari asabhui?" (Hello gentlemen, how are you today?), asked Wilson, walking with energetic steps toward the vehicle.

"Ni nataka pombe baridi sana! Pese-pese!" (I want a very cold beer! Quick, quick!), said Edgar, greeting his friend and contract pilot.

Two black men dressed in ponchos appeared from a small outbuilding and garage, quickly off-loaded the vehicle, and began toting the duffels into the house. Wilson, Bazaan, and the Sanchez brothers walked into the house, already laughing and riding each other about one transgression or another. The door shut as the last duffel was spirited away into the house by the servants. The rain pattered softly on the ground and the thatched roof of the house. One of the buffalo cautiously nosed the cool mountain air and walked nonchalantly back to again graze on Wilson's front lawn.

Bazaan, Jesus, and Edgar stalked down the red track beside the Ewaso Ng'iro River. Armed with intel from Wilson, they marched through the co-op farm looking for the old man named Terrari. Edgar held his taser unit in his left hand, his right hand cradling the pepper spray. Jesus and Bazaan carried subtler forms of persuasion. They came to the three huts they were looking for and began shouting for Terrari. An old woman with three teeth in her head issued out of the first hut, a cook pot held in her arms. Her head was shaven and she wore a sarong-like garment held together with a single knot. The old woman was vigorously shaking her head and kept repeating the same phrase over and over. Edgar grabbed the crone and asked in a voice of repressed anger, "*Wapi Terrari? Pese-pese!*" (Where is Terrari? Quickly, quickly!)

Suddenly, a young woman dressed in a Western skirt and blouse with cheap plastic shoes came running from another hut, a look of concern on her broad, obsidian face. She spoke excellent English.

"Please, gentlemen, may I help you? I am Terrari's newest wife. He is not here today, but I expect him in about five days. May I communicate anything to him on your behalf?"

Bazaan, to take devastating control of the situation, produced a Kabar knife and held it at the throat of the older woman. He smiled at Terrari's young wife, and the feral look in his eyes communicated his dangerous nature.

"I will take this woman's life if you are not shooting square with us, *bibi.*" Bazaan referred to the young woman as "wife." "Is that clear?"

Anger shined in the woman's eyes as they narrowed, her nostrils flaring slightly. She stared directly into Bazaan's eyes—clearly challenging the *mzungu.* Obviously, this was not a docile Kyuke *mama.* This one had some pride, and her own form of danger.

"Take the cow's life now for all I care. She is my husband's first wife and she does not share in the labor. Go ahead, take her life, we would thank you, *mzungu m'baya.* As to my husband, he is unavailable at present and unable to talk with you."

Bazaan had not expected such levelheaded aggression. He looked to his side and saw that both Edgar and Jesus had smirks on their faces and were looking at the ground, toeing the red dirt of the yard.

"Where is your husband?" asked Bazaan. "How can he be reached so the five days is only one or two?"

"He went to meet with his brother at the Mutindua market over Chogoria way. They are making arrangements to sell honey. There is no way to contact him. You should come back in a week. I'm sure he will be able to meet with you then."

If this sassy woman was telling the truth, it would be an easy thing to find Terrari at Mutindua. However, he had to be sure her words held the truth. He lowered the knife from the old woman's throat and shoved her down to the ground. The old woman quietly grunted, but did not utter a word in protest. Bazaan walked to the young woman. Their eyes locked. He could see the hate the woman had for him and that she would need some convincing before she truly feared them. Yes, this was one saucy *bibi,* probably liked it on top, too. *No missionary position for this one,* thought Bazaan. Bazaan's war face manifested itself and he could see the woman's eyes widen, yet she stood still and offered no retreat.

"Woman, I will tell you what we'll do if you are lying to us." Bazaan's eyes became insane and cold all at once as he stared the woman down. "I will kill a *nugu* (hyena) and cut off its penis. I'll stretch that penis and let it dry in the sun. Then I'll find you and I'll *tombwa* (fuck) you with that dead *nugu*'s dick—first in your ass, then in your cunt. Last, I'll put it down your throat and then gut you from cunt to throat. Your last seconds of life will be spent with a dead hyena's cock in your mouth."

The woman's eyes shined with fear now—yet only for a moment. The next moment the curtain of the African came over her eyes, and they stared blankly at Bazaan. She then turned away from Bazaan and the Sanchez brothers and walked back to her hut. The old woman still lay on the ground, protectively sheltering her cook pot in her arms.

The trio drove to the east side of Mt. Kenya—past Nanyuki and on to the Chogoria entrance—and the Mutindua market. For the most part, the drive was silent, each man focusing on his own thoughts. Edgar spoke first concerning their plan for the old man named Terrari.

"Now if we find this *pendejo,* what do we do with him? Where do we take him to do whatever it is we have to do to him? Just say the words, *mi amigo,* and I will do. But be talkin' to us."

Bazaan said, "If we find this old man we'll coerce him into coming with us to camp. In public, we'll hire him to lead us up a difficult area south of the Chogoria Track. In reality, we'll lean on him and sweat everything he knows of Dream Walking. I have good intel he knows much and has a lot to offer. We simply convince him to share what he knows with me."

"How will we know if we actually find him?" asked Jesus. "Do we just start going door-to-door in Mutindua, asking for some old wog *chingazo* who can disappear and pop a cap in your ass without a sign?"

"The Mutindua market is made up of only a half dozen houses. An N'dorobo will be easy to spot. He'll stick out among the Kikuyu interlopers like a sore thumb."

They drove on, and the afternoon clouds closed in on them as large dollops of rain splattered the windshield of the Suzuki. The blacktop of the highway glistened like an Apache teardrop, and the narrow highway became a tunnel in the lush green of the forest. The windshield wipers laid down a syncopated beat as the tires sang on the asphalt. Bazaan continually sipped from a water bottle. Edgar and Jesus were biding their time, humoring their friend and benefactor. After all, they had little else to do, and if this was part of an Alpha job, so be it.

They turned off the B-5 and soon found themselves coasting into a settlement amid the green of the forests of Mt. Kenya. A Coca-Cola sign adorned a shed-like merchant's stall. The proprietor seemed to be asleep, his head on the crook of his arm.

The Suzuki rolled to a crunching halt as Bazaan walked over to the backcountry *duka*. The proprietor was passed out or dead—Bazaan could not ascertain which. He gently cuffed the man, which elicited a bleary-eyed stare and a hoarse *"Jambo"* from the backcountry entrepreneur.

"*Wapi M'zee* Terrari? *Wan'dorobo. Wapi?*" (Where is the old man Terrari? The N'dorobo. Where?)

"*M'zee* Terrari *hapanna, sahib. M'zee* Sendeo, *n'dio. Wan'dorobo, n'dio.*" (The old man Terrari, no sir. The old man Sendeo, yes. N'dorobo, yes.)

Bazaan turned to the Sanchez brothers and said, "There is an old N'dorobo here named Sendeo. Terrari appears not to be here. I bet the old man, Sendeo, is Terrari's brother that the bitch talked about. We'll find him, and he'll lead us to his brother. If not, since he is N'dorobo, we'll see what he knows."

Bazaan addressed the *duka* owner, "*Wapi M'zee* Sendeo?"

The proprietor pointed to a small hut not thirty yards away. The trio walked up to the hut and, once outside, Bazaan barked out, "Sendeo, *m'zee. Jambo.*"

An impossibly black old man with tufts of white hair issued from the hut and looked for the source of the noise.

"I speak English. What do you wish of me? Do I know you? What is your business with me? I am quite busy, so please state your business, *sahib.*"

We're looking for your brother, Terrari. You do have a brother by that name, do you not?" asked Bazaan in a perturbed manner.

"*N'dio, sahib.* (Yes sir.) Yet I have not seen him for quite some time. He lives very far from here, and I have no vehicle and the *matatu* rates are very high. I have not seen him."

"His youngest wife said he was setting up a honey-selling deal here with you. If that is not true, how is it you are here at Mutindua?"

"My brother has had nothing to do with honey for decades. For that matter, I tend only to my needs. I have traded here in Mutindua for years. His wife must have had her reasons to lie to you. I have not seen my brother in some time, nor do I particularly care to see him. We have gone our separate ways. I am sorry, I cannot help you."

The shadows were lengthening and the clouds were on the march. The Nithi Valley filled with gray cotton balls of mist as the cold air sought the colder air of the alpine peaks that loomed above the valley. Bazaan considered his options.

He conferred with Edgar and Jesus, keeping his voice down, turning his back on the old N'dorobo who called himself Sendeo.

"Take this old man and pitch camp three or four klicks from here. Fall back on your training. I'll be back early the morning after tomorrow. Weaken him, have him ready to talk to me. You know what you need to do. If your methods kill him or make it impossible to interrogate him, I'll dock your pay for the upcoming job twenty percent. So be careful, but be effective. I'll be back in thirty-six hours and I expect to squeeze this old man of everything he knows."

"Where are you going?" asked Edgar.

"I'm going to find and shoot a hyena and pay a visit to a certain *bibi* on the Ewaso Ng'iro," answered Bazaan simply.

Edgar replied, "Man, you gonna chase that grounder? She's only a wog cunt. Why waste the time and energy?"

Bazaan fixed Edgar's gaze with steely eyes.

"Always do what you say you'll do. That's the way of strength. Get lazy, soft, and let your word slide—you can never be strong again. I'm going to fuck that sassy bitch with a hyena's prick just as I said I would. Your words are not grounders. They're everything."

Bazaan motored the Suzuki through the upcountry highways of Kenya in the late-afternoon golden light. Intent on his mission, he parked the SUV outside Nanyuki by the public dump and waste fields. The grays of dusk gave way to the indigo of night. He fished his Maglite from his pack, along with his Glock. He placed the gun in his belt and the flashlight in his mouth. Bazaan went around, opened the back of the vehicle, and hefted the ten pounds of cheap stew meat he had purchased from a flyblown butcher's stall in the Nanyuki market. He walked about fifteen yards from the vehicle and scattered the meat about the ground. Then Bazaan attached the silencer to the Glock, turned off the Maglite, and waited. The smell of human garbage and waste was overpowering—the now-rotting stew meat adding to Bazaan's aromatic chum. His eyes burned with the putrid smell as it shifted across his face with the gentle breeze of the White Highlands.

The first moaning whoops began after only a five-minute wait and grew closer and closer to Bazaan, who was perched on the fender of the SUV. He was certain he could smell the creatures from this distance—the devil dogs of Africa. The whoop started low and got increasingly higher in pitch, with a low-octave moan seemingly issued at the same time. When it seemed as if the source of the surrealistic moaning was only a few yards away, Bazaan turned on his Maglite and pointed it at the noise. The hyena's eyes reflected in the light like mirrors against an inky night, its strong jaws and the spots on its hindquarters showing in the intrusive light. Three other hyenas were skulking behind the most aggressive and careless beast, all within twenty yards of Bazaan.

Calmly, Bazaan pointed his silenced Glock and took the head shot. The skull of the closest hyena exploded like an overripe pumpkin thrown down on the street on a hot August evening. The three other hyenas flinched and retreated cautiously amid mournful cries.

Bazaan quickly went to the carcass and kicked its belly over so it lay on its headless back. He put on latex surgical gloves and positioned the beast, seeing its short hair was filled with small mud balls and its hide was full of ticks and scabby sores. With his Kabar knife in his right hand, Bazaan grabbed the flesh of both scrotum and penis of the beast with his left and sliced away with his right, freeing the mass from the body of the animal. He placed the bloody prize in a plastic ziplock bag.

Bazaan drove from Nanukyi and into the forest reserve outside Nyeri. Pulling off onto a rough track, he parked and locked the Suzuki and lay down in the storage space, wrapping a light fiberfill bag over himself as a comforter. The forest night swallowed everything, including the dreams of Ralph Chang Bazaan.

Bazaan came awake, his throat and mouth dry and parched. The light was still the gray of predawn. Finding the water bottle, he drank deeply. He stepped outside his sheltering SUV and pissed on the lush forest floor. He fished in his pack for his essentials bag and found the paraffin-coated fire starter. He then gathered small twigs and then branches no larger than his index finger. He placed the lit fire starter in the center of the four walls of twigs and branches. Soon the fire was crackling and warming Bazaan's hands, which had grown cold in the damp forest morning. The smoke of the fire cut lazy spirals—gray ghosts—against the deep green of the forest.

Bazaan retrieved the hyena treasure from the SUV and, again using gloves, placed the organ on a longish green stick. He gently stuck the stick in the dirt at an angle, the hyena's pride almost a foot above the small cook fire. Bazaan chuckled as he sang to himself a parody of a Christmas carol, *"Hyena cock roasting on an open fire, Kyuke bitch taking it up the bum."* The organ smoked slowly and became as stiff as leather. *Not as big as I thought it'd be,* thought Bazaan. *Oh well, it'll serve its purpose.* Satisfied, Bazaan removed the stick from the ground and set it aside, allowing the organ to cool. He placed it back in its bag and kicked the fire out, pouring a bit of water over the glowing coals. Storing the rest of his gear in the pack, he sat in the driver's seat and started the Suzuki. He drove back down the track and entered the main road to the Ewaso Ng'iro River and the hut of the old N'dorobo shaman Terrari.

Parking the Suzuki off the side of the road beyond the line of sight of the huts, Bazaan walked with the smoked, dried hyena organ in his left hand and his right hand empty and ready. Bazaan saw Terrari's new *bibi* before she saw him.

"Jambo bibi. Wapi Terrari? Wapi m'zee?" (Hello, wife. Where is Terrari? Where is the wise, old man?)

Upon identifying who it was speaking, the nostrils of the young woman flared in a mixture of anger and fear. The woman assumed the universal position of female aggression, her hands propped on her hips, glaring at Bazaan.

"He is sleeping now in his *thanga* and must not be disturbed. I will tell him of you when he awakes to drink his *pombe*. He will see you then. He is an old man who needs his rest, so it may be many hours before you can see him."

Bazaan studied the young woman with a smirk on his face. She was clearly a proud one—a modern *bibi* with an attitude. He began to anticipate how she would react to being buggered by a dried hyena dick. He held the hyena penis behind his left leg. The woman had not noticed it. They spent the next ten seconds staring at each other, the woman growing more fearful and Bazaan becoming more dangerous. Bazaan held up the hyena organ for the young woman to see as he smiled broadly.

"Well, I imagine old Terrari must get pretty tired trying to service a saucy bitch like you, *bibi*—no wonder he needs his sleep. I'm gonna help the old boy out and take a time with you myself. 'Course, then you're gonna have to take a time with *nugu* here. I always keep my promises, *bibi.*"

When Bazaan brandished the hyena organ the young woman instinctively took a step back, fear overcoming the hate she held in her eyes. She backed up to the *thanga* thinking to wake the old man, but realized the old man could do little to stop this dangerous man.

"Why don't I wake up the old man myself? Don't want to leave him out of the party," Bazaan said as he slipped his gun into his hand and held it pointed at the woman while making obscene thrusting movements with the organ.

Bazaan motioned with his gun for the young woman to stand about ten yards away from the *thanga* as he dropped the organ in the dust beside the entrance, which was nothing more than a sheet of cheap fabric hung over the hole in the wattle hut. Bazaan's eyes quickly adjusted to the lower light, and he saw the old man lying on his right side on the floor, his knees slightly drawn up, his right arm forming a pillow or headrest. The old man was gently snoring.

Bazaan felt a familiar sting as the blade of the knife cut through his clothing and entered the large, hard latissimus dorsi muscles of his back. Without thinking, he threw himself forward onto his own arms, his body outracing the plunging knife. He kicked back strongly and felt his heel bury itself into the groin of his attacker. He spun onto his back like a gymnast on the pommel horse, allowing his right leg to execute a crescent kick to his attacker's head.

Thinking the young woman had attacked him as he entered the hut, Bazaan was stunned when he looked at the form of the old man, now lying in the doorway, the knife still loosely held in his hand. The old man was out, and moaned quietly. Bazaan looked around to see Terrari still asleep on the floor, moaning replacing the old man's snoring. Bazaan again turned to the doorway of the hut and stared in disbelief—only the knife lay on the dirt. The old assailant had disappeared.

Bazaan rushed out of the hut and saw the young woman had also disappeared. Feeling the sting of the cut, Bazaan felt the warm, wet blood soaking the back of his shirt. The wound was difficult to treat given its location, yet Bazaan probed the cut and found it to be not critically deep. It would no doubt ache and hurt like hell for the next two or three days, but he would soak it in Betadine and it would be fine. He looked back at the old man who now sat quietly, his eyes on Bazaan as he rubbed his crotch, which elicited more moans from the old man.

"Did you attack me, old man? How was it you were there, and then, there? Was it you who tried to stab me or was it your young *bibi?*"

"What do you think, *mzungu?* Don't you wake up from your sleep with aching privates? Don't you always wake with a swollen seed sack?"

"But you were asleep, lying by the fire." Bazaan pointed to the old man's place in the hut. "I was attacked from behind."

"I was not sleeping, you ignorant *mzungu*—I was dreaming."

Bazaan and the old shaman studied each other silently for some time in the warm, brown shadows of the hut. The smell of fresh-cut hay and charcoal smoke hung in the air. Insects buzzed outside, and the cloth door gently flagged, billowing in a whisper of sunlight. Bazaan noticed he was in need of a shower, his young, vital body exuding its strong male odors. In contrast, the old man, who wasted little energy and whose body worked slowly, with few wastes, was as clear of odor as a boiled rock.

The old man continued to massage his lower stomach and crotch, making tight grimaces. Bazaan squatted down beside the cook fire and idly toyed with his Kabar knife, sticking its point into the packed earth, his gaze not wavering from the old man's eyes. The shaman lowered his squat as if to settle in for the duration. However, Bazaan detected a change in the his energy and shifted his focus to the cleft of the shaman's throat. Eyes could betray an opponent's intent, as could hands or feet. Watching the cleft of the throat allowed one to see the whole body.

The old man's thrust was as quick as a mamba's—the small blade reflecting a spark of sunlight as it arced toward Bazaan's throat. Bazaan left his knife stuck in the ground and executed *shionage,* a basic disarming aikido technique. He cupped his hand over the shaman's blade hand and bent the hand and wrist back. Quickly, Bazaan shot his left leg back and, using his hips, threw the old man on his back, with the knife flying free. Bazaan deftly reached back and found the handle of his knife. Pulling it from the dirt floor, and without hesitation, Bazaan forced the old man's hand flat onto the floor, cut off the little finger, and nonchalantly threw the digit into the cook fire. The old man stared dumbly at his four-fingered right hand.

"We'll start with that part and move south until you cooperate with me, old man. I'd hate to separate your manhood from you for the sake of that saucy young *bibi* you must service. But that is what I'll do if you continue to resist my friendly company."

The old man fished a small stick from the cook fire. The tip of the stick was an orange ember that left spirals of smoke as it moved in the air of the hut. Silently, he placed the ember on the stump of his little finger, cauterizing the blood vessels. The sweet, sickly smell of burning flesh filled the hut as the old man stared intently into Bazaan's eyes, the hint of a smile playing across his ink-black, wrinkled face.

"If I lose my manhood to you, *mzungu,* my young wife can use the plaything you made for her. Of course, it is a bit small for her liking and I fear she may prefer you to fashion such a toy from my privates." The old man chuckled to himself, apparently more amused than frightened by his situation.

The old man produced a bit of clean cloth from his greasy trousers and tied it over his cauterized stump. He then found a plug of tobacco from a pouch under his shirt and tore off a piece with his few remaining brown teeth. Like an old, black zebu cow chewing its cud, the old man enjoyed his tobacco in silence, studying the shape of his newly altered hand. Unconcerned, he squatted and spit a brown stream of tobacco juice into the fire and, again, rubbed his groin and lower stomach.

"What do you want of me, *bwana m'baya* (Mister Bad)? I have much to do and must leave again soon. What do you wish of me, *mzungu?"*

Bazaan considered the shaman in a new light. This old boy was definitely not your typical old wog. This old man did not scare easy. As old as he was, he was as dangerous as a viper, and had no compunction about killing. *Indeed,* thought Bazaan, *killing and death were old friends to this one.*

"Did you fight with the Freedom Fighters, *m'zee?"* asked Bazaan in a more polite tone.

"I did little fighting, for I was old even then. But I did see to the business of the Freedom Fighters. My means were much more subtle and refined than were those of my Kikuyu friends. I bothered only with the more important of our would-be masters.

Occasionally, I would have to deal with a Kikuyu or Luo who sought the graces of our enemy, yet that was usually of little effort or consequence."

"Were you the Dream Walker assassin, *m'zee?*"

"What matter of that is yours? You were an *mtoto* on your mother's teat during the fight for freedom. Why bother the ghosts and old men now, *mzungu?*"

"I want to know what you know, *m'zee*. I want to—"

The old man interrupted Bazaan, laughing openly.

"Then live my years and perhaps you will know something. You *mzungu* are like our young people—not courteous to time. Time is the Mother as N'gai is the Father. There are only the ideas and intentions of the Father, and then the time of the Mother to accomplish a world. We may worship the Father, but we are rude to the Mother."

Bazaan was somewhat taken aback by such philosophy issuing from the lips of the old savage. Another puzzle piece began to form a picture of this N'dorobo shaman named Terrari.

Bazaan said, *"M'zee,* I share your past. I am, as you were, a solver of human problems. I help great men retain their country's stability and also help others gain countries to lead to stability. I have the same trade as you did during the freedom fighting. I wish to learn your skills in this regard."

The old man replied, "You wish to know of dreaming, *mzungu?* That is not possible. No *mzungu* has been taught such. It is the secret of the N'dorobo. We keep our secrets, *mzungu.*"

Bazaan flatly stated, "If it is not possible to teach me of the dreaming, then it will not be possible for you and your wives to live. It is that simple."

11

MT. KENYA, 2005

GABE, FOCUSED ON HIS COOK FIRE, BARELY HEARD THE HUMAN scream in the gathering dusk. The clouds were marching up the Nithi Valley like columns of legionnaires. Here, on the Chogoria Track, Gabe was more concerned with his curry than he was with heroics. Yet he cupped his ears in the direction of the scream and thought he heard a low moan. His intent was, then, only action. Without thinking, Gabe gathered up his alpine hammer and ice ax—they would have to suffice no matter what peril he faced.

He traced the Chogoria Track in the dim light, walking in his stealthy mode. He flared his nostrils and kept his eyes on the move, looking out of their corners, better able to discern things in the deepening gloom. He heard a metallic thunk followed by a scream cut short, and then another deep, guttural moan. Heel and toe, quietly, with quickening strides, Gabe made his way through the bamboo and lush undergrowth.

Gabe smelled them before he saw them. He crept to the periphery of a low-burning campfire. Here, gathered in a rocky cul-de-sac, he discerned an old black man tied up and suspended—almost crucified—on a camphor tree. Gabe studied the scene and saw two other men, apparently Hispanic, with thick, spiky hair, sitting, talking without caution, perhaps drunk or high on ganja. The old man, with hooked heels and obsidian-colored skin, was naked. It took Gabe some time to see and understand what he was looking at. The noisy men had tied a thin nylon cord around the old black man's scrotum. The cord was, in turn, tied to a bucket. It appeared that, at random and upon their personal determination, the duo would throw a rock into the bucket. The old man's scrotum was already severely distended and had stretched almost to his knees.

Gabe had seen this form of torture perfected in Uganda. Idi Amin would have his political enemies crucified on the sides of highways outside of Kampala, with an invitation for passersby to place a rock in the bucket. The victim's scrotum stretched until it would finally come free of the body, and the victim of the torture bled to death in his agony. Such torture could last for days.

The old black man was wringing wet with the sweat of such pain. Gabe assessed the situation and decided he needed to take action. He saw the Heckler & Koch MP-5, 9mm submachine guns lying beside the antagonists. He gathered up his Lowe alpine hammer, which was tied to a fifteen-foot piece of nylon webbing. He secured the hammer to his body with a quick bowline. His plan was to use the hammer as a *suruchin*—a martial arts weapon of deadly application. Gabe had studied under Gakiya-Sensei, the successor to Matayoshi Kobudo, an ancient weapons tradition of Okinawa. Gakiya-Sensei had taught him over the years how to kill with almost anything that could be tied to a long rope. However, here in the thin, cold air of Mt. Kenya in the presence of such real danger, the warm, laughter-filled afternoons after training in the dojo, full of Kirin beer and soba noodles, were stripped away to reveal only Gabe's deadly training.

He began to swing the alpine hammer over his head in a five-to-six-foot circle, holding the line secure with his right hand.

There was a six-to-seven-foot loop of webbing between his left and right hands, so that he could launch the deadly hammer like gauchos did their bolas.

He stepped forward to close the distance and let the hammer go, aiming it at the head of the antagonist closest to his H & K. The hammer's pick end lodged in the man's neck. Gabe quickly pulled on the webbing, careful to use his hips, and was splattered by dark arterial blood as the hammer's sharp, serrated edge severed his enemy's carotid artery. The ice hammer flew back to Gabe's right hand like a falcon takes to the glove. He gripped it securely.

The other man responded quickly, automatically reaching for his machine pistol. Gabe faced the man and looked down the barrel of the weapon. Without thinking, Gabe leapt forward off-line, forty-five degrees at the man. He performed an awkward *ukemi,* or roll, and with a reverse grip buried the ice hammer in the perineum of his enemy, who dropped in a heap as the pick deeply punctured his body cavity.

Gabe had entered *mushin,* or state of "no mind" honed and cultivated by his years of martial arts practice. As a result, he was almost surprised himself to see what he had wrought. Strangely, he was not even a little bit tired and his heart continued its measured beat as though he had been watching a rerun of *Gilligan's Island* rather than dispatching gun-toting killers.

Gabe rushed to take down the old man, first carefully removing the bucket with the few pounds of rocks in it from the lashing to the man's scrotum. He found a damp sleeping bag thrown onto an Ensolite pad near the campfire and engulfed the old man in it. He gently carried the man back to his camp. The *m'zee,* with a blank expression, eyes closed, accepted his release from pain with more moaning.

Gingerly, Gabe inspected the old man's scrotum. It was purple and blue with purple clouds rising to his lower belly. Lacking extensive medical training, Gabe simply filled a plastic food bag with the cold, clear water running in the stream by his camp. The water had been snow just a few hours before and was bone-chillingly cold. He placed the bag of ice water on the old man's groin and wrapped the rest of his body in down and pile. He then lay the man down gently on the floor of the tent.

Gabe nestled into his Ensolite pad, which he placed against the snag of a downed camphor tree. He covered himself with a poncho and stood vigil in the dark. The wet dripping of the forest engulfed them both.

Gabe woke up cold and wet in the gray of morning. The condensation coating Gabe's head dripped fat beads of water off the visor of his balaclava and onto his poncho, which was draped over his body core. His first sight upon waking was the elephant grass, its tussock coated with shiny jewels of water droplets. He looked to the tent flap, wondering how the old man had fared through the night. Frankly, Gabe had fallen asleep despite his resolve to monitor the old man's health throughout the night.

The tent flap was open and hung lifeless as a funeral shroud. Gabe crawled over and saw that the cocoon of pile and down that had wrapped the old man was lying in loose husks, like the shed skin of a snake. The old man was gone.

Shrugging, Gabe prepared breakfast. Boiling water doused with iodine, Gabe found the rolled oats and began to spread peanut butter on a chapati. He then threw a loose handful of tea into another pot and dumped most of the hot water into it, making proper British tea. The reserve of hot water was poured onto the rolled oats in his enameled bowl. Gabe thought, *I would give my soul for some honey to slather on this fry bread.*

Promptly, a honeycomb plopped onto the blue nylon of Gabe's breakfast food bag and oozed its golden treasure. Gabe looked up, surprised at this manna from heaven. There stood the old man.

"Finding honey comes easy for the N'dorobo," said the old man. "May I take my breakfast with you?"

"Sure," said Gabe. "Let me put on some more chapatis."

The two men squatted by the MSR stove and contemplated the chapatis browning in the hot butter. They noisily slurped their tea. Gabe had put dried milk and sugar into the cup he offered to the old man—now full of the tan-colored, sweet chai of Africa.

"Chai m'zuri sana" (Very good tea), observed Gabe.

"N'dio, sahib" (Yes, sir), responded the old black man.

"I am Gabe Turpin." He spit in his right hand and offered it to the old man.

"I am called Sendeo," said the old man in soft, almost Indian English, as he, too, spit in his hand and clasped Gabe's.

Spitting and sharing such a life force in a handshake was a statement quite significant among most of the Nilotic tribes of Africa. The act showed you were willing to share your vital life's water.

Gabe stood and flexed his aching knees as Sendeo squatted on his ebony heels, and they both slurped their chai in silence. Sendeo studied his chapati with interest and then devoured it with relish, licking the raw honey from his fingers. Gabe studied Sendeo out of the corners of his eyes. He squatted like a stick-thin gargoyle, chewing his chapati, eyes focused on the low brush and fronds around camp. Sendeo gently burped and smacked his lips one last time.

It was impossible to age the old man. His ebony face was deeply creased and spottily covered with white whiskers. His nose was thin rather than broad, hinting at Nilotic ancestry.

His eyes were shot with the red of the third world. He was tall compared to the Bantu tribes of Kenya and carried himself in a unique manner. When he walked, Gabe noticed, he seemed to barely touch the ground, as if he were floating lightly over the grass and stones. Now, he just sat there, his bony buttocks on his heels, like a cultural fossil in the dappled sunlight.

"How is it you speak English, *m'zee?*" asked Gabe quietly, his voice barely above a whisper.

"Many of our group chose to spend time with the whites. I chose a good man, white or not—a man named Seamus. We had many good *shauries* together—hunting game in the Northern Frontier, and then hunting men on this mountain."

Sendeo allowed himself a slight smile as he obviously remembered his master and student—all the same. He focused on the cooling tea in his cup as though reading the leaves of the past that was once, for him, a future.

"You say you hunted men on this mountain. Were you involved in the Emergency?" asked Gabe.

"N'dio, bwana. Seamus lead a group of *mzungu,* some very hard men, soldiers from America. We lived only to kill and stay alive in those days. I can't remember how many times my *kisu* tasted Kikuyu blood. I remember the soldiers had such terrible guns, yet they thought I was terrible to kill in so close with my *kisu.* They didn't understand the cold evil they carried, like a *bibi* would carry a *mtoto* (child). When some of their guns yelled, a whole hut could be knocked down. They carried the *thahu* of cold death, not I—I was dignified and proper in my killing."

Gabe remembered the declassified situation report issued by military intelligence that mentioned a Seamus McLevin in charge of a team of UDT frogmen during the Mau Mau revolt. Gabe wished he'd had more time to follow up on that report on before his departure for Kenya.

Gabe gently asked, "Did you ever meet someone named Jimmy, an American soldier, when you and Seamus were on Mt. Kenya?"

Sendeo abruptly placed his cup of cold tea on the ground and effortlessly rose on his haunches. He was clearly stricken, and took quick glances at Gabe out of the corner of his eye.

"Are you a witch or shaman, *Bwana* Gabe? How is it you know of the soldier Jimmy? So many years ago, how is it his name is spoken now on this mountain? Explain how it is so, *Bwana* Gabe. You bring back such an old memory at this time. Do you, too, walk in my dreams?"

Gabe quietly answered, "Sendeo, I have read reports from our military about Jimmy and the Dream Walker assassins. I know bits and pieces of what happened up here. I'm here to study this Dream Walking. I'm a professor of anthropology—a teacher of students. I am a spectator into your past, Sendeo. But I am a most curious spectator. I want to know of your Dream Walking. I want to know of it then, and now. Will you help me, Sendeo? Will you help me understand the Dream Walking you speak of?"

"This, too, is what those two bad men and their leader wanted. You don't tear off my manhood, *Bwana* Gabe—but instead, you may be offering me a honeycomb of lies. Why would a *mzungu* want to understand Dream Walking?"

Gabe thoughtfully considered the question, and responded simply, "I want to understand about what's possible—what's real—what's not. Perhaps then more can walk in dreams, or choose to not waste the time in this endeavor. I simply try to uncover possibilities in order to grow."

Sendeo considered this. Without pretense, he began, "Dream Walking is as honey gathering—a part of life for the N'dorobo, *Bwana* Gabe. But I doubt that even if I revealed the nature of dreaming and walking within those dreams you would understand. You are a *mzungu*. You have the noise of your beliefs that will drown out the whisper of dreaming. You are trapped in this dream." Sendeo spread his arms to indicate the here-and-now.

Gabe motioned for Sendeo to again relax by the fire, drink his chai. Sendeo slowly lowered his thin, whippet-like frame back onto his haunches. He took the mug of chai in both hands and finished it. They spent the time looking at each other. Gabe knew that talking was often only a Western means for dealing with insecurity. In his years of dealing with the world's cultures, he had little need for talk anymore.

Sendeo studied Gabe with his dark eyes as his face took on a puzzled or perplexed look.

Sendeo spoke softly, "*Bwana* Gabe, you have a hole in your heart—the emptiness that is the way of the Dream Walker. You know of dreaming; you know of what little is real, and how so much is not. You have walked in your own dreams. You have taken the longest walk, I feel. Looking at your eyes, I see you have dreamed yourself back from death itself. Very strange, your death, your dreams are from here on this mountain, *Bwana* Gabe. Have you been taught the Dream Walking by my brother, Terrari?"

Gabe smiled and shook his head, saying, "No, *m'zee*. I was a young and strong climber so many years ago. I almost ran up the Sirimon Track to North Liki. Sprinted up to Kami Tarn. Forged to the Amphitheater on the North Face, below Firmin's Tower. It was there I became ill. It was there, and after days of crawling, that did I find my death. I realized at that time the reality of dreams. I had an infant daughter, a beautiful wife. To die would break commitments. I dreamed myself back to life. Even now, the dreaming and reality have hazy lines—and I guess I am waiting to wake up and die, these decades later—in reality, those decades being only a few minutes of dreaming."

Gabe's stare became unhitched, and he lazily asked, "Sendeo *m'zee,* are you a dream? Am I still dreaming? And when I awake, will I find myself dead below Firmin's Tower, on this mountain? Have I really lived, raised a family, and taught thousands of students? Or is that, too, only part of my dream?"

"No more talk of dreaming now," said Sendeo. "Your hold on your dreams is that of a child. It is no good to speak of that now. There will, perhaps, be another time. But not now."

Without speaking, Gabe cleared up after their breakfast as Sendeo fished through an old cloth bag and found a plug of market tobacco. He gnawed a bit off the plug and silently offered it to Gabe, who declined, saying, *"Hapanna, sitaki tobacco"* (No, I don't want tobacco).

Gabe sat cross-legged, and the old N'dorobo continued to squat as both silently studied the forest around them. Without speaking, Sendeo pointed with his chin at a break in the green wall of bamboo. Gabe saw a dik-dik cautiously peer out of the game trail. The dik-dik was a forest antelope no larger than a long-legged cocker spaniel. Its black muzzle tasted the air. Tightly ridged, small horns adorned its head.

The dik-dik, seeing Gabe and Sendeo, froze against the curtain of bamboo, and then simply disappeared. Sendeo chuckled.

"See, *Bwana* Gabe, even antelope can dream themselves invisible."

For the next three days, Gabe and Sendeo quietly got to know each other. Sendeo would appear like a will-o'-the-wisp in time for morning tea. He always allowed himself to be talked into sharing Gabe's fry bread. They mused at the wonders of the forest. Sometimes they walked silently, Sendeo pointing out the natural wonders and oddities with his chin, the sweep of a hand, or even just the intent of his gaze. They never spoke of dreaming and Dream Walking. Content to just be with each other, they were the consummate odd couple on the slopes of Kerrinyaga.

Gabe was concerned and asked after the health of the old man, having been witness to the severity of his trauma. With a gentle smile and uncharacteristic modesty, Sendeo talked to Gabe about his injuries. "As an old man, I have little need for my privates other than for passing water. All the same, I have grown used to having them, and am glad they did not leave me. They are just a little sore. No worse than when I was tracking a *kifaru* (buffalo) with Seamus and a stalk of bamboo assaulted my privates."

Gabe was in total amazement at how Sendeo seemed to be an integral part of the forest. He moved quickly, yet without haste, down the game trails and made nary a sound. He floated through the green tunnels of bamboo and would often be found waiting for Gabe to catch up, a slight smile on his lips as he squatted on his hooked, obsidian heels.

On the fourth morning, Gabe was washing breakfast dishes. The enameled bowls and cups made hollow clunking noises as Gabe cleaned them in the big pot full of hot water. Sendeo had taken a load of tobacco and was silently masticating the plug as he studied the cloud patterns of the mountain, already dark and gray, a wet veil over the main peaks.

"You wish to know of dreaming," said Sendeo quite suddenly. "You wish to understand the dreams of the N'dorobo. For what purpose, *Bwana* Gabe?"

Gabe answered, "Yes, I wish to understand the dreaming of the N'dorobo. As to why—that is my nature. I am a teacher, and every good teacher is a curious student."

Sendeo took some time to process Gabe's statement and smiled. He looked intently, though with kindness, into Gabe's eyes—assessing all the same. The morning promised rain. Sendeo looked around camp and quietly said to Gabe, "Come. We will talk more of this in my *thanga* (bachelor's hut)."

They silently walked the game trails over swells and waves of green forest. Gabe began to sweat as the foliage of the forest seemed to close in around him, his lungs finding little purchase in the thin air of these highlands. The bamboo gave way to the camphor, and then lower-growing trees and shrubs. Suddenly, beside a waterfall, amid elephant grass and basalt boulders, Gabe and Sendeo entered a village of two dozen mud-and-wattle huts. Cook fires traced lazy patterns of smoke in the thin air. The village was silent, and the deep greens and browns of the huts were framed and filled with dark shadows.

"I have been in this valley and did not see this village, Sendeo," said Gabe, quite confused.

Sendeo replied with a smile on his face, "Our dreams were not for you that day, *Bwana* Gabe. For you, we were not here. Our dreams had us elsewhere. You were not in our dreams, and our dreams were not yours."

Sendeo stooped and entered a hut on the outskirts of the settlement. He motioned for Gabe to follow. Gabe, bent nearly double, entered the hut and breathed in deeply the aroma of cool dirt and thatch. It was quite dark in the hut. Gabe could hear Sendeo settling into a squat as he sounded a contented sigh. Gabe sat cross-legged, feeling the packed dirt with his hands, cool and smooth.

Gabe and Sendeo said nothing as their eyes adjusted to the shadows of the hut. Sendeo, Gabe saw, was rubbing his whiskered chin as he lowered his squat, settling in for the duration.

Sendeo spoke quietly, in a strange singsong voice, "Dreaming has always been a part of the N'dorobo. We understand the nature of this dream that most others cling to with the strength of a hungry *mtoto* as it grasps for the teat of its mother. Who is to say what is real and what is a dream? We do, *Bwana* Gabe. We take control of our dreams."

Gabe reflected on the old man's words. A quiet voice issued from outside the hut. Sendeo responded in a clipped, quiet voice. After a few minutes, a young woman in a sarong-like garment sat two huge gourds of liquid on the floor and quickly shuffled out of the hut.

"Is that your daughter?" asked Gabe.

"No, that is one of my wives," responded Sendeo. "She is the youngest of my wives and is hoping to provide me with a male *mtoto*. All the others have given me daughters or empty nests. I have yet to sire a son." Sendeo added with a wry smile, "Perhaps the actions of those two bad men will change that, *Bwana* Gabe."

Gabe reflected on his family of females. He was always able to take safety in the differences of gender as he parented his only daughter, although he tried to raise her as a person, rather than by gender. He and Sendeo were strangely kindred spirits in that regard.

"Tell me more about dreaming," said Gabe. "I feel I have this secret I have always known, yet have not learned. Tell me of the secret of dreaming."

Sendeo slowly unfolded his tobacco pouch and took another plug. Gabe could hear quiet chewing, could feel the silent contemplation.

"This, you know, is not necessarily . . . real," said Sendeo as he gestured to the here-and-now. "We can dream all this, if we are in touch with our dreaming."

To Gabe, this made a special type of sense. His life had included both a death experience and many near-death experiences. The transient nature of reality was old ground for Gabe.

"Is there a ceremony to the dreaming of the N'dorobo?" asked Gabe.

"*N'dio.* When an N'dorobo comes of age and is circumcised, his training in dreaming begins. We take the initiate to a quiet place and have him fast for two days. Then, we give him the smallest bit of the *Kidogo Kifu,* the Small Death. This is, for most, their first dreaming."

"What is the Small Death, *m'zee?*"

Sendeo noisily slurped the sweet honey beer from his gourd. He hawked and spat on the floor, clearing his throat, continuing to rub on his whiskered chin. Clearly, they were on difficult ground—attempting to span cultural gaps of immense distance. Sendeo took another long drink of honey beer and continued in an even quieter voice.

"The Small Death is one of the great secrets of the N'dorobo. It has never been discussed with a *mzungu.*"

Sendeo and Gabe studied each other without talking for nearly a half hour. As before, Gabe was not in a hurry for words. He felt close to a breakthrough and held his ground of reserve. He did not ask and he did not say anything. Gabe only met the eyes of Sendeo and laid himself bare, knowing any hint of insincerity would be construed as artifice and the relationship would be over.

"My eyes see your heart, *Bwana* Gabe, and it is not truly that of a *mzungu.* Your heart is that of a traveler—not an N'dorobo, most certain, but one who has traveled so far from home as to not have a home. I think it is not improper for me to discuss this matter with you."

Gabe remembered haggling for jack mackerel in the furnace-like markets off Mombassa. He had been in the country for months and was sunburned as dark as a Somali. His hair was full of dust and his eyes were bloodshot, empty, and distant. The locals referred to him from that point on as a "traveler." Not a *mzungu,* tourist, or even an American. He was seen as a "traveler."

Sendeo shuffled his feet and squatted down lower as he gently adjusted his genitals—the cross-cultural behavior shared by men worldwide.

"The Small Death is a combination of things we find in the forest, mix together, allow to grow, and, when ready, we take only a bit, for it is very strong."

Not wanting to push things, Gabe balanced his understandable need to be quiet with his desire to know this secret—this thing called the Small Death. He, too, cleared his throat, slurped his beer, and gave an appreciative sigh, wiping his lips with his hand. The honey beer was cool, and its sweet fermentation with the oaky taste of the gourd was not unpleasant. The hut was cool and dark—a cocoon of quiet veiled from the afternoon heat of the equatorial sun.

"What things from the forest are used to make the Small Death?" asked Gabe gently.

"Flowers, roots, honey, and, of course, the power of the serpent."

Sendeo, in a raised voice, clipped off some of the Maasai-like words of the N'dorobo, apparently talking with his young wife, who remained outside the *thanga.*

A few minutes later, as both of them sat in silence, the woman came into the hut and placed between Gabe and Sendeo some plants and roots that were sitting in a large, waxy leaf. Gabe studied the leaves and noticed a white flower that seemed familiar. He also saw a root that was gray with mold. Gabe offered a questioning gesture as to whether he could study the plant stuff. Sendeo made a pushing motion with his hand to signify the affirmative.

Gabe keyed the flower quite quickly as a member of the *Ipomoea* genus, commonly referred to as morning glories. The parts and seeds of morning glory species were often used in primitive cultures as hallucinogens and a part of arcane ceremony and sacrament. He then saw the dark brown nodules of ergot growing on the roots and leaves, looking like a mold. Contained in ergot was nature's original of the base of LSD. Gabe remembered back when in Tom Crepple's basement they would take marijuana leaves and hashish, when they could get it, and soak it in brandy, letting it ferment in a wrap of waxed paper. The ergot lacing supercharged the cannabis high with vivid hallucinations.

The woman again came into the hut after offering a greeting to Sendeo. She placed a basket made from fibers—banana leaves, it seemed. The basket had a small lid with a handle made from a piece of leather, or sinew. Then she quietly took her leave.

Sendeo took the basket in both hands and sat it down between his bony knees. He carefully removed the lid and hesitated, as though studying the contents of the basket. Like an egret claiming a fish, Sendeo's hand shot into the basket and produced a gray coil of snake. Gabe unconsciously scooted back, recognizing the Hines viper. The snake looped and coiled its small body around Sendeo's wrist, fighting for purchase and escape.

Gabe was visibly frightened. The Hines viper was the consummate "I Got" snake. That is, one had time to issue only an "I got . . . ," never completing the sentence, ". . . bit," before one died.

Sendeo chuckled. He grasped the small snake, which was no more than a foot long, by the head. He squeezed on the side of the snake's head, causing it to open its small mouth. Then he took the ergot-coated root and pressed the snake's head into it, milking the venom to mix with the ergot and root. Sendeo gently placed the viper back into the basket, gingerly covering it with the lid. Sendeo crushed the morning glory blossom, scraped off the ergot and mold, and mixed it with the venom from the Hines viper. It formed a pasty substance that coated the waxy-green leaf. To this pasty mixture, he added a few splinters of bamboo.

"The Small Death," said Sendeo as he offered the wide leaf for Gabe's inspection.

Gabe studied the mixture, analyzing it with a scientist's perspective. The mechanism was clear to Gabe—hallucinogens and a strong neurotoxin that were taken into the bloodstream in small amounts via the small piercings of the mouth created by the bamboo splinters in the mix. This mixture would basically unhook the frontal cortex, allowing the mid-brain and basal ganglia to have a heyday.

"A young N'dorobo male of fourteen or fifteen years will take larger and larger doses of the Small Death. Eventually, they are trained to die, but dream on past their Small Death. After years of such practice, some have no need of the Small Death in order to dream. Neither my brother nor myself have had to take of the Small Death for years, yet we dream daily."

This talk of dreaming and a priori reality made Gabe reflect back on the seventies, when he was in Switzerland.

During a climbing holiday in Leysin, Gabe was staying at the Club Vagabond, which catered to English-speaking climbers. Alex MacIntyre—a Scott with a penchant for white chocolate, bitters, and big-chested women—and Gabe had just done a splendid route on the Tour d'Ai and were slowly walking to the quarry outside town. There they were going to eat their dinner of white chocolate bars and crusty French bread. Gabe had acquired a bottle of wine from one of the kitchen workers at the Vagabond and had it all to himself. A buxom Australian gal was going to meet Alex for an early-evening climbing class, so Alex had to forgo the wine and be satisfied with beer at the Vagabond afterward, shared with his well-endowed client.

Walking past the American School, Gabe noticed a poster announcing a weeklong meditation session to be led by the guru of Transcendental Meditation, Maharishi Mahesh Yogi. Gabe had dabbled in TM, as it was called, at about the same time the Beatles were seeking spiritual guidance from the Maharishi. Gabe was curious about what the grand master of TM was really like. He told Alex, "I'm going to take a rain check on dinner. I'm going to see if I can wrangle an audience with the Maharishi."

"All right, mate," said Alex. "Anyway, I'll feel more at ease when I fasten this Aussie bird's chest harness without you gawkin' at me."

Alex walked onto the quarry, and Gabe peeked through the French doors of the American School, seeing a handful of people setting up a platform on which they were piling cushions and placing dozens of flower arrangements. He let himself into the meeting hall and saw the diminutive little guru sitting like a hairy gnome.

The Maharishi sat calmly, smiling broadly as his entourage fussed about the cushions, pillows, and flowers that surrounded him. The Maharishi saw Gabe and nodded a welcome. Gabe introduced himself and told him of his initiation into TM by Bill Witherspoon some years before.

Gabe was accepted warmly by the group, and it was not long before he joined the others in a casual conversation with the Maharishi. The tiny guru seemed to thrive on the attention and questioning of his followers. The conversation shifted naturally to the issue of transcendent versus relative reality—what is real, and what is not.

The Maharishi said, "What we refer to as reality is as a huge sheet of gossamer—the sheerest of silk—translucent. It offers only a delicate barrier between us and that we cannot think about. We fold and fold our sheet of silk and it becomes tangible and strong. Soon it can support the weight of a human mind, and most cling to it with tenacity. From the moment of our birth we begin to fold and fold our mind's tapestry, creating a lifeline, an anchor in what many would call sanity. Over a lifetime of folding, we are sometimes remiss here and there, either too lazy or not diligent, and the sheet becomes thin—too weak to hold the weight of our mind. Some break through their reality's web. These are the lurkers in our asylums. These are the ascetics roaming the power places of the earth. These are sometimes the religious leaders of the world."

The Maharishi drew an analogy on gaining cosmic consciousness by saying that meditating regularly was like dipping a white cloth into dye. Gradually, the white cloth of reality would become the permanent color of the cosmic-mind dye in which it was continually dipped.

With a characteristic giggle, the Maharishi leaned over and whispered to Gabe, "That is perhaps a small fib on my part. Meditating is not so much a dye as an acid that weakens the fabric of the reality we have made for ourselves. Even a reality that has been tightly folded many, many times can become weak if it is continually

> *dipped in acid. Finally, the mind falls through the web of fabric and becomes one with that which is not yet real. Therein lies the way to being truly aware."*

Gabe began to synthesize the nature of Dream Walking and the Dream Walker assassins. With day-to-day life for him a sometimes fuzzy image, Gabe intuitively understood the nature of dreaming. It was the ultimate expression of a priori thought—pure intent. Dream it, and it is so. He remembered back to his dreaming on the North Face of Mt. Kenya. Then, he had dreamed back his entire life.

Gabe and Sendeo sat in silence in the hut, studying the ground. Gabe quietly asked Sendeo, "Tell me of the Dream Walking during the Mau Mau."

Gabe heard Sendeo's exhaling as a long sigh. The old man was obviously uncomfortable with this whole matter. All the same, Gabe persisted in his best collegial manner.

"The Dream Walkers of the Mau Mau did not reflect the good heart of the N'dorobo. They used the old secrets to kill others. That was bad, wrong. Regrettably, my brother Terrari was one most active in this. The colonials tried their best to capture him, yet it was for them like trying to capture a ghost—killing one already dead."

"How did they kill so many so closely protected, Sendeo? How did it come to be? Is that also part of the N'dorobo's dreaming?"

Gabe heard Sendeo rustle around in his toga-like garment, apparently searching for something. He looked up to see him take a plug of tobacco and bite off a piece using the sides of his teeth, his face almost a grimace. He chewed in the silence of the hut.

Sendeo said, "When one dreams, and if one chooses so, one is not seen by those not dreaming. The only time one is seen by those not dreaming is when one does something directly to the one not dreaming. The dreamer cannot dream the other unaware, for we can only dream for ourselves. However, we can dream ourselves invisible, dream ourselves here or there—even over large distances, for, in dreaming, distance is nothing. But when we decide to take action in the world of the nondreamers, we are, for them at that time, real. We can be seen. We are then of their dream, as well as our own."

As Pacific islanders do with poi, Gabe used two fingers to scoop a large dollop of the Small Death mixture into his mouth. The taste was bitter, yet not altogether repulsive. There was a dry, acidic taste to the concoction, and he could feel the bamboo splinters ignite small tracks of pain that were quickly forgotten as the paste coated his mouth and throat. He swallowed the last of the paste and looked over at Sendeo as he, too, partook of the Small Death.

Sendeo said quietly, "Although I don't need it to dream, its taste is like an old friend. Now, *Bwana* Gabe, as you drift away, concentrate on holding on to your own hand. This is very important. You will be deeply asleep, but remember to hold on to your own hand, for that is all that will keep you here. If you don't hold on to your hand, you will drift away and your dream will disappear."

Gabe was unusually sober and alert. The Small Death was subtle, it seemed. Gabe was reflecting on his alertness and sobriety when he became aware that he was staring at himself as if from ten feet above camp. The image of his body lazily shifted as he tried to focus. His body was seen through a fuzzy film—dark brown and viscous. He puzzled on this, for Gabe felt himself to be awake, yet shut off from all but the sight of his own body in the hazy brown world of dreaming. The brown haze became dirty brown cotton clogging his throat, his lungs. The brown precipitated death. Then, the brown cotton became only the benign, transparent brown of sun tea brewing in a Nebraska summer.

He felt as if he were floating, lazy, drifting. There were then huge iridescent, green swells—waves hundreds of feet high tugging and flowing around Gabe. The waves were like water in benzene, slowly flowing, miles high. Gabe was a spot of light in this sea of iridescence. Gone was the fuzzy brown, the hazy world—gone was his body. The green swells turned over on themselves and formed a pipeline—a tunnel of fantastic proportion, its current roaring silently with soothing calm. Gabe remembered to hold on to his hand. He grasped it tightly as the light changed to amber and finally to the rose of alpine glow on cowboy mountains. The tunnels of green water and world-sized waves flattened, and he was, again, reclining against the log in the forest, holding on to his own hand in a death grip.

Sendeo was there, quietly staring at him, a look of concern on his face. Then the hard edges of concern softened into a small smile. From Gabe's vantage there was only the camp and a rosy, surrealistic sky—a Salvador Dali landscape. Sendeo's speech was guttural and garbled.

"What do you wish now, *Bwana* Gabe? Where do you wish to go? There are no limits in the world we are in now. We are dreaming. We are in the dreams of the N'dorobo."

Gabe focused his attention and kept hold of his hand.

"I wish to go to Malindi. Is it possible to go there in this dream?"

As an immediate answer, Gabe saw the flat surf and dhows anchored in the bay. The pretty German sunbathers lay sprawled on the heating white sand, their ample breasts baking in the sun. The geckos gathered heat from the dark paint of the door frame of a *banda*. Gabe floated uncontrolled and found himself inside a holiday *banda*. The sleeping couple in the *banda* noisily adjusted their positions in bed, draped in mosquito netting—gauzy sheets of white. Gabe dreamed himself outside.

Sendeo was squatting in the sand, silently chuckling to himself. Gabe floated amid the bathing beauties, unseen, a voyeur of reality. He walked down the beach, Sendeo shadowing him. They walked unnoticed.

"Sendeo, how is it they do not see us?" asked Gabe.

"Because we are dreaming our dream, and our dreams are not theirs. If you choose to sample the goods of one of these maidens, however, you choose to have your dream blend with theirs. They will see you. Choose to just look and we are ghosts. Choose to act, and we are of their dreams, and real."

"I wish to test this dreaming. If I were to pinch this buxom German frau here and then I wish to dream myself onto the upper slopes of Mt. Kenya—would that be possible?"

"Depending if you are quick in your dreaming," replied Sendeo with a chuckle.

Gabe leaned over and pinched the beautiful, bountiful blonde on the thigh. A shriek was issued as Gabe thought of the senecio and groundsel of Mt. Kenya.

Gabe saw the sunbirds flitting against the green of elephant grass. Snow had nestled into the spaces and outlined the cupped, circled layers of leaves of a lobelia—stark white against the deep green of the plant. A stream wound its way down through the elephant grass amid basalt boulders covered with wildly colored bracts of lichen—the oranges, reds, and yellows as bright as a vandal's art. Gabe recognized this spot. Years before, on this deadly and often dark mountain, Gabe had found this one gentle place. He had spent hours here, lazing around this soothing oasis, reading, dozing, and writing in his journal. In a small amphitheater made of rock framing a deep, dark pool lay a large deposit of feldspar crystals, like rough jewels to the finder. Gabe had placed a fistful of the brown-gray crystals in a blue ditty bag—the mountain, like a witch, giving up her jewelry of fire.

The images of the mountain appeared to Gabe as through an amber filter. He looked to his left and saw Sendeo squatted beneath an overhanging boulder, loading a plug of tobacco into his mouth.

"I remember this place," Gabe said. "It is the one and only place on this mountain that was peaceful and gentle—everywhere else seems to have an edge or a hidden darkness."

"Many people remember this place, *Bwana* Gabe. It is called N'gai's *Thanga* (God's Bachelor Hut). Every man needs the peace and quiet of a *thanga*. It is our escape from the meddlesome ways of women, which are the sources of our joy and sorrow in life. I am comforted that even God, N'gai, needs to escape from the witch of Kerrinyaga from time to time. N'gai's peace is what you find here."

Gabe mused on N'gai's *Thanga* and looked up at the main peaks of Nelion and Batian. Clouds layered heavy and wet over the snaggled teeth of Kerrinyaga. Gabe had never successfully climbed to the top of Batian. So much trying for so little achievement. So much paid for so much pain.

"Sendeo, I am going to dream myself on top of Batian. I must, somehow, see that which I have tried so hard to see through a force of my will. I must see the reality of that place—the top of Kerrinyaga."

Gabe felt he was suffocating as the cold air on the summit filled his lungs—yet did not satisfy. Air here was desperately thin, and one was always left wanting. The summit was littered with human debris, and Gabe saw abandoned gear, slings, and fuel bottles. He saw the crypt-like bivouac shelter just off from the summit. He could not see the twin peak, Nelion, because clouds drifted up the Gates of Mist, a couloir that meandered down and became the treacherous Diamond Couloir—the standard of the mountain for ice climbers, the Eiger Norwand of this tropical, icy summit.

Gabe felt empty as he looked down from the summit—this square meter of rotten rock a decades-long challenge that had taken much of his strength and left, for the most part, only desperate memories. Even the good memories had a melancholy about them. Mt. Kenya was a dangerous mistress. She gave sparingly, yet took everything you had.

Gabe was weary from his dreaming. Perhaps just weary of the emptiness he felt having seen the transitory reality of one square meter of rock for which he had paid so much to stand on. Gabe found himself lying on his side, as he had been, out from the camp off the Chogoria Track. The amber light gone, Gabe opened his eyes and met those of Sendeo. The old N'dorobo smiled and offered some chai from Gabe's own enameled cup. A bushbuck coughed from inside the green wall of bamboo around camp. Night was coming. Wisps of vapors were floating like banshees to fill the spaces between cloud and ground. The air was wet—chilly and humid at the same time. The night promised to be long, wet, and cold. Gabe went to his cache of dried tinder. He coaxed a fire out of wet wood, and the camp became a shadow as the sun retreated from the mountain. Sendeo had disappeared. *That's okay,* thought Gabe. He needed to be alone anyway, after this, his first dreaming. As with most journeys of inner growth, there appeared to be a spiritual price of admission.

Gabe opened a Power Bar and ate it, chasing it down with unsweetened tea, cool from condensation in the early evening. He brushed his teeth, using a bottle of iodine water to rinse. With his flashlight held in his mouth, Gabe went to the tent, unzipped the opening, and reached inside to fluff his sleeping bag, then crawled into the cocoon of nylon and Polartec naked, having shed his clothes on the tent floor. The nylon was slightly damp and made Gabe shiver as he contracted muscles to warm the bag up with his body heat. In the dark of the mountain forest, Gabe sorted through the past twenty-four hours. *Impossible* was one descriptor—*affirming* was another. Gabe stared at the dark inside of his tent and was startled by the cry of a tree hyrax. He was then strangely comforted when he heard the bark of a bushbuck. He forced himself to re-create N'gai's *Thanga* against the screen of his closed eyes and smiled broadly in the dark as he experienced, again, the deep peace of this power place. Smiling, hearing the small cascade, seeing the deep pool in the moonlight, Gabe found an unusually deep sleep.

12

KENYA, 2005

TERRARI AND BAZAAN SAT IN THE WARM, HUMID WOMB OF THE hut. Bazaan reached behind his back and produced the Glock in an almost ceremonious manner. He made much of attaching the silencer to the weapon and calmly pointed it between Terrari's eyes.

"I will surely kill you, old man. If you will not help me in this business, I have nothing more to gain from you. Choose quickly and be smart. I am not bluffing. As you have not meant anything to me up till now, why should you mean anything hereafter? Choose, old man."

Bazaan kept the gun pointed at Terrari's forehead. The old man studied this hard man—a source of hate and calm, all the same—and found only a dead look in his eyes. Terrari knew he was seconds away from his own certain death.

"I will give you a supply of the *Kidogo Kifu* that we depend on to dream. With this, you will be able to have the dreams of the N'dorobo—many dreams. I will do this and then you will leave this place."

"Will you explain and guide me in the use of the *Kidogo Kifu?* Or will the *Kidogo Kifu* only be a poison given to me with a knowing smile and a wink of the eye? No, you will partake of the *Kidogo Kifu* with me. At least that way we will balance the account."

The old man looked at the packed dirt of the floor and wiggled a toe in it, forming a zigzag design. He began to smile and looked up at Bazaan, again assessing the hard man who sat across from him with so much violence so near to the surface. Terrari thought, *Dealing with this man is like trying to handle a very sharp double-edged* kisu—*it is very easy to get cut, for that is all there is to this man's life, killing, sharp edges.*

"*Sow-sow, mzungu,* so it will be," said Terrari.

The old man rose to his feet and slowly walked out the front of the hut, holding the piece-of-cloth door aside as he sought to find his youngest wife.

"Shalita, *pese-pese. Kidogo Kifu,* Shalita. *Pese-pese bibi,*" said Terrari.

Bazaan had put his Glock back into the waistband of his pants and was waiting to see how this situation would play itself out. The young *bibi* appeared inside the hut, giving Terrari an assortment of woven bags and baskets. Terrari organized the various weavings in front of him. He began his work as Bazaan watched, the cook fire dying into orange embers in the darkness of the hut. Green leaves and pale yellow pastes were mixed and spread. Bazaan reached for his Glock as Terrari produced a small gray snake from one of the baskets. Terrari milked the venom from the snake and mixed it with the rest of the concoction with a forked stick. He then placed a large, green leaf covered with a three-inch smear of paste in front of Bazaan and quietly said, "*Kidogo Kifu.*"

Bazaan studied the paste on the waxy-green leaf in front of him. He was unsure as to the nature of the Small Death and felt somewhat vulnerable about this bit of paste placed in front of him now. Yet he studied the dollop all the same.

"You first, *m'zee,*" said Bazaan as he offered the leaf and the Small Death to Terrari.

Terrari scooped a couple of fingers' full of the concoction

and licked it off his digits with no hesitation. In turn, he offered the leaf and half of the paste back to Bazaan. Bazaan carefully sopped up the remaining paste with his fingers and placed the mixture inside his mouth. He sat in the darkening shadows of the hut and waited.

Terrari watched Bazaan and chuckled a bit as he said, "*Mzungu,* during the first part of your dream, hold on to your hand—it will anchor you to life. Then again, as you may think, perhaps it is a trap to grasp your hand. Who knows, eh, *mzungu?*"

Bazaan realized he was in a cat-and-mouse game of deceit and death with the old shaman. Clearly, he could not trust the old man and must evaluate and make his own decisions concerning this "dreaming." He deemed the old man's instructions of grasping one's hand as not being a lie with a deadly outcome. He quickly grasped his right hand with his left.

Bazaan watched his own body, almost as if he were not aware of the impossibility of doing such. The light of the hut had become an eerie, tequila-sunrise rosy color as Bazaan seemed to float over his prone body. The body was lying beside that of the old shaman on the packed-dirt floor. Then, impossibly, Terrari was squatting beside him, looking at Bazaan with a smile on his chiseled, obsidian face. Terrari downplayed the nonreality of it all by spitting a stream of brown tobacco juice onto the dying cook fire.

Bazaan began to collect his senses and realized he was thinking clearly, despite the impossibility of what was happening. He asked Terrari, "How does one move in this dream? What are the rules, old man?"

"There are no rules," replied Terrari. "Dream of where you want to go and you will find it so. I will follow you. Where do you wish to go, *mzungu?*"

"Mutindua," replied Bazaan quickly. "I wish to pay a visit to my friends. They will shit when . . ."

Bazaan saw the dirt track leading out from the shacks at Mutindua. Thought begot movement along the track, and Bazaan scoured the area just off from the Chogoria Track that led up the mountain. He saw the two dome tents pitched in an island of grass among bamboo and camphor trees. The camp appeared to be deserted.

The dreaming was not unlike playing a video game, with directed thought as one's controller. Bazaan hovered over the camp, and his heart started to beat wildly as he saw the bodies and the beast. Edgar and Jesus were both slumped over in the unique postures of death as a leopard enjoyed the soft tissue of Edgar's rectum and lower belly. With blood and bile coating its whiskers, the big cat was purring deeply as it dined. Bazaan, disgusted and angered by this vision, reached for his Glock by reflex and found it tucked safely in his belt. Without hesitation, Bazaan shot the leopard in the head. The cat let out a loud hissing sigh.

"Piga!" said Terrari. "A fearsome shot, *mzungu.* And with no more noise than a *bongo* passing gas. Is it your friend that the *chui* was eating? And what of the other man? Surely this was to be quite a feast for *chui."*

Without responding to the old shaman, Bazaan inspected the bodies of his friends and onetime lieutenants. He could not find any wounds on Edgar other than the leopard's feeding and wondered how he was killed. Jesus, on the other hand, had a large, terrible gash on his neck and lay in a pool of black, pudding-thick blood in which a swarm of flies and other insects were feeding. The ashes in the fire were cold. Clearly, someone had killed the Sanchez brothers quite soon after he had left them at Mutindua with the old man, Terrari's supposed brother, Sendeo. *And where is he?* wondered Bazaan as he scoured the camp for clues. *Perhaps the old man Sendeo killed the two brothers? Quite inconceivable, but, perhaps, possible.*

Bazaan began to dream of the area around him—scouring it for signs of the old man and any clue as to what had befallen his friends and would-be troops. His attention was almost physically jerked into order when he saw another solitary tent over a mile away from the Sanchez camp. It was a Jansport Expedition dome tent sitting like a toadstool in a field of dark green. Bazaan dreamed closer and saw a single body, apparently asleep inside the tent, which was pitched just shy of a game trail. The figure was clearly not an African. His head nestled in the crook of his elbow and his knees slightly drawn up in his sleeping bag.

Bazaan floated around the stranger's camp and tried to assess the intent of its owner. He saw no Perlon ropes or climbing equipment and ruled this out as a mountaineer's camp. He drew closer to the sleeping man in the tent. The veins in Bazaan's neck pulsed, and he saw with tunnel vision. The man he had seen on Kenyatta Avenue in Nairobi some days before—the same person who, he was certain, had left the list of Dream Walker notes at the Norfolk—lay before him. Bazaan felt the goose flesh start as he peered down at the sleeping man. Should he kill the man now? Restraint coupled with curiosity stayed Bazaan's hand as he studied this somehow familiar man, searching for something to explain his presence here. Clearly, the Small Death would allow Bazaan greater scrutiny and study in the future. *Hell,* thought Bazaan, *if I can kill a leopard at five yards without him sensing me there, I will not need any help in my job at Keekorok.*

He continued to study the man. He knew that, somehow, this man lying on the floor of the tent was linked with his own destiny. Strangely, Bazaan felt a remembrance of this man whose appearance evaded his memory banks. Who was he, and why was he here?

"Kill him, *mzungu,* for he would surely kill you." The gnome Terrari spoke to him amid the dreaming. "Did he not kill your friends?"

"Possibly your brother Sendeo did the killing. Do you cover for him, old man? He was the only one to have been with my friends. Is this a spider's web of lies and deceit, old man? Perhaps I should be killing you now instead of this *mzungu.*"

"Kill who you wish, *mzungu.* It was not I who killed these men. I was too busy trying to kill you, if you remember."

Bazaan almost smiled at the old man's words. Most certainly, Terrari did seem to have been preoccupied with such activity. And at the same time, it would not wash to allow this man in the tent to live in the face of building doubt. Bazaan put little stock in happenstance and felt the prickles of conviction. He must kill this man sleeping so soundly in his tent.

Bazaan was totally focused on his approach to the sleeping man's tent. He slipped his Glock out of his waistband and crouched—centered down—and almost tiptoed to the tent. The sleeping man lay on his back on top of a Polartec sleeping bag, his head nestled into the instep of a giant climbing boot.

Bazaan leveled the barrel of the Glock and took aim at the head of the sleeping man—the target made hazy by the tent's netting. The bark of a bushbuck startled him, and he squatted stock still outside the tent. Out of nowhere, a fist-sized piece of basalt hit the juncture of the thumb and forefinger of Bazaan's gun hand. The pain was excruciating as the rock squarely hit the nerve bundle. Bazaan involuntarily let go of the Glock, and it tumbled out of his hand.

The man in the tent sat up bleary-eyed and saw Bazaan looming inside the vestibule of his tent. Bazaan grabbed for his gun. Instantly, the man in the tent crabbed onto his back, supported by both arms and feet, and thrust a kick at Bazaan's face directly through the mosquito netting. The man's heel buried itself deep in Bazaan's eye socket, knocking him backward ten feet outside the tent. Bazaan gripped his Glock tightly, trying to focus through the pain and needlepoints of light that dazed his vision. With amazing speed, the man was now outside the tent, grabbing Bazaan's gun hand.

The man was performing a technique called *shionage* on Bazaan, pointing the gun inward as he forced the wrist back on itself. Bazaan head-butted the tall man, who then let go of his wrist lock. Bazaan sprung off the ground like a cat as the man held his nose and eyes and collapsed, his knees folding under him. Bazaan again pointed the gun at the man's head. A callused black hand reached around from behind him and pulled his head back, exposing his throat. In the moment he felt the cold of cutting steel, he saw Terrari to the front, his eyes wide in surprise.

If Terrari isn't doing the cutting, who is? wondered Bazaan. He quickly hammer-fisted his assailant in the groin, spinning within the outstretched arms. There was the old man, Sendeo, bent over, favoring his groin. He held a knife pointed at Bazaan's eyes.

The old man shouted a command to the man, who was still on his knees, blood flowing between his fingers, which cupped his nose. "Quickly, *Bwana* Gabe. N'gai's *Thanga!*"

Then the old man simply disappeared. Bazaan spun with his gun ready to shoot the man who had been sleeping in the tent. There were only drops of dark, red blood splattered like a crimson Rorschach test on the grass and small rocks of the forest floor. The man was gone.

Terrari squatted beside the tent, looking like a desiccated corpse made of tar. He was casually chewing a plug of tobacco, and spat a stream at the drops of blood, testing his accuracy and nodding as the brown stream hit its target.

"Where the hell did he come from, and where the hell did they go?" snapped Bazaan.

"They are dreaming as we are, you stupid *nugu.* My brother Sendeo has taught the tall *mzungu* to dream, as I was forced to do with you. You became of his dream and were real enough—you have your bulging eye to prove it is so, *mzungu.*"

Bazaan muttered rubbing his left eye, which was throbbing and swelling closed. "I know that tall fucker. I can't believe it, but somebody that tall with the name of Gabe—it's gotta be Gabe Turpin. I haven't seen that motherfucker since my mom and us moved from that hick town in Nebraska when I was a kid."

Bazaan was pacing and rubbing his eye. He slipped the gun back into his waistband. "How long does this dreaming continue to work?"

"A bit longer, *mzungu.* Where do you wish to go now? I tire of this dreaming with you, *mzungu.* I wish to go back to my *thanga* and sleep without dreams."

Bazaan continued to rub his eye and asked, "What if I am dreaming elsewhere when it ends?"

"Well, if I were you, I would dream yourself back to my *thanga* and your vehicle, unless you wish to walk for a long time."

Bazaan consented, and thought of the old man's bachelor's hut. He found himself inside the hut and saw his own body lying beside the unmoving form of Terrari—still on the packed dirt floor. The cook fire had burned itself down, showing only small flecks of orange embers under the gray ash. His dreams and thoughts grew clouded, confused, and mixed. He was again a young man, armed with a knife and fighting a tall white boy in an old neighborhood. He remembered the chants of young boys crying, "Gabe!" He felt the hits and the kicks. He was floating in his dreaming—his reality. The tall white boy, who was unarmed, was kicking his ass, despite the knife. The white boy locked him up—hit him and kept hitting him. The boy then stomped on his crotch.

Gabe. The name brought a shudder of reality to Bazaan. Gabe Turpin. So many years ago. So much history heaped on history. Bazaan remembered the day he fought Gabe Turpin, some thirty-odd years before. His body had never healed. The stomp on his privates had ruptured the vas deferens in his scrotum. He now had some difficulty maintaining an erection during normal intercourse. More and more, Bazaan had to rely on oral sex and intercourse supercharged with sadism in order to satisfy his sexual needs. For years, Bazaan had hated Gabe Turpin for stealing a part of his manhood from him. Now he was certain this man was again involved in trying to ruin his life.

Bazaan's hazy reality revealed Terrari sitting in the hut, studying him in an openly unfriendly manner. Bazaan's vision of reality shifted and glided like a kaleidoscope. The old black man sat there amid Bazaan's confused maelstrom of thought and memory and continued to study him.

"*Jambo, mzungu.* Have you enjoyed your dreaming? Why is it you protect your privates? Are your memories so real?"

Bazaan regarded the old man and maintained his silence as he continued to adapt to the realities of reality.

"Meet someone in the dreaming you wished you hadn't?" asked Terrari.

Bazaan continued to be silent, garnering his strength, marshaling his breath. He stared at the old man Terrari. He cared not for this old man.

Later, Bazaan heard the quiet conversation between Terrari and his young wife and felt the early-morning sun cast shafts of warmth through the cloth door of the hut. Like a persistent cat licking his face, the sun steadily showered Bazaan's face with rays of wakefulness. He lazily rolled over, testing his joints and muscles, and realized that he was totally alone. There was just the cooing of rock doves and the sun filtering through the cheap *merikany* cloth of the doorway.

Bazaan found the leafy package of the *Kidogo Kifu* in the middle of the doorway. The old man had delivered as promised. Hefting the package, Bazaan estimated he had enough of the paste for more than twenty dream sessions. Ducking down and exiting the hut, he had to nearly close his good eye in the sudden brightness of that clear morning on the Ewaso Ng'iro.

Terrari and his *bibi* were nowhere to be seen. Cautiously, Bazaan walked toward the SUV and found it where he had parked it, under a huge fig tree. The roof and hood of the vehicle shimmered with dew and looked alien in this arboreal setting, like a giant, metallic beetle asleep on the forest floor. The sun was now growing warm and blunted the bite of chill in the highland air.

He found the keys, stiffly sat down in the driver's seat, and rested. Bazaan was dizzy, and it seemed his brain was still somewhat muddled. He absently tapped his fingers on the steering wheel, waiting to feel better. His eye was now a living, throbbing thing, and he wondered if he didn't have a slight concussion. He thought to look in the rearview mirror to see if both pupils were evenly dilated, but couldn't open his left eye enough to see the pupil. Wondering about his driving ability with no depth perception, Bazaan started the vehicle and carefully nosed it back down the track to the highway. He pointed the Suzuki toward Nyeri and drove slowly. He hoped to find a pharmacy in town, as well as a good supply of ibuprofen and a cold-pack compress for his eye.

The wooden foldout store shelves of the Indian *duka* sported an unusually complete supply of over-the-counter medical supplies. The ibuprofen was between the chloroquine used for malaria and the Good Baby antiseptic eyedrops used for the frequent eye infections spread by the ever-present flies of East Africa. Surprisingly, Bazaan also found an old chemical cold compress next to the Ultra Sheen hair pomade. The blue ink on the plastic bag of the compress was faded and peeling.

Bazaan gave the *duka*'s proprietor a one-hundred-shilling note and waved away the change. The old Indian barely nodded his head in thanks and slowly blinked his hooded eyes, looking like a fat brown chameleon. The horns of the passing *matatus* sounded above the growling of lorries and country buses.

Bazaan wanted to find a pair of sunglasses to hide his injured eye—to make himself less conspicuous. He passed by a number of the hucksters who arranged their goods on dirty sheets that lay on the dusty red ground. He saw a number of sunglasses, but all were garish and bordering on ridiculous—a misguided attempt at Western cool.

Bazaan found a pair of simple aviator glasses that were displayed along with cassette tapes that included *The Best of Roger Whittaker* and *The Classics of Zamfir, Master of the Pan Flute.* He paid for the glasses, put them on, and walked to a curry restaurant for an early lunch.

Sitting at the small wooden table in the flyblown restaurant, Bazaan took four ibuprofens and chased them down with a Tusker beer. He quietly belched and downed the rest of the beer in one long pull. The restaurant owner, who looked like a brown chameleon, walked the few steps from the kitchen to Bazaan's table and offered a yellow, torn, one-page menu obviously produced by an ancient typewriter. Meat curry and vegetable curry were available, along with yogurt and the ubiquitous Samosas. Bazaan would have asked what type of meat was used in the meat curry, but deferred, knowing that was probably dependent on what sort of animal had been killed on the road that morning.

Glad he'd had a hepatitis shot recently, Bazaan ordered the vegetable curry and the Samosas made with peas and potato. He was leery of the yogurt and ordered another Tusker. The proprietor shuffled behind the counter and back to Bazaan's table, presenting the Tusker. Bazaan drank deeply and muffled another belch.

The handful of ibuprofens and the two beers had put the pain and throbbing of Bazaan's eye in check. The brown chameleon served Bazaan his lunch. The vegetable curry was potent and had a backbeat that cleared Bazaan's sinuses. The Samosas were hotter than the center of the sun. Bazaan bit into the first one and had to open his mouth and let the biteful roll out of his mouth and back on the plate. He quickly grabbed his Tusker and coated his mouth with the cool, yeasty brew.

Bazaan considered his options in view of the turn of events. He absently munched on the fried vegetable pockets and opened his throat to receive the flood of Kenya's premium *pombe*. The Samosas were now only warm and spicy, their mint taste blending wonderfully with the peas and potatoes and the cumin and peppers. He sopped up the vegetable curry with warm chapatis and continued to let his plan of action assemble itself. Bazaan ordered a third Tusker, as he realized it most prudent to start preparing for the Alpha job, even though it was some weeks away. He figured he'd stage his recon from the Serena Lodge, about fifty kilometers from the Keekorok Lodge. With the Small Death, the distance was irrelevant.

⟡⟡⟡

The Mara Serena Lodge was a white stucco monstrosity built near the base of the Esoit Oloolo Escarpment of the Great Rift along a western tributary of the Mara River. One dirt road connected the Mara Serena with the other major lodge in the reserve—the Keekorok. Both lodges were a spitting distance from Tanzania's border with Kenya. Although the animals knew no difference, Kenya's Maasai Mara Game Reserve melted into Tanzania's Serengeti National Park. The wildebeest and zebras ran in their typical zigzag patterns and crossed national boundaries dozens of times a day, not knowing the difference between the acacia, the stands of grass, and the anthills in democratic Kenya and those in socialist Tanzania. The heartbeat of Africa was very old here, and not disrupted by the cultural and political flatulence of the last century. Here, the same story of life was told day after day, never ending. Here, in this vast sea of grass and forested riverbeds, was the tree where man was born. The very bedrock of the land was ancient.

Bazaan would stage out of the Mara Serena and, with the Small Death, visit and recon the Keekorok Lodge. With or without the help of the old N'dorobo Terrari, Bazaan felt confident he could manage this recon and gather intelligence using the *Kidogo Kifu* to keep him in stealth mode. He would dream a presence in the old man's hut on the Ewaso Ng'iro and press him into a chaperoning function at the very least. With or without the old man, Bazaan was confident the *Kidogo Kifu* would allow him to pull off this Alpha job by himself. With his newly found killing capability, he no longer needed the Sanchez brothers—or anyone else, for that matter. Bazaan could kill invisibly, and no walls or security could keep him from the performance of his chosen job.

The curry was served with chapatis and a bowl of yogurt, which came unordered. Bazaan ordered another Tusker. Thinking, *What the hell,* Bazaan spooned the raw brown sugar from a crusted bowl into the yogurt and gave it a taste. Meaning to reserve the sweetened yogurt for dessert, he focused back on his curry. The saffron and cumin flavors of the curry went well with the rice.

Bazaan sopped the curry gravy from its bowl with his chapatis.

Bazaan's eye no longer troubled him. The four beers and ibuprofen had seen to that. He finished the last spoonful of brown sugar yogurt and ordered a *kahawa* (coffee). He ladled in the raw sugar and dosed the dark mixture nearly half and half with goat cream. Bazaan smiled, anticipating being five million dollars wealthier. The security services of President Odinga and Vice President Baker were not prepared to deal with the witchcraft of the N'dorobo. Bazaan planned to perfect the use of the Small Death in order to raise the bar of political and military assassination. *How does one stop the wind from blowing? How does one confine a cloud at sunset? Such are the paradigms with which traditional security must now deal. How does one stop another's dreaming?*

Bazaan left a handful of shilling notes on the table and exited the café, walking slowly across the dirt road and on to his SUV. He would drive to Nairobi that afternoon and stay at an out-of-the-way hotel, the Fairview, before he went on to the Mara Serena. Feeling a little too drunk to negotiate the upcountry roads of rural Kenya, Bazaan dozed in the driver's seat of the Suzuki and woke an hour later to the multitoned honking horn of a garishly painted *matatu* as it rounded the curve and plunged on to the market area. Shaking the cobwebs from his mind, Bazaan started the vehicle and picked his way slowly toward Nairobi on a road bordered with ribbons of red footpaths and framed by arbors of dark green. His eye was, again, throbbing with intensity. He took another five ibuprofens and choked them down dry. Bazaan was on his way to the Mara and had mentally clocked in on the job.

13

MT. KENYA, 2005

GABE HEARD THE COMFORTING SOUND OF CASCADING WATER and smelled the clean, thin mountain air laced with the duff smells of soil and grass. He saw Sendeo squatting on a basalt boulder adorned with toupees of moss and splashes of lichen. He wondered at his presence there. N'gai's *Thanga* was safety for the moment. Gabe squinted as he focused back through the haze of memory on the man who had head-butted him and had come armed with bad intent into Gabe's camp. The coarse hair, the drawn features, were somehow familiar.

"Sendeo, what's happened? I thought my dreaming was done. I slept the evening and into the early morning. How was it I was able to dream without taking of the Small Death?"

Sendeo answered, "Your mind was not yet organized. You weren't alive enough to know you couldn't dream. So, you could dream. I told you to dream of N'gai's *Thanga*. You did. If you had been awake and fully alive in the world, your mind would have told you you could not dream your way to N'gai's *Thanga*. Think not about this, *Bwana* Gabe. We are safe now in N'gai's *Thanga*."

Gabe mused on the reality of this nonreality. Clearly, the real world was made up of realities with faint borders. Reality and nonreality were all the same. Gabe gripped a tussock of elephant grass to test its reality. It held fast against his efforts—as real as a pinch to one's self.

"Sendeo, I'm tired and somehow disturbed by this dreaming. I want to go back to camp and spend some time by myself. Possibly go away for a bit."

"N'dio, bwana. We can go back and, if the bad man is gone, pack up your gear. Remember, we are visible and real to others only when we choose to act on another. Let us dream of your camp, *Bwana* Gabe."

Gabe saw the dome tent and could not detect any interlopers or enemies. He quietly dismantled his tent, taking its rain fly off and stuffing the tent, the fly, and the three fiberglass poles into a long nylon tube. He stuffed his sleeping bag and the flotsam and jetsam of his gear within the confines of the Lowe Expedition pack. The camp was quickly compressed into the pack, the only evidence of Gabe's presence the matted-grass outline of his tent—a circular design on the forest floor.

Sendeo silently watched the ritual. Gabe could break camp unconsciously and with remarkable efficiency. It appeared almost like a grand illusion. One second a thriving place of occupancy, the next second no sign of anything.

Gabe shouldered his pack and turned to Sendeo.

"Sendeo, I'm off now, and no worries. I will be back in a few days. I need to rest and think a bit. I'll wish to do more of the dreaming with you when I return, but have no more stomach for it now. I'll be back sometime next week."

"N'dio, Bwana Gabe. I can feel the weight of your dreaming. Go rest. Go to a gentle place to think. I will wait for you. I will find you, *Bwana* Gabe. When you are ready, just walk up the Chogoria Track. I will be at your side as you walk in the mist."

Gabe hiked to the Mutindua market and found transport to Nanyuki. From there, he paid for passage to Nairobi on a *matatu* and found quite useful the "emptiness of being" when the infant of a fellow passenger pissed all over Gabe's pants. Mama M'Binga cut up on the tinny-sounding speaker mounted in the camper shell of the *matatu*. Gabe's eyes were as blank and empty as were his African counterparts'.

The countryside of Kenya melted into the cityscape of Nairobi. Getting out at River Road, Gabe walked on stiff legs toward city center. The baby's piss had dried on his pant legs, and Gabe shouldered his huge pack in search of a cab. A cab driven by a toothless old man skidded to a halt inches away from Gabe. Gabe off-loaded his pack in the front seat and nestled into the back, feeling soul-weary. He told the cabbie to go to the Hotel Tropic first and wait there for him, then they'd go on to the Fairview Hotel west of city center. The old man nodded his understanding and drove.

Gabe exited the cab at the Hotel Tropic and glanced into the Jevanjee Gardens on Moktar Daddah Street. The shiftless afternoon had claimed the city. The toothless cabbie closed his eyes and rested his chin on his chest as Gabe went into the hotel. Gabe claimed his duffel, paid the chit, and tossed the green bag into the backseat of the taxi. He wedged himself in the backseat beside his duffel and directed the cabbie to the Fairview Hotel. The cabbie drove south off of Moktar Daddah and on to Moi Avenue. The cab went southeast down Moi to Kenyatta Avenue. It turned west and continued to Valley Road and the Fairview.

Gabe had the cab idle outside the Fairview while he made certain there was a room. Receiving a confirmation, Gabe went to the cab, placed a fistful of shilling notes into the cabbie's hand, and walked back to the lobby of the Fairview as doves cooed in the jacaranda trees and the smell of charcoal fires grew omnipresent. Gabe dumped his pack and duffel in his second-story room. After he toted his duffel, he sought out the communal toilet and relieved himself.

Gabe went into the formal dining room and ordered dinner—grilled Nile perch and a bottle of chardonnay. Gabe shuffled from dinner to his room and collapsed.

It was the city air that woke Gabe first. No longer was he smelling the soil and vegetation of the mountain. The air was also alive with sound. Although the Fairview was sheltered from city center, the buses and traffic on the A-2 provided a background to the doves and other tropical aviary of this urban forest.

Gabe wearily pulled himself from the small single bed and went to the communal bathroom. He splashed his face with water, brushed his teeth, and tried to comb out the spikes and plates of his thin, matted hair. He took breakfast on the lawn. The tea was served from thermos urns and the eggs and sausages were adorned with cooked tomato. The toast was offered with incredibly yellow butter and a crystal dish of orange marmalade. He slathered the toast with huge dollops of the golden marmalade with its yellow flecks of orange peels. He sipped his tea, which was diluted by nearly half with cream and included two huge spoonfuls of sugar. The jacarandas were full of rock doves, and the cooing worked as nature's mantra. Gabe began to become human again. Gabe's goal was the Maasai Mara Game Reserve and Fig Tree Camp. He had spent magical times at Fig Tree Camp and looked forward to healing himself there again. The first time he was embraced by Fig Tree Camp, he had been severely dehydrated from giardiasis he had contracted at the meteorological station on Mt. Kenya after a three-week climb. He and his friends Joe and Ted had drank deeply of the water there and had, through the night, continually sprayed their fecal offerings to N'gai. At first, their offerings sought the target of the dark outhouse hole. Later, their offerings adorned all four walls of the outhouse. At five o'clock in the morning, Gabe had little strength left and had crawled out of the *banda* they had rented at the met station, cocked his ass over the porch, and let go. He could no longer stand or squat, and the *banda*'s outdoor toilet was too far, given the immediacy of his need and his physical debilitation. The early hours found all three men shitting on the grounds around the *banda,* or on themselves. The next day, they had driven pell-mell through the chuckholes of the B-3 Highway through Narok and found themselves at Fig Tree Camp. After a dinner that was cautiously consumed by all three, the loo, or tented bathroom, was occupied throughout the night. Gabe and Ted applauded a more-than-minute-long fart Joe issued into the bowl of the toilet. The tent at Fig Tree was like a leper asylum. Gabe had crawled out of the green tent before the morning tea and coffee service. The waiter had come in white robes. "*Chai, kahawa, sahib. Asante*" (Tea and coffee sir. Thank you).

The smell of the tent damned near dropped the waiter as he entered with the tray. Quickly, he unlashed the window flaps, clearly in an attempt to breathe. He issued himself from the flaps of the tent, quite shaken. Gabe settled into the folding safari chair and felt sorry for the man's trouble. A hippo grunted from the nearby river, and Joe, in a diarrhetic stupor, asked Gabe, "What was that?"

Gabe replied, "They have a tape program of African wildlife. That was a recording of a hippo."

Quite satisfied, Joe said, "Okay, so it's a tape?"

Gabe quietly chuckled.

The air outside the tent was so clearly decontaminated, and Gabe sat there and watched a chameleon crawl up the taut line of the tent. Joe and Ted had either died or were sleeping soundly, their bowels clear of all traffic. Birds called from around the tent. Gabe had come home again—so many years ago.

Gabe wanted to do R and R at Fig Tree. He finished his breakfast and paid his room chit. He checked his large Lowe Expedition pack and duffel at the desk of the Fairview, then carried only the summit pack with its two changes of clothes and minimal toiletries and personal gear. With the blue summit pack slung over his shoulders, he nodded his agreement to a taxi outside the white colonial exterior of the Fairview. They went to River Road, where Gabe found a *matatu* bound for Narok. At Narok, Gabe bought a White Cap at a bar that offered a rooftop view of the only road through the town. Gabe sipped his beer and watched the tourist traffic going to the Mara or Amboseli National Park. To his dismay, he saw a fellow Nebraskan-turned-white-hunter pull into the bar-restaurant and issue forth as a personal assault on Gabe's solitude. Gabe was rude and pointed. The *mzungu* white hunter disappeared and troubled Gabe no more.

From Narok, Gabe hired a Peugeot taxi and proceeded down the B-3 to the Maasai Mara Game Reserve and the turnoff to Fig Tree Camp. From Ewaso Ng'iro, the road branched three ways. Gabe instructed the driver to take the middle road toward Fig Tree, past Cottar's Camp toward Keekorok, and then north to Fig Tree. At the juncture of the three roads Gabe stopped briefly at the Maasai handicrafts booth manned by Gabe's old friend Peter.

Peter had hardly any teeth left in his skull. He was a young Kikuyu. He was, for all intents and purposes, a Maasai handicraft wholesaler. Women came from miles around to consign their handicrafts to Peter, who, strategically placed at the juncture to every lodge in the reserve, sold his wares at a fraction of the price commanded in Nairobi.

Gabe had imported a few tins of Kodiak—an American chewing tobacco. Peter loved Kodiak. Over the past years he had foolishly traded wonderfully beaded calabashes, spears, and *kisus* to Gabe when under the influence of the freely given Kodiak chew. Gabe stepped out of the Peugeot and silently offered Peter three tins of Kodiak.

Peter silently gestured at his array of genuine Maasai handicrafts. Gabe, just as silent, shook his head in denial and simply grasped Peter's hand in friendship. Gabe got into the taxi, and the Peugeot took off into the golden afternoon haze of the African rift.

The Maasai Mara Game Reserve closed its gates at sunset. In the back of the Peugeot, Gabe fretted they would be too late and he would have to return to Narok and spend the night in a vermin-infested hotel. The sun was a huge orange plate in the west, and its edges shimmered as it touched the escarpment. Giraffes loped alongside the Peugeot, and Gabe could see the tan silhouettes of the beasts bobbing alongside the green of the Talek River basin just past Cottar's Camp. At the reserve's entrance, just as the last golden rim of the sun plunged into the dark of the escarpment, Gabe met some resistance, but was waved on as the *askaris* closed the gates. Gabe would have to pay for the driver's room and board for that night. Little matter—he would be staying with workers in their poor quarters.

They passed the Sarova Mara Camp and continued toward Keekorok. Just before Keekorok, Gabe instructed the driver to turn north to Fig Tree Camp, just outside the small village of Talek. There, perched on the Talek River, Fig Tree Camp was a veritable oasis for the soul. All of the camp's appointments were tents—wonderfully green, spacious tents with a bath and a toilet walled in stone at the back of each. Fires burned under the series of fifty-five-gallon drums of water connected to the tents in a spiderweb of rubber hoses, which supplied the tented camp with hot water. Gabe checked in and gave his driver some drinking money.

"Asante sana, sahib" (Thank you very much, sir), voiced the driver, already wetting his lips in anticipation of the *pombe* of his hosts.

Dinner was a half hour away. Gabe had off-loaded his small pack on the cot of his tent and splashed water on his face in the tent's loo. He walked past the suspension bridge strung over the Talek River and took a seat at the bar. He ordered a gin and tonic and nursed his drink as he watched a baboon breach camp security and push open a gate on the bridge carelessly left open by one of the guests or an incompetent staff person. The baboon was intent on making his way to the food tent and gave Gabe only a quick, guilty look as he headed for the smells of the canvas kitchen. Baboon barks and human shouts were punctuated by the sound of pots and pans being thrown at the primate interloper. The baboon raced along the path, gave Gabe a quick, frustrated look, and scampered back across the bridge. A kitchen boy gave pursuit and closed the gate on the bridge, content the culinary assault was unsuccessful.

Chuckling to himself, Gabe walked into the main dining tent and ordered the roast guinea hen and saffron rice. He went to the appetizer table and picked through fresh vegetables and fruits, along with breads, chapatis, and water biscuits. His dinner came with a gin and tonic, and he quietly enjoyed the food among a minor din of tourists—mostly German—who had come to see for themselves the wilds of Africa. After the main course, cheese and salads were offered. Here, in the depths of East Africa, prevailed the European tradition of cheese and salads served as the last course, even after dessert. Gabe enjoyed a ripe

Stilton and washed it and the tomato vinaigrette salad down with a glass of South African chablis.

Gabe reflected on a trip after his discovery of Fig Tree Camp. On that very special trip, he, his wife, and their daughter had also experienced the magic of the Mara, here in this idyllic corner of the continent.

Gabe, Cindy, and Malindi had come back to Nairobi after a week on Mt. Kenya, and Gabe, going on the cheap, had consumed a three-day-old cheese sandwich made for him by the Naro Moro River Lodge as a picnic lunch. Malindi and Cindy had eaten well at the African Heritage but Gabe chose the suspect cheese sandwich for his repast. By late afternoon, the rotten cheese had claimed Gabe's gut, and he could eat no more than tomato soup at the Norfolk that evening. After eating his soup, Gabe had silently proceeded to the toilets of the Norfolk and puked his guts out. He washed his mouth and face and went back to join his daughter and wife on the verandah. He reported his problem to his wife and eight-year-old daughter. They got a taxi and went to their room in the New Stanley and, upon entry, Gabe, with great intestinal upheaval, instructed his wife to turn up the radio really loud. Cindy informed him there was no radio in the room and Gabe issued a subdued, "Too bad."

Gabe puked his guts out again and curled into a fetal position as his wife and daughter wondered about their fate in Africa, with the "King of Kenya" out of commission and in the hospital. Gabe, in the quiet of the night and the strangeness of the New Stanley, made his stand. Morning dawned and the three drove on toward Fig Tree in a rented Suzuki compact. Regrettably, the recent rains had erased the roads between Narok and the Mara. Gabe improvised and drove for miles in the bush, keeping the Loita Hills to his left and focusing on the natural breaks that were, at one time, the road from Narok to the Maasai Mara.

At one point, a torrent poured across their path to Fig Tree, and Gabe got out of the vehicle to assess the situation. He waded knee-deep into the torrent, guessing at its depth. He placed a cairn at the edge of the water, knowing he could gauge future negotiations of this new river by looking at the water's edge and its relationship to the stone cairn.

Gabe slipped the vehicle's transmission into low-range four-wheel drive and began to grind across the torrent. Cindy clasped her hands over her ears, screaming, filled with fear.

Malindi had begun to sing the lyrics of a John Wayne movie soundtrack and whistling "Hatari," *which meant "danger" in Swahili. The Suzuki successfully deposited the family on the far side of the torrent. The water had come only to the middle of the door—no more than two feet high.*

After negotiating some steep, muddy washes, the family issued into Fig Tree Camp in a stately manner. German tourists grounded by the torrents of road-washing rains asked, "Where did you come from?"

"Nairobi," Gabe replied.

"That's impossible! There are no roads open between here and Nairobi!" responded the Germans on holiday.

"Don't need roads if you know where you're going," said Gabe.

The tourists were in shock as the American family got out of their mud-spattered four-wheel-drive truck and into the safety of their green tent. Unlike the professional combi *drivers, this family from Nebraska didn't know they couldn't make it.*

The following week, the Fig Tree and the Mara offered daily miracles to Gabe and his family. Perhaps the most precious for Gabe was the afternoon, after an early-morning game viewing, that Cindy had sought the relaxing comforts of the tent for a nap. Gabe and Malindi ventured forth onto the plains of Africa. Fortified with two gin and tonics from the bar, Gabe parked the Suzuki and walked with Malindi through the high grass of the African plains, ignoring all of the rules of the reserve. A rainbow from a nearby torrential downpour south in Tanzania spread across the sky. The end of the rainbow enveloped an old thorn tree less than a quarter mile away. Gabe urged his daughter into the vehicle and they sped to the end of the rainbow. There, amid the golden glow of the rainbow, Gabe and his daughter gazed at the waves of golden grass and the menagerie of African wildlife going about their lives on the plains, as they had before mankind.

Gabe sat in the poorly lit dining tent of Fig Tree as it registered on him how much he missed his wife and daughter. Although Malindi no longer lived at home, she was still a vital part of their lives. He and Cindy had embraced their empty-nest status with resignation. Theirs had been a life often defined by separations, some heartbreakingly long.

Gabe threw down the last of his drink and walked out into the inky darkness of the camp's grounds, where gas lanterns on poles cast blotches of light here and there. He found his way back to his tent and drew a bath of hot water. Breathing in deeply the unique smell of canvas, he reclined in the hot water, and the dust that coated his skin congealed in the soapy water.

Then Gabe opened the flap of the tented bathroom and entered the cooler confines of the green tent. The sheets on the bed, a military cot, had been turned back. No mint, however—after all, it was Africa. He could hear the gentle moaning of the hyenas beyond the camp. The Talek River served as background for a menagerie of wildlife sounds. The moon cast shadows on the front window fly of the tent. Gabe sought rest. He nestled into the stiff cotton sheets and dreamed of nothing at all.

14

KENYA, 2005

GABE'S EYES OPENED AS THE GENTLE WORDS OF THE SERVANT broke through his slumber. *"Jambo bwana. Chai, kahawa?"*

"Kahawa, tafadhali," Gabe mumbled into the pillowcase.

Gabe smiled as he heard the soft, tickling sound of coffee being poured into a porcelain cup.

"Mziwa?" (Milk?), asked the voice in the darkness of the early morning.

"N'dio. Asante sana." (Yes. Thank you very much.)

Gabe heard the trickle of milk poured into the steaming cup. He rolled out of the bed and slurped the first taste of strong Kenyan coffee in the shadows before full light. The canvas floor of the tent was cool and only somewhat damp. Gabe went out into the gray dawn, collapsed into the safari chair, and slurped half of his coffee as the landscape of green unfolded before his sleep-clouded eyes. He sat there and quietly took in the landscape as he sipped the Kenyan coffee.

The cool of the morning was broken by Gabe's bellyful of hot coffee. He could smell the bacon frying in the cook's tent. He was ravenous. He poured another cup of *kahawa* from the silver service, along with a third-of-a-cup of milk and three spoons of sugar. A zebra barked near the river. He heard the hippos grunting and drank his third cup of coffee before seven o'clock.

The *combis* were loading the European tourists. Gabe walked over to the camp's office and found his driver already consuming his breakfast of maize meal and gravy, along with smoky milk from zebu cattle.

"Jambo, habari?" asked Gabe.

"M'zuri, bwana."

"First I will have breakfast and then, *pese-pese, safari."*

"N'dio, bwana."

Gabe idled over to the cook tent. He took up a heated porcelain plate and filled it with scrambled eggs and maize meal porridge. He ladled on three sausages and a grilled tomato, grabbed a handful of toast, and went to a table underneath the green canvas. There, the orange marmalade and cubes of fresh butter held station. A starched, cotton-clad waiter served Gabe his fourth cup of coffee of the day. He drank this one sans milk and sugar.

Mist and steam were rolling off the greens and yellows of the Rift's foliage. The purple of the escarpment loomed distantly, like the afterthought of a Kenyan morning. *This,* Gabe thought, *was what ancient man saw. This was the cradle of mankind. The world is clearly old here.*

Gabe beckoned his driver and the two set out on the road that went south from Fig Tree, pulled shy of the Keekorok Lodge, skirted the Tanzanian border northwest across the Mara River, and arrived at the Serena Lodge. A little west of the Keekorok, Gabe motioned his driver to follow a track up an old riverbed. They plied on among red anthills, thorn trees, and scrub until the gray dollops of elephants appeared. Gabe instructed the driver to stop and got out of the vehicle. He slowly walked toward the herd. The females on the outer periphery were trying to scent him. Ears flared, one or two young males bowed at the tail end of their charges. Gabe, knowing something about elephants, did not move and enjoyed the bravado.

Gabe smiled broadly as he assessed the herd. The elephant was his favorite African animal. He bowed in respect to the herd, and they no longer seemed threatened. Gabe continued to smile as he went back to the vehicle and sat on the bumper of the Peugeot. The elephants continued their gentle, rhythmic forage. He sat not more than forty yards from the herd and seemed content to share his thoughts with the large creatures.

Gabe got back into the Peugeot and the driver motored on toward the Mara River, the taxi vibrating over the washboard ruts in the road. Upon arriving at the Mara River, Gabe again told the driver to stop, got out of the vehicle, and sauntered to the edge of the riverbank to gaze down on a bend that produced a huge eddy in the river. There, the hippos floated like huge, brown turds in the tawny-colored water. The steep, fluted banks of the river looked like polished jasper in the morning light.

A huge, splashing commotion disturbed the sleeping hippos as a string of wildebeest careened down a gully and into the water, noisily swimming across the river. The herd galloped up a steep draw not thirty yards from Gabe—a mass of wet fur, clacking hooves, and ungulate flatulence. Their long, shaggy heads bobbed up and down as they sprinted away from Gabe with surprising speed.

The entire herd was soon swallowed up by the shimmers of hot air that hung like liquid bands of light, shifting and contorting in the hot equatorial sun.

Gabe saw the hippos settling back into the cool, shaded waters of the eddy. Their wiggling ears and snorted spumes of river water were offered as a gruff reaction to the affront of the unsophisticated wildebeest. Gabe smiled broadly. The Mara seemed to cradle him in a primal comfort, drawing out of him pure wonderment, as well as wonderful memories. It was getting on toward noon and Gabe thought a lunch at Keekorok and a visit to the nearby Maasai *manyatta* and his *Laibon* friend, Olioke, could provide not only a pleasant afternoon, but also possibly information on the nature of the N'dorobo dreaming. The *Laibon* was the senior man of a Maasai tribe—a chief of sorts. The *Laibon* dutifully learned and documented the history of the tribe and, to some degree, the very history of man in Africa. The Maasai, like the N'dorobo, were a Nilotic tribe and, hence, had longtime dealings and histories in common with the tribe they referred to as the "poor people"—the N'dorobo.

"Keekorok, *pese-pese,*" said Gabe as he climbed into the Peugeot.

Gabe reveled in the landmarks and scenery that were, for him, like old friends. Lost in the beauty of it all, he slouched back in his seat and let the warm air blow into his face as the vehicle crunched down the road. Turning south on the road to Keekorok, the Peugeot had to slow down to avoid a herd of giraffes as it floated across the road and out onto the plains of the Mara to the north. Their characteristic gait gave the illusion that the beasts were running in slow motion.

Parked at Keekorok, the driver melted away into the outbuildings that housed the lodge's workers. Gabe ambled through an open-air foyer and found the swimming pool being used by a handful of German tourists, apparently a family, the patriarch and matriarch wedged into deck chairs, sunscreen daubed on their Aryan cheeks, noses, and foreheads. Papa was sweating profusely and thirstily gulped his large glass of beer, pursing his lips with satisfaction. He belched mightily and went for another drink to fill the void. His nubile daughters—like inspirations for Rodin—cavorted in the pool, squealing at every occasion.

Gabe entered the bar off the pool deck and noticed an old man—*an American,* he thought—sitting in a wheelchair alone in the corner. Two empty martini glasses were dead soldiers that stood watch over an uneaten steak sandwich and chips. The old man was delicately sampling a third martini as if it were a magic elixir. He saw Gabe walk into the bar and waved, smiling that devil-liquor grin.

There's a happy drunk, thought Gabe. It was odd to see such an infirm old man with such a healthy thirst for gin.

"Jambo mzungu! Habari?" (Hello white man. How are you?), bellowed the old man, speaking Swahili with a southern twang.

Gabe grinned and replied, *"M'zuri, m'zee mzungu"* (Good, wise old white man).

Gabe walked over to the old man's table and noticed the oxygen tank and its tubes lying limp as hyacinths in November in a tangle behind the wheelchair.

"Gabe Turpin. Glad to meet you," said Gabe, taking the old man's hand into his own. The man's grip was cool, dry, and surprisingly strong for someone with so many years resting on his slender shoulders.

"Friends jus' call me Jimmy," declared the man, who still sat ramrod straight in his wheelchair, not succumbing to circumstance. Here was a proud and able old warrior.

Gabe motioned at an empty chair at the table and Jimmy loudly told him to "sit his cheeks down." A waiter appeared, and Gabe ordered a White Cap.

"Care for another martini, Jimmy?"

"W'all certainly would, boyo. Much obliged. Another Bombay, please, and thank you."

Jimmy delicately drained his third martini and chased it down with the olive. He sat there munching, smiling to himself. Quickly, he focused his attention back on Gabe.

Jimmy carried the conversation. "What brings a *mzungu* to these parts, *mzungu?*" he offered with a big southern-boy grin.

Gabe said, "Just touring the zoo. Been here quite a few times, but it's still good to renew old friendships with the country."

"Been here some myself, boyo. Though not with all these here fancy amenities. Yep, this old frogman got landlocked upcountry about when you were suckin' on your mama's titty."

Gabe nodded in interest. "You were a frogman in the service?"

"Yessiree, boyo, UDT-21—a-poppin' wogs for fun and profit. Did a lotta shootin' and lootin' up on Mt. Kenya during the Mau Mau. Cold motherfuckin' place—and always wet. Shit, I was so cold my dick went north for the warmth, if ya know what I mean."

Jimmy, thought Gabe. *No way.* Yet this had to be *the* Jimmy he had read about in the situation report. Gabe couldn't believe the synchronicity and decided to go for broke and see what information he could draw out of the old frogman.

"I have to tell you, Jimmy, I'm a college professor of anthropology and I'm mixing my business with pleasure on this trip. Amazing as it may seem, you appear to figure into both."

"What the fuck could I have to do with your business, boyo? Studying the mating behaviors of geriatrics?" Jimmy let out a loud guffaw.

Gabe smiled at the old man. "No, actually I'm researching the Dream Walking of the N'dorobo and its cultural implications to Nilotic tribes. As strange as it seems, I have reason to believe Dream Walking was utilized in the Mau Mau, but hard facts are thin. I'm most curious as to the Dream Walker assassins of the Mau Mau and their true origin, as well as their dispersion after the Emergency."

Jimmy sat silently, yet Gabe saw the dancing of his jaw muscles. He looked squarely into Gabe's eyes and said, "Dry hole, boyo. Watcha' doin' wastin' your time chasin' that juju shit?"

Gabe responded, "UDT-21? You were a member, were you not?"

Jimmy threw back the martini in one gulp and signaled the waiter for another. He silently munched on the green olive he had slipped off the plastic sword. He studied Gabe for a long time.

"Leave it alone, boyo. Comes to nothin'."

Gabe, hardly believing this coincidental turn of events, touched Jimmy's arm with his open palm.

"Tell me what you saw, Jimmy. I've reviewed your sitrep. And what the hell are you doin' here now?"

Jimmy took two draws on his martini. He grimaced deeply both times.

"Fuck you, puss nuts. You weren't even a pup when I was runnin' in them jungles. Just leave this old man to his liquor and a kindhearted woman to blow him. Move on, boyo—there be dragons here."

Gabe pursued the topic, refusing to let it go despite Jimmy's reluctance to talk about it.

He asked, "Did you see the small, gray snake Jimmy? I have. I have even partaken of the magic paste myself—flew all over the goddamned countryside as invisible as a clear day. Sneaked up on a bevy of German fraus. Grabbed a handful of thigh with no problem, for I was dreaming."

Jimmy's eyes narrowed slightly, "You use that juju shit yourself? Damn. How the fuck did you get into that shit?"

"An old N'dorobo is my teacher in this dreaming business. I've seen him prepare the mixture—they call it *Kidogo Kifu*—and we have used it together. It seems very safe, although challenging to one's order of reality."

"You're dealing with some very bad people, boyo. Killed a passel of my mates—killed 'em hard. So, now, here you are—Professor Indiana fuckin' Jones, fraternizin' with the bloody-handed wogs so he can figure out how this shit affects the patterns of their fuckin' basket weavin'. You're dumb, boyo—gonna end up with a slit belly and no dick, playin' cutesy with that bastard. That old man, if he's still alive, is more than any twelve of you can handle. He'll float up to you one night and turn ya into a fuckin' smorgasbord with his blade. Drop it now, son. Put that shit down and enjoy life, like me."

Jimmy drank deeply, dropped a wad of shillings on the table, and wheeled off without so much as looking at Gabe.

Gabe spoke softly, saying, "I trust Sendeo. He is not who you say he is. I saved his life, and he will honor that."

Jimmy stopped, slowly turned his wheelchair around, and faced Gabe with a blank look on his face.

"Sendeo? Did you say Sendeo is a-teachin' you this shit?"

"Yes. He is teaching me of dreaming."

Jimmy offered a chagrined smile. "Shit, boyo, that's a pig pipin' a different tune. Sendeo ain't no bloody fuckin' wog killer—why, he was part of our team on my last sortie on that piece-of-shit mountain. Why, shit, I slept cuddled up with him and the others like spoons when it got butt-cold on that hill. He's one hell of a man—don't say much, though. Mostly just a-thinkin' all the time. Didn't know he was into that juju shit like his killin' fuckin' brother. Now there's the dickhead I thought you were messin' with, if not his son or some of his people. Hell, Sendeo's gotta be lookin' at eighty-five years old, or older."

Gabe responded, "Who knows how old he is? The only thing I know is he can still get around like a thirty-year-old."

"That's good to know," said Jimmy. "Well, I'd say this happy reconcilin' calls for another bit of Bombay—and I'll pop for your next White Cap. Want this here sandwich, Gabe? Didn't so much as even breathe on it."

"Sure, I'm not above eating off strangers' plates. My good old mountaineer friend Willi Unsoeld did that all the time, and he was famous; he was on the first successful American Everest expedition back in the sixties. We shared many a lunch together that way at conferences."

Jimmy seemed to have taken a liking to Gabe. "Hey, Gabe, you say you actually have taken a taste of that juju mixture that turns ya into a fuckin' spook?"

"Yes, it was really pretty simple—nothing to the dreaming, really. Just think of where you want to be, and there you are. Can't see a downside other than it kind of tweaks your perception of what's real and what's a dream."

Jimmy shook his head and looked at the center of the table as a crooked smile spread over his lips, "A bellyful of Bombay is enough dreamin' for me, boyo. Don't much go into the snake spit—but to each his own."

"Jimmy, can you fill in the information I saw on the situation report? It was pretty thin. Basically, they didn't know how the assassins were doing their wet work with so much security. Just kept mentioning inconclusive tribal legends—saying you had an experience consistent with those tribal legends."

Jimmy grunted, "I don't know about any fuckin' tribal legends—just know what I saw and felt. There the old man was, lying on his side, passed out by the fire a hundred yards away, and the next thing I know he comes up from behind me and tries to slit my throat, a-wavin' this knife around, acting nuts, howlin' at me and lickin' the blood of my friends off his knife. How he did it, don't have a fuckin' clue—but if you're a-tellin' me you can move around all instantaneous as hell with this native dreamin' concoction, why, maybe that's what he did."

Gabe asked, "Did this old shaman mix up roots and stuff with the venom of a small snake?"

"Yeah, I saw this snake come outta the basket—probably a foot long. Looked to me like he was milkin' the venom out of it into this fruit or a root—I don't know. Saw it all through the scope on my Weatherby."

"You said Sendeo was with you on this mission?"

"Yep. He was Seamus's shadow all the time. They appeared really tight. Sendeo was a tracker for Seamus's big-game hunting business before the Mau Mau. I guess they had been a song-and-dance routine for years. Seamus ate it that night. I was runnin' through the jungle just tryin' to save my skin. Ran into Sendeo down toward the track early the next mornin'. It was there he told me the puss-nutted voodoo spook that killed my team and tried to kill me was his brother. Can't remember the fucker's name."

"Terrari. Sendeo's evil brother," replied Gabe, smiling, looking at the floor of the bar. "Both old N'dorobo shamans—one seemingly dreaming on the dark side, the other dreaming himself immune from being part of this country's history."

Jimmy and Gabe silently sat in the bar of the Keekorok and drank their Bombay and White Cap.

"Do you figure it was Terrari doing the Dream Walker assassinations?" asked Gabe.

Jimmy appeared a tad uncomfortable. He adjusted his shirt a couple of times and looked over his shoulder, almost unconsciously, as if someone could be listening. He let out a big sigh and reached for his martini. He almost killed the drink in one prolonged gulp. Licking his lips and partaking of one of the olives left on the plastic sword, Jimmy slumped into a posture that smacked of resignation.

"Mr. Turpin. I've been around the horn a few times in my life. Gotta tell you now, can't tell you much about myself. But, yep, I think that was Sendeo's brother doin' all those poor fuckers back then. It's the only explanation. And subsequent to my frogman days, well, I've been mixed up in, well, the weird shit-per-mile index is way high. Not very good at chitchat unlessin' you're a bunch prettier than the likes of you, Mr. Gabe."

Jimmy guffawed loudly and finished his last olive. Somewhat bleary-eyed, he pondered the ordering of another martini.

"Jimmy, just never mind. I think I understand a bit about you. I will never pry into such a bag of maggots," Gabe responded, wearing an earnest smile the whole time.

"There you go, boyo. That's showin' some smarts. You know? I really like you, Mr. Gabe. Like your style. Like how you are lookin' for some fuckin' good out of the bad juju I've tried to forget all these years. Got a phone number? Could stand talkin' to a straight shooter like you, sometimes."

Gabe answered, "Well, I have a satellite phone. Not carrying it now, but I can get it out of my kit at the Fairview when I go back to Nairobi. And, hey, I've enjoyed meeting you, too. In this equation, you're somewhat of a legend—the only one to have escaped the Dream Walker assassin."

Jimmy offered Gabe a long, silent look before saying, "Fuck you, boyo. Didn't 'scape nobody. Just shit myself and ran like the wind. Why, hell, that juju fucker probably slipped in my shit. Now there's some dignity for you." Jimmy guffawed again and drained his martini.

Gabe smiled and watched Jimmy finish his drink. Clearly, he would learn no more from him of the dreaming or the Dream Walker assassins. Jimmy was a fossil—an antiquated paradigm who knew nothing about more than one form of reality than could be defined by the barrel of a gun. Regardless of the man's lack of theosophical breadth, Gabe liked the old sea dog. The man was the real thing.

"Jimmy, stay in touch. I don't really give a rat's ass about what happened fifty years ago. I've got my hands full of what's happening today. But please, do keep in touch."

"Gimme that cell phone number," said Jimmy.

Gabe scribbled the number down on one of his business cards and handed it to the old frogman. Jimmy took it in both hands and studied it, turning it over and studying the credentials on the card.

"Well, Professor, if I see any spooks floatin' around—well, I'll call you directly."

"Thanks, Jimmy," said Gabe, smiling broadly. "Care for one last toddy before we split ways, Jimmy?"

"Hell, yes. Your parents raised you right good, son. Respectin' your elders is the first sign of a balanced soul. Realizin' someone's thirst is—why, hell, boyo—is revealin' an evolved spirit."

Another Bombay martini and White Cap appeared on the table. Gabe realized there was a lot of information about Jimmy that would not be forthcoming. He smiled to himself and wondered what such an old man was doing here. Clearly, Jimmy smelled of America's shadowy acronyms. Yet the man was so original he seemed to defy such a sterile world of deceit. The two silently finished their drinks and Jimmy looked no worse for the wear from the half dozen martinis. Gabe definitely felt the handful of beers buzzing in his head.

Jimmy slammed down his glass, resolutely, and, like a punctuation mark, said, "Gotta go take a little Betty Ford nap now, boyo. And I gotta go pee. Been good talkin' with you, son. Give me a call if ya have the reason. Damn, boyo, gotta drain this dragon—my back teeth are floatin'. Hey, finish the fuckin' sandwich so the kids of Africa don't starve."

Gabe reflected on the afternoon's enlightenment. Clearly, this Jimmy was deep in the shit of black ops and deniability. The man was haunted by what he had seen and done. Yet there was a strange sense of patriotism Jimmy clung to—an iron will that protected him. This was clearly one wild old man. Gabe smiled, snatched the remaining sandwich half from the plate, and tossed it down, chased by the last fourth of his White Cap. Moderately lit, Gabe made his way back out to his waiting driver and the Peugeot.

Gabe instructed the driver as they drove over barren tracks toward Sand River Camp. Olioke's *manyatta* was always in this area, out from the Mara. They drove on, the Peugeot bucking and slipstreaming in the washed-out tracks. Zebras and wildebeest, along with occasional herds of Cape buffalo, sought escape from their vehicular assault.

The island of thorns presented itself against the grass of the Mara. The Maasai *manyatta* was a piece of indigenous genius and simplicity. Thorn branches like razor wire were laid out on the periphery so as to dissuade even the most bold of African felines or devil-dog hyenas. Out from the *manyatta* were a number of women and children. The women were, for the most part, beautiful and sported beaded jewelry to rival even the most ambitious of Western debutantes. Of course, the flies were everywhere around the *manyatta,* since the Maasai kept their cattle—their currency—safely within their huts at night.

Gabe asked after Olioke and found him to be within the *manyatta,* although he was playing a game of *Mankala.* Gabe smiled and shook his head. *Mankala* games could last for hours, or even days. Olioke would probably not appreciate the break in his concentration. *Mankala* was a game of the Maasai elders. As *Laibon,* Olioke was the most senior of the elders. Gabe shuffled his toe in the red soil and squatted down to wait for the convenience of the *Laibon,* his friend.

An hour later, a Maasai with woolen locks shuffled toward Gabe. When they saw each other, they both simply smiled.

"*Jambo, m'zee,*" offered Gabe.

"*Jambo, rafiki,*" countered Olioke.

Gabe reflected back on first meeting Olioke. It was 1974, and the Kikuyu-dominated government was busily outlawing everything Maasai.

> *Gabe had found the plains west of Narok and perched his tent among the acacia at the bottom of the Loita Hills.* Eunoto *was the Maasai rite of passage from* morani, *or warrior, to elder. The hills were alive with the reddish brown of Maasai warriors. Many wore the outlawed lion-mane headdresses. They came in a spiritual frenzy—hundreds, thousands. Warriors came in columns that stretched to the horizon, red clouds of dust a halo of their passage. Their religious fervor was manifested in the frothing and tremors of the participants, so common during an* Eunoto. *They came to grow from warriors to wise old men.*
>
> *Gabe remembered seeing Olioke for the first time. He wore a lion-mane headdress and was painted white, with finger-painting smears adorning his naked body. The milky froth of spittle seeped out of the corner of Olioke's mouth. The man was clearly at his life's epiphany. Gabe was merely documenting. Olioke collapsed and began to spasm. Gabe rushed to the man, held him closely, and, with a singsong English lullaby, calmed his spiritual fevers, soothed the man's anxiety. Olioke went on to become* Laibon.

Olioke spoke relatively good English.

"*Rafiki* Gabe, I have been missing you all these years. Will you share in the hospitality of my *manyatta?*"

Gabe smiled and retained hold of Olioke's hand, continuing to shake it in a gentle embrace. He stared straight into the *Laibon*'s eyes and continued to smile.

"Olioke, can you take time away from your duties and talk with me?" asked Gabe, making sure to convey his respect for the seriousness of *Mankala.*

Olioke responded, "*N'dio,* Gabe, I have soundly defeated my opponent. He wishes no more chances at being beaten. Let us go to my hut. It is cool there and we may talk in comfort."

The women and children reflected toothy smiles that hid their confusion. Clearly, it was unusual for the *Laibon* to escort a *mzungu* to his hut. Flies danced on the eyeballs of children cradled in reddish brown slings wrapped around the bony shoulders of their mothers.

The hut was very dark. The smell of zebu cattle was everywhere about the confines of the hut. Olioke and Gabe sat around a charcoal brazier as the cool of the hut seeped into Gabe's skin. Flies seemed to not invade the keep of this mud-and-wattle fortress.

They silently sipped on their libations as their eyes adjusted to the gloom.

"How have you been, Olioke? I take it you are well."

"My bones ache in the cold mornings and my knees are stiff, but it is good that other of my parts can be stiff at my age," said the old *Laibon* with a knowing smile and a wink to Gabe.

The two sat in the cool of the hut and talked of the time Gabe and Olioke had hunted eland farther to the south. They both laughed openly, remembering the determined warthog that attacked them viciously, running the hunters up an acacia tree, where they remained for over four hours, their hunt ruined for the day.

Gabe innocently asked if Olioke's village traded with any of the N'dorobo who lived to the south into Tanzania. The old *Laibon* nodded his head, swallowing his beer at the same time.

"*N'dio,* Gabe. We trade milk and leather goods for honey and wax. Since they are such poor people—they don't own cattle—they are in need of products from our zebu. They are as strange a people as they are poor. Very strange, but their skills of finding honey are like magic."

"What do you know of their magic, Olioke? Are there any, you know, legends or tales told about the strange abilities of the N'dorobo?"

"Well, they can talk to animals. That is widely known among my people. I have seen them do so with these eyes," Olioke said gesturing at his eyes as he took another drink of *pombe.*

"What did you see that made you think the N'dorobo can talk with animals? What did you see, Olioke?"

"Many years ago, my uncle and I were invited to stay for a while with an old N'dorobo about two days' travel from Sand River east into the Loita Hills. One morning, we were to go hunt for honey. The old N'dorobo made much of his preparation and said he must call the *Euchoshoroi* bird and set him to work."

Gabe had heard of the *Euchoshoroi* bird somewhere in his research. He tried to place the reference as Olioke continued.

"The old N'dorobo began to call the bird and, suddenly, my uncle and I saw the small thing come flying out of the sky from a group of fig trees near the village. The old man continued to talk with the bird and told us he had told the bird to take us to a good honeycomb. We followed the old man and could hear him talking to the bird. The bird would fly a bit and would stop, waiting for us to catch up. This went on for over an hour. The whole time, the old man and the bird talked to each other."

Olioke stopped his tale to finish off his mug of *pombe*. He wiped his lips with the back of his hand and, satisfied, smacked his lips loudly.

"After some time, we saw the bird sitting above a hive of bees. Most certainly, the N'dorobo could talk with the bird."

Gabe remembered his prior exposure to the *Euchoshoroi*. In an advanced ethology course, the symbiotic relationship between African honey hunters and the *Euchoshoroi* was detailed. It appeared to be a conditioned response of the bird to the stimulus of the N'dorobo, a conditioned response that was initiated some time in the shadows of the distant past. Through some form of genetic memory, the birds knew by their discovery of a beehive they would eventually feast on the wax and larvae left from the N'dorobo honey gatherers.

"Have you heard any stories of how a N'dorobo can disappear and appear in another place as a ghost?"

"*Mtatugo Mafukizo*. Smoke Walking with long strides. Yes, the N'dorobo are known for their *Mtatugo Mafukizo*, Gabe. Because of this Smoke Walking, our people have never sought to war with the N'dorobo. Anyway, they have no cattle, so there would be no profit in doing so. But even so, trying to capture and hold a N'dorobo is like trying to hold the cloud of one's breath in cupped hands in the cold morning."

Gabe mused on this Smoke Walking, as Dream Walking seemed to be referred to among the Maasai. Clearly, dreaming was endemic to all N'dorobo—a cultural element of this small, splintered tribe. Perhaps the dreaming of the N'dorobo explained how they maintained a consistent tribal culture despite their wide dispersement from the mountains of Kenya to the Serengeti Plain of Tanzania.

Olioke continued, "Yes, Gabe, the N'dorobo are not like our people. They seek the shadows of the trees and they keep to themselves. They care not about their poverty, their lack of cattle. They talk to birds and come and go like clouds in the sky. Strange people, indeed."

Gabe nodded and finished his *pombe*. A beautiful woman walked into the hut and placed new bowls of *pombe* in front of both Olioke and Gabe. The woman's pert breasts pointed up, and her fine features were breathtaking. Olioke noticed Gabe's long stares at the young woman and smiled to himself.

Gabe asked, "That is not one of your wives, is it, *Laibon*—even though I am not saying you are not worthy of such a treasure."

Olioke widened his smile.

"No, *rafiki* Gabe, she is the daughter of my nephew. If your seed sack is swollen and you are in need of relief, I can see that such relief is given. She is quite comely, and even arouses my old, worn-out parts—though I will deny such to everyone."

Olioke laughed openly and drank deeply of his *pombe*. Gabe followed suit. The afternoon was aging as the two old friends sat in the shadow of the hut and exchanged and recalled stories well into the evening. Gabe was happy to have a driver, since after a half dozen graciously offered bowls of beer, he was quite unprepared to drive anywhere, even in the outback of the Mara.

Gabe and Olioke issued from the hut. The waning light offered a challenge to both of them, making each of them squint after hours in the cool dark of the manure and mud-and-wattle shelter. Gabe tottered to the Peugeot with Olioke, who was laughing as he escorted him past the throng of curious Maasai women and children. Flies circled Gabe's head, and the smoky smell of milk and blood being prepared filled the air. Both Gabe and Olioke spat in their hands, then grasped palms and forearms, using both hands. The Peugeot galloped off in the ruts of the track as the sun grew large and sat as heavy as a giant pumpkin over the hills to the west of Sand River.

The driver dropped Gabe off at Fig Tree just at dark. Gabe, still tipsy from the *pombe,* focused on his steps toward his tent. Still dressed, he collapsed on the cot and fell into a deep sleep.

The grunting of hippos in the Talek River awoke Gabe just before the quiet salutation of the servant.

"Jambo, Bwana. Nataka chai, kahawa?"

"Chai tafadhali. Asante sana."

Gabe took his chai out in front of the tent and sat down in the canvas chair. The early light of the morning turned the greens deeper and rendered the shadow lines between grass and forest a darker shade of black. The hippo continued to claim his place in the pool as the birds began to make claim, as well.

Gabe determined another couple of days in the Mara would heal him and fortify his spirit so he could, again, enter the N'dorobo world of dreaming. He finished a second cup of tea and quickly went for a light breakfast at the dining tent. He collected his driver and told him to drive west toward the Mara Serena Lodge. He was reenacting the bush barhopping regimen he and Bill would follow to wile away the warm Mara afternoons after two weeks of cold and challenge on Mt. Kenya. Bush barhopping was a gentle endeavor.

The Peugeot would slow here and there as Gabe marveled at the menagerie that spread itself across the plains. The lightness of having no schedule and no responsibility was wonderful, and Gabe found himself smiling broadly without any specific reason.

He saw a group of hyenas slowly and doggedly following a herd of impala. The herd had a number of young, no more than three days old. Each spindly-legged antelope shadowed its mother as it navigated the tall grass. An African kite lazily circled in the air over the purple of the Loita Hills west of the Mara River. Every animal was either avoiding the hunter or pursuing the hunted in this ancient place. Gabe reflected on how such intent violence, such purposeful killing, manifested itself in a dance of such grace and beauty.

Around noon, the driver entered the grounds of the Mara Serena Lodge. Gabe didn't particularly like the Serena. Sterile and clean compared to the green tents of Fig Tree, it seemed to Gabe not to be—Africa. He studied the lunch crowd in the dining room. Two-thirds were European, the rest Americans, along with a lone Japanese couple, obvious pioneers from a culture that avoided such individuality.

He ordered fish-and-chips and a White Cap. The order came promptly, and Gabe devoured the greasy fries and sweet ketchup. He swallowed the last of his beer and paid his chit. He walked down to the patio beside the swimming pool and failed to notice the man sitting in the corner of the dining room. In this setting his incongruous Hispanic features and thick, black hair offered a unique warning; his dark glasses worn in the shadows of the dining room added to the danger that was there for anyone to see. Gabe did not see the warning, did not see the danger.

Sitting behind the heavy, dark, high-backed chairs, the man quietly ate his salad. Having dropped his napkin, he retrieved it at the same time that Gabe walked between tables twenty feet away and into the sun on the patio, away from view.

Gabe and his driver plied their way back toward Fig Tree, exiting the main road and following many a whim along the way. Gabe addressed the driver. "John, we will go back to Mt. Kenya tomorrow, first thing. Will that be okay with you?"

"We are going home tomorrow?"

"Well, in a way, I suppose both of us are. But, for certain, you will be having *pombe* in your own home in Narok late tomorrow night. I hope you don't mind the trip north before you're free to go back to Narok."

John offered Gabe a warm, wide smile, "I am your man, *bwana*. You have treated me well, and I have enjoyed your company. You are not like most *mzungu*—excuse me, *bwana*—most whites, who seem to not know I breathe the same air as they. I look forward to my *thanga,* my *pombe,* and even my wives."

"*Sow-sow.* I will be packed and waiting at the parking lot by eight o'clock. I need to stop by the Fairview in Nairobi for a half hour to pick up my stores. After that, we will go straight away to Mt. Kenya. We should be at Mutindua market by mid- to early afternoon. There, I will pay you and go up the Chogoria Track for a bit."

"*N'dio, bwana.*"

They drove into Fig Tree Camp, where Gabe had two gin and tonics prior to dinner. After his smorgasbord dinner, Gabe had a whiskey nightcap, the fire of the cheap liquor burning his throat yet relaxing him at the same time. He thought to order a second drink, but decided against it.

Tomorrow will be a long day, Gabe thought as he brushed his teeth and stumbled into the tent's sleeping quarters. He anticipated again spending time with Sendeo and looked forward to the days in the forests of Mt. Kenya spent in such good company. The air in the tent was chilly. Gabe snuggled into the linens and wool blankets and breathed out, deeply satisfied and totally relaxed. The Mara—this cradle of mankind—had again healed his wounds. This was the nature of such ancient memories.

15

KENYA, 2005

BAZAAN WAS TIRED OF DRIVING. SOMEWHAT DRUNK AT FIRST, he had driven straight through from Nyeri to the Mara, opting to not spend a night at the Fairview in Nairobi. Since the Mara Serena Lodge was inside the Mara reserve, which closed its gates at sundown, Bazaan could not press on to the lodge. Instead, he rented a tent for one night at the Kichwa Tembo Tented Camp just shy of the reserve border and an easy hour's drive to the Serena.

He slept fitfully. His eye, still puffed and engorged, throbbed painfully throughout the night. He awoke late and ate breakfast after three cups of strong Kenyan *kahawa*. He fished the ibuprofen out of his kit and downed several with some passion fruit juice. After paying his chit, late in the morning Bazaan motored slowly south along the Esoit Oloolo Escarpment and enjoyed the fine, sunny day. The pain of his eye was numbed by the dose of analgesic.

Bazaan pulled up to the Mara reserve gate, where a relatively sharp-looking *askari* asked to see his papers. Upon closer inspection, the guard's eyes reflected the boredom of spirit so endemic to modern Africa. Bazaan showed him his Ralph Chen passport and was duly waved into the reserve. Cruising down the gravel road, Bazaan reflected on his confrontation on the

Chogoria Track with his old nemesis, Gabe Turpin. He processed all the variables as to why Gabe Turpin would be chasing the same ghosts he was. Turpin was clearly off the radar screen with regard to every element of Bazaan's life. He had never run into his name, nor even his description, in his years as a merc and "ultimate problem solver."

It has to be a fluke, thought Bazaan as a herd of zebras zigzagged in front of his SUV, leaving a wake of dust as they plunged off the roadbed and into the scrub. *Flukes cannot be counted on,* thought Bazaan. The sure fix would be removal of the variable. The next meeting between the two would be a reflexive solution. *Death removes all questions,* thought Bazaan as he smiled to himself and continued down the gravel road in the golden morning of the Maasai Mara.

Bazaan turned off the road into the grounds of the Mara Serena Lodge. The stucco walls reflected white-hot in the noonday sun of the Great Rift. Bazaan entered the dark-wooded, shady cool of the lodge's lobby. There, a cute woman dressed in a *kitanga* cloth sarong greeted Bazaan with a toothy smile—brilliant, white squares evenly framed by a chocolate-brown face. Her hair was pinned in a bun, and she asked Bazaan for his confirmation in pleasant, almost musical English. High-quality batiks were hung throughout the lodge's lobby. All of the furniture was heavy, dark wood, which worked with the heavy wooden beams on the ceiling and the white stucco walls of the interior.

Bazaan checked in and found his room with no problems. The room was clean and adequately appointed, yet somehow sterile. In fact, Bazaan found the whole lodge to lack earthiness. It was almost too clean, too white, too . . . empty. After storing his meager kit, Bazaan walked around the grounds of the Mara Serena. Over at the salt lick near the manufactured water hole, a herd of zebras was slaking their luncheon thirst. Baboons ran around the base of the acacia trees and were barking noisily. Bazaan went out on the deck by the lodge's swimming pool. The pool, like almost all of the Serena, was abandoned.

Bazaan sauntered up to the bar adjacent to the dining room. He ordered a Pimm's and nursed it, musing about his recon protocol. He expected advance security would be building at the Keekorok. Even though his dreaming was a new paradigm and immune to the variables of modern security, Bazaan maintained his ritualistic regimen of analysis and intelligence gathering. Bazaan always contended he should know two hundred percent more than he thought he should know. Only through such diligence could one survive the odds of this profession.

For the next week and a half, Bazaan would survey the lay of the land at the Keekorok. He would also enlist the old man, Terrari, to handhold him through his next dreaming. The old man didn't know it yet, but they would meet again, quite soon. Bazaan went to his kit and found the bundle of *Kidogo Kifu*. Late that afternoon, or perhaps early in the evening, he would partake in the Small Death and go looking for his dreaming mentor, Terrari. After one more guided dreaming session, he would have no need for the old N'dorobo devil and would remove him as a variable, as well. Bazaan smiled grimly and ordered another Pimm's.

In the fading afternoon light, Bazaan removed the leaf wrapping of one dollop of the Small Death. Without hesitation, he plopped it into his mouth and masticated the matter thoroughly. Soon, the rosy tequila-sunrise light bathed the interior of Bazaan's room. He was dreaming, clearly. He thought of the hut on the Ewaso Ng'iro and had to wait for his eyes to adjust to the darkness before he understood clearly where he was and what he was looking at.

The scrawny old man was taking his young *bibi* from behind, his whippet frame lunging rhythmically back and forth as he played the ancient game of procreation. Bazaan nearly laughed out loud, realizing the old man was knocking off a piece without being aware of his presence. Beside the copulating couple were a gourd of *pombe* and some *ndizi* and porridge.

"How romantic, old man," said Bazaan in the darkness of the hut.

The old man whirled around and faced Bazaan squarely, still on his knobby knees, his erect member glistening in the firelight.

"Is this what you have come to, *mzungu?* Watching other true men take their women honestly because your talents are wanting?"

The old man has a mouth on him, thought Bazaan. "Finish up and come outside, old man. I have need of your assistance."

Wearing a sneer, Terrari said, "Why, *mzungu,* I may not finish up here for some time. I know that may seem strange to you, but I tend to please my women more than once or even twice. I realize you probably lack such skills."

"Cut the banter, old man. Come if you want, quit if you want. I'll be waiting outside and so will you be in five minutes—and no tricks. The gun will be drawn and ready."

Some rustling sounds came from the inside of the hut, along with a greedy grunt from Terrari. Then, with much dignity, Terrari adjusted his wrap as he ducked out the door of the hut. He sat silently and stared at Bazaan. They sat that way for nearly five minutes—the animosity between the two palpable in the cooling air along the riverbed of the Ewaso Ng'iro.

"I wish to have you as my chaperon on this next dreaming in case I have missed something."

Terrari leveled his gaze on Bazaan and replied with an air of dismissal, "You seem to be dreaming fine without me, *mzungu.* You need not any further counsel from me. Leave me to mine. I have given you a goodly supply of the *Kidogo Kifu,* as I said I would. That is all you seek. With the *Kidogo Kifu,* you have all you need for your purposes."

Bazaan persisted, "All the same, I want you with me as I take my first dreaming reconnaissance of Keekorok. You must come with me now. Quickly, we must go to Keekorok."

The lights of the swimming pool at Keekorok Lodge hung like lamps filtered through dusty water. The bubbler on the purification system offered a near-silent abstraction of the water as it surfaced, with small bubbles bouncing about the floating leaves in the pool. The air around Keekorok was cool and filled with the smell of softwood smoke as the lounge chairs were abandoned to the dark and cool of the Kenyan evening. Bazaan glided effortlessly inside the scene.

Bazaan and Terrari floated like invisible wraiths outside the bar at the Keekorok. Doing his recon, Bazaan scanned the bar and then the dining room, sifting through the faces and demeanors of the patrons and looking for those who could be advance security, who were doing the same thing as Bazaan. He saw the typical mix of Europeans and a salting of Americans. The pilots of the hot-air balloon flights over the Mara were also working the rooms. For about three hundred dollars, one could view the game of the Maasai Mara from the vantage of a hundred feet above the deck. Floating silently over the plains, one could be witness to a panorama of Africa's primeval past. The terminus of the balloon flight was a champagne brunch served with crystal, china, and silver. Miles from support, a Land Rover chased the balloon, the tureens and platters of food jostling in the back, clinking against the bottles of cheap champagne and serving china. The balloon pitchmen were dressed in World War I aviator garb and lingered at the tables of attractive, bored European housewives—birds kept in a wonderful cage.

Bazaan studied the people in his professional mode. No stone would be left unturned, no blade of grass not looked behind for the presence of an enemy. Such vigilance was the source of Bazaan's longevity in a vocation with short windows of survival. Bazaan physically shuddered as his recon took in an improbability. Sitting at the bar in a wheelchair was a man he knew. When Bazaan had met him a number of years ago, the man was old beyond his years and bordering on infirm. Here, he looked impossibly old and fragile. Jimmy. Sitting in the shadows of the Keekorok's bar was the man who first told Bazaan of the Dream Walker assassins—the ex-UDT frogman who had made it through the shit of the Mau Mau and became a successful arms merchant and supporter of mercs and professionals, such as Bazaan. Bazaan studied the old frogman. He knew he was not clean and was there for a reason. It was clear the old frogman was linked somehow with one of the government's alphabet-soup agencies whose purview included advance cabinet-level security. Obviously, there were no arms deals going down at the Keekorok. Jimmy was a U.S. government player.

Balancing the possible breach of his security with the chance at more intelligence was a gamble Bazaan was ready to make. After all, killing the infirm old man could swiftly and easily negate any breach of his own security. He dreamed himself closer and knew he must somehow engage the old arms dealer to make concrete his reality.

He put his hands on Jimmy's shoulders, bent over next to the old man's right ear, and quietly said, "Long time no see, Jimmy."

Jimmy slowly turned his head to see who was offering the salutation. "Well I'll be a son of a bitch—Bazaan, ain't it? What the fuck you doin' in the Dark Continent, boyo? Last time I saw you we were both watchin' a Thai bitch smoke ciggies with her cunt."

Jimmy had a Bombay martini in his left hand and had already eaten one of the three olives. Bazaan saw the oxygen bottle tucked into the pouch of Jimmy's wheelchair. The oxygen mask dangled, abandoned, like an ornament on the wheelchair.

Bazaan asked, "Whatcha doin' here yourself, Jimmy? Far from your point of sale, isn't it?"

"Just fuckin' natives, boyo. They love this *mzungu* meat. Why hell, 'cause of the beta-blockers, I gotta inject my dick with saline just to make it come alive, large and in charge. The women love it, they surely do. You all know that I got two pieces of hardware in me now. One to bang my heart back into rhythm when it goes astray, the other to bang it back if it goes too quiet. Just last night I was servicing this Maasai bitch and, you know, I got a-goin' pretty hard, sweatin' like a fuckin' pig. Well, my fuckin' heart stops, and the implant jolts the shit outta me. Being all sweaty and belly-to-belly, well, the bitch got a gutful of amps too. She thought it was some *mzungu* sexual juju. Hell, she was begging for another jolt. Now I'm a legend here among the Maasai, as adulterous as they are. Gotta watch my p's and q's though. Those *morani* still fuck burros. STDs at my age are a bitch, boyo."

Bazaan ordered a Pimm's Cup and shook his head. This old man was the real thing. Wild as a spring thunderstorm, as concerned with his actions as a corpse. This old man was trouble.

Jimmy sat there in his wheelchair, a Hudson's Bay blanket thrown over his lower body, protecting the old man from the chill of a Rift evening. Jimmy sipped his martini and ate a second olive, leaving only one on the plastic sword offered by the bartender.

"Well, I've had my salad and will now drink my main course. Bazaan, who're you fuckin'?"

"I'm fucking no one, Jimmy. I don't have the benefit of a saline-supported dick as you do."

Jimmy guffawed and took another sip from his martini.

"Hell, Bazaan, we're all grownups here. You gonna do whatcha gotta do? Let me have one more martini and then we can throw down our shit. Join me, boyo?"

Bazaan studied the old frogman. He seemed to know the score and, at the same time, not care a shit about Bazaan and his mission. He'd humor the old UDT rogue.

"Sure Jimmy, I'll raise a glass to you."

"Much obliged, puss nuts," replied Jimmy, signaling the waiter.

Bazaan was quickly calculating his risk/reward equation. He made a decisive action plan, and that plan involved counsel with Terrari.

"Hold on, Jimmy. I gotta drain the dragon. I'll be right back."

"Go ahead and wring your root, boyo. I don't move much anymore," said Jimmy, chuckling.

Bazaan went out onto the lawn of the Keekorok and dreamed of Terrari. The old man was squatting beside the pool, reflectively chewing on his plug of tobacco. The rosy filter of light of his dreaming was the only noticeable difference from Bazaan's everyday reality.

Bazaan addressed Terrari with false respect. "Old man, we have a problem with an old man here. You must give me counsel. I am almost certain he is one of the advance intelligence gatherers for Vice President Baker's security force. He is old and infirm, however. He is not a formidable adversary; he gets about in a wheelchair and needs much medical attention. Yet his mind is the most dangerous. Will you study him and lend me counsel? I feel I must kill him, most certainly, but seek your wisdom, old man."

Terrari simply disappeared from the lawn of Keekorok. He studied the invalid as the *mzungu* was poured another martini.

Terrari smiled broadly. He would have laughed out loud, but reserved himself from early celebrations. He continued to study the old man, perched in his wheelchair. He saw the shadow of death on the man. Terrari dreamed himself back to the front lawn of Keekorok. There, he saw Bazaan stiffly awaiting his return.

Terrari told Bazaan, "I know of this *mzungu, mzungu.* I have seen the color of his spirit many years ago. I will act as your second. I will kill this old man myself. Why, it would be an insult to have a young, strong boy such as you engage such an old man in the last moments of his life. I will do the honors, *mzungu.* I know of this man and would not mind to wash my hands in his blood."

"You know Jimmy? How is it so, old man? Or is this another snare lying in wait for me?"

"The first time I saw this man, he was intent on killing me. The last time I saw this man, he was intent on killing me. Both times, he failed to put me down. Now, I will return the favor with a smile. Perhaps I'll be more successful than he."

Terrari went into the lounge of the Keekorok and locked his intent on the old man in the wheelchair just off the bar. The old man was laughing heartily and had two stunning blondes hanging on his every word. He was gently stroking the thighs of each woman, leaning over to first one then the other—whispering in their ears and then laughing at his own words. The women were mesmerized.

Jimmy sat upright in his wheelchair, his military bearing still obvious regardless of his age and health. An oxygen tank lay slung in a pouch over the back of the chair, the tube and nostril aerators hanging haphazardly over one of the handles. Jimmy leaned up to the bar and retrieved his gigantic martini. The Bombay exhibited the benzene-like ripples of alcohol amid the three olives skewered on the small, garish plastic sword. Over

Jimmy's legs lay a thin woolen blanket of a drab brown color, the wool pilling on the edges.

Jimmy's intent was clearly to bed one or both of the blondes—obviously two German fraus on holiday. He was talking loudly, the gin decreasing his volume control.

"Why, hell girls, I got one pacemaker to jump-start my heart if it quits and another to calm it down when it gets a-racin' like it is right now." As he winked at the women and took a long pull on his martini, he continued, "Well, last week I was doin' my civic duty, if you know what I mean, and I was a sweatin' like a pig and belly-to-belly with this Ingrid gal. Well hell, one of these here pacemakers went off, don't know which one—hell, shocked the shit out of both of us. She thought it was some ancient tantric sex technique. Boy howdy, she let go with an orgasm that damned near killed me. Who knows, gals, maybe it'll happen again!"

The old *mzungu* disgusted Terrari. He had disdain for most *mzungu,* but for this one he reserved a double dose of derision. Terrari maneuvered behind Jimmy and placed himself directly behind his wheelchair. The blondes were glancing up at the old black man, who was positioning himself into their verbal party, and their attention was not wasted on Jimmy, regardless of his three-martini dinner.

Terrari grabbed both handles of Jimmy's wheelchair and leaned down to whisper in his ear.

"How is it you have grown so old, *mzungu?* Why, wasn't it yesterday you soiled yourself and jumped from the tree and the arc of my *kisu?* It seems the young cub has lived past his prime. Perhaps I should have saved you from this insult many years ago, *mzungu."*

Without looking back, Jimmy, in an even yet serious voice, said, "Girls, gotta tend to this old friend here. I'll meet you tomorrow morning for the balloon ride—remember, my treat."

The two women, puzzled looks on their faces, made their small talk good-byes and strode gracefully, if not voluptuously, out into the cool Kenyan evening, amid a halo of body heat and clouds of heavy breathing.

Terrari, without talking, wheeled Jimmy out into the open-air bar around the pool, abandoned due to the evening chill that always settled on the Rift at night. He violently spun the old *mzungu* around in his chair, almost upsetting the chair, and faced Jimmy with a wicked grin.

"Do you remember me, *mzungu?* Do you remember how I killed your friends and tasted their blood? Do you? Do you remember their screams, *mzungu?* You were such a coward. First you soiled yourself, and then you ran. What a warrior."

"Fuck you, puss nuts," said Jimmy evenly and without a touch of fear. "I shoulda popped your ass when I had the chance. Whatcha have in mind, you no-load pencil dick?"

"So much bravery now, *mzungu.* Where was it that early morning so many years ago? I have just come to finish what I left undone. Pity to kill such an invalid. Tell me, *mzungu,* how does it feel to smell death's breath now? Am I doing you a favor, *mzungu?* Are you more than ready to die?"

Jimmy started to laugh. This obviously inappropriate humor was an affront to Terrari, who produced a small, sharp knife and held it at arm's length, pointing at Jimmy's eyes.

"Now you will die!" growled Terrari.

"Just like a fuckin' wog to bring a little pig sticker to a fuckin' gunfight," said Jimmy as he produced a 9mm Beretta with a silencer from beneath his worn woolen blanket. *"Salama* (good night), motherfucker," said Jimmy as he double-tapped two rounds into Terrari's head.

The back of the old N'dorobo's head blew open like a melon hit with a sledgehammer. Gray matter and blood, mixed with shockingly white cranial bone, sprayed over the deck of the pool and on the deck chairs. The impact of the hollow points knocked Terrari back into the pool, and a psychedelic cloud of pink floated and played about the old N'dorobo's head—the pool's underwater light helping document the loss of blood and life.

"Fuck you," said Jimmy as he wheeled his chair back into the Keekorok lounge. Into his hidden transmitting mike he mouthed, "One bad Indian down in the pool. Scrubbers, empty the garbage."

Jimmy breathed in and out deeply only once. *Well, that piece of history is history,* he thought. *Gotta go find some pussy and another martini.* He wheeled his chair into the dining room of the Keekorok, smiling broadly. There, he spied the two blondes, cocked back his head, and laughed. The two babes covered their laughing lips with their tanned, manicured hands.

"Darlin's, let Uncle Jimmy order for you both. Why, hell, I'm as thirsty as a polecat in the Sahara. Care for a little drink before we have the lobster?"

In the dark and chill of the Mara evening, Bazaan watched as men in jumpsuits retrieved Terrari's body from the pool and quickly off-loaded it into a black van with no plates or markings. He watched Jimmy reveling in the attentions of the two blondes, both of whom were stroking his jaw and running their long, slender fingers through his hair.

Bazaan understood what he now must do. Terrari had let his ambition and ego get in front of his intent. Such was always a fatal mistake in Bazaan's trade. Bazaan floated above the Keekorok's pool and dreamed of the Serena Lodge.

Amid his dreaming and in the dark of the Mara, Bazaan heard the grunting of lions and the moaning of hyenas. He walked down alongside the white stucco wall and into the heavy wood and iron of the Serena dining room. An American couple was just starting on their course of Nile perch. Bazaan ordered a Pimm's and a roast beef sandwich with horseradish. The spot-lights of the Serena Lodge shone on the salt licks beneath the dining room, and Bazaan saw the menagerie of the Rift, their eyes like mirrors in the African night. Bazaan was now alone and without help in his work. He smiled crookedly, content, knowing this is how he operated best. He ordered another Pimm's Cup and heard the low, moaning grunting of a lion out in the salt lick. The softwood fire of the lodge reminded Bazaan of the sagebrush fires of the Sonora when the Mexican cartel had hired him to remove a middleman in the Medellín. The fire crackled, the lion grunted, and the moans of hyenas could be heard from the verandah, all converging on the salt lick.

Bazaan drained his Pimm's Cup. He pinched off one last piece of sandwich and dredged it through the horseradish. Content with his repast, Bazaan paid his chit and went out into the cool evening to his small, stucco cabin to sleep, listening to the grunting of the lion out from the salt lick. The moon was a Saracen's saber rising over the escarpment in the night—a sickle of death that reflected silver off the Loita Hills to the east.

16

MT. KENYA, 2005

GABE WALKED UP THE CHOGORIA TRACK. ITS MAIN PEAKS WERE already blanketed with thick clouds, and it was well before noon. The forest was alive—the green vervet monkeys nosed close to the track to study the noisy, smelly interloper. Sunbirds and colobus monkeys streaked through the forest canopy. Gabe's pack rode high over his head and softly creaked at each step, the clevis pins straining against the grommets in the Cordura nylon. Back from his respite in the Mara, Gabe was intent on studying the role of dreaming and its cultural and philosophical ramifications among the N'dorobo. *What structure could exist to sustain a tribal tradition if everything was a dream?* thought Gabe as he slowly marched up the muddy track on the north side of the mountain. His plan was to find Sendeo, or—more accurately—have Sendeo find him, and delve deeper into this business of dreaming.

A bushbuck barked somewhere from within the green wall of bamboo off to Gabe's right. Gabe continued on up the track, slower now as he peered through the lattice of canes and bowers to find the source of the noise.

From his left came a voice. "*Jambo, Bwana* Gabe, *habari?*"

Gabe barked out a nervous laugh, startled by the old man's presence. There, on the knobby stump of a rotted camphor tree, sat Sendeo, slowly masticating a plug of tobacco. He looked at Gabe in a reflective and evaluative manner—making judgments as to Gabe's spiritual angle of flight.

"Jambo, m'zee. Habari?"

Sendeo offered a paternal smile to Gabe and softly said, *"M'zuri."*

Gabe smiled and warmly shook the old man's hands with both of his. It was very good to see the friendly face of this *m'zee.* Sendeo also smiled and returned the warm handshake with both of his gnarled, callused hands, which felt cool and dry.

"*Bwana* Gabe, I have made arrangements for you to stay in our village tonight. No need to pitch your tent. My middle wife has prepared a hot dinner of porridge, *ugale,* and chapatis with honey. Of course, the *pombe* will loosen our tongues so we can discuss the important things of this world," said Sendeo with a broad, self-deprecating smile.

The two shifted into the slow, methodical gait of the mountaineer. Never out of breath, the duo gradually made their way up through the bamboo and mountain forest to find the haven of the N'dorobo village. Gabe's pack squeaked and made other sounds as the two moved up the mountain.

"You've moved your village again, haven't you, Sendeo? Why, it is for all intents and purposes an African Brigadoon."

Sendeo looked confused and simply asked, "What is a Brigadoon?"

"*Brigadoon* was a motion picture, Sendeo. In this movie, a whole village and all of its people would appear and disappear, seemingly at the will of the people. So, it seems, is the case with your village. First it is here, then it is there. Then it is gone altogether. Just like in *Brigadoon."*

"No, *Bwana* Gabe, it does not go away. It is always here for us. It is just not always of others' dreams. That is the way of the N'dorobo. We stay, yet our dreams may be different. This is our way."

It was getting dark as the two bent over and entered Sendeo's *thanga.* Two large gourds of *pombe* were sitting across from each other by the fire. Without talking, Gabe removed his Ensolite pad and sleeping bag and spread it at the side of the hut, out of the way. He placed his personals in a blue ditty bag on top of the sleeping bag, next to his flashlight. Sendeo silently watched Gabe go through his organizational ritual, contentedly slurping his honey beer. The small fire played shadows on the hut's walls as it snapped and crackled, its smoke offering a slight sage smell that was not at all unpleasant.

"You are a very careful man, *Bwana* Gabe."

"Why do you say that, Sendeo?"

"With you everything is in a line, everything has its place. I noticed when you took down your camp before you left your bag and torch were placed along the same line of your sleeping bag."

"Sendeo, such deliberate behavior has saved my life, and others', on more than one occasion. One must know where everything is, in case one needs it. What good is a first-aid kit if you can't find it in the dark because you also can't find your flashlight?"

"Fair enough, *Bwana* Gabe."

Gabe held his gourdful of *pombe* with both hands and took a big swallow of the sweet, yeasty brew. He saw Sendeo in the dim light of the hut, droplets of beer impaled on his gray stubble as he chewed off a load of tobacco. He had squatted beside the fire, smiling and content. He spat on the dirt floor and took another drink of *pombe.*

"I see you are well rested and the hole in your spirit is scabbed over, *Bwana* Gabe. Do you wish to continue your study of dreaming?"

Gabe wiped his lips with the back of his hand and studied the old N'dorobo before he answered.

"Yes, I wish to continue my study. Yet, Sendeo, it is still very difficult for me to truly give way to the reality of dreaming—since that reality is, at the same time, not real. This is bothersome for me to think about. How can one live in a world that is not real, but only a dream? Aren't you afraid that at any moment, your dreaming quits and you are no longer real? It is like having death looking over your shoulder."

Sendeo spat on the floor again and took another large swallow of *pombe,* smacking his lips slightly as the brew began to lubricate his tongue. He sat there and considered his response quite carefully.

"No, *Bwana* Gabe, it is like N'gai—God—looking over your shoulder. Is it not taught to you as *mtotos* that the world is nothing more than N'gai's dream? When you are no longer of N'gai's dreaming, you die. Yet, as long as you are of N'gai's dreaming, you are free to dream, as well."

Gabe thought about this. He realized he and Sendeo had fallen back into their ways of discussion. Neither was hurried, all words considered carefully, both those spoken and those heard. Gabe was in awe of the wisdom of the old shaman. Despite having no formal education, Sendeo could teach a lesson to even the most learned of existentialist scholars. His explanations of complicated concepts were always elegantly simple.

The conversation made Gabe reflect on an exercise he had done when he was a kid. At night, Gabe would look at the stars and try to think of a time before he was alive. He would always wonder, *Where was I?* Then, still looking at the stars, he would think to a time beyond his death. Would he find himself reborn with no knowledge of his previous life? Wrestling with such weighty concepts, Gabe formed a belief that death and rebirth would be like waking from a dream. Waking from the dream of death to the dream of life.

"So, I cannot dream myself if N'gai, or God, is not including me in his dreams? Then how was it I did so on this very mountain, *m'zee?* For a while, I was not of God's dreaming."

Gabe's death experience on Mt. Kenya back in 1978 left him greatly changed. To dream back one's entire life was, on one hand, monumental, and on the other, quite simple. Gabe had to let go of his entire understanding of life and reality in order to live. He had to take the most insane leap and actually *believe* he could dream back his life.

"Perhaps N'gai forgot you for a bit, *Bwana* Gabe, but you were soon again of his dreaming, for you, yourself, then began to dream."

"M'zee, this was the only time I have dreamed, until knowing the *Kidogo Kifu.* Why was it I could dream then? I could not do so thereafter."

Sendeo continued to masticate his tobacco and stared into the fire, a sad look on his face telling of his empathy for Gabe. He took another drink of *pombe,* smacked his lips again, and sighed.

"Bwana Gabe, the seriousness of your situation made your dreaming much more necessary. Every man, when faced with his death, will do anything to preserve life, even things thought to be not possible. You had to acknowledge your dreaming, for N'gai's attention was not helpful to you, and your situation was desperate. Yet you could not have dreamed unless you were of the dreaming of N'gai. It appears, since you are here talking to me now, N'gai's dreaming is not done with you yet, *Bwana* Gabe."

Sendeo smiled, finished off his gourd of *pombe,* and belched softly. He raised his voice so as to be heard by his *bibi,* who was tending a cook fire outside.

"Ninataka chakula, bibi. Asante." (I want food, wife. Thank you.)

As soon as the request was made, Sendeo's young *bibi* entered the hut balancing a number of bowls in her arms and hands like a coffeehouse waitress serving a large group. She set down the bowls on mats of woven grass. The food smelled wonderful, and set Gabe's mouth watering. He saw the chapatis and maize meal, over which was poured a porridge with meat and vegetables. Honey for the chapatis was in abundance.

As soon as Gabe and Sendeo began to eat their banquet, Sendeo's *bibi* brought two more gourds of *pombe* for washing down their repast. Gabe felt a slight buzz from the beer. All in all, he was immensely enjoying Sendeo's company and hospitality. As well, the weighty philosophical issues of dreaming were gradually sorting themselves out a bit for Gabe.

The two men finished their *chakula,* adjusted their sitting, and grew visibly more relaxed. They both nursed their *pombe,* and Sendeo did another load of chewing tobacco. Gabe yawned, as did Sendeo. The *pombe* and warmth of the fire were taking their toll on Gabe's wakefulness. He was strangely tired and very calm. He knew he would find a peaceful night's sleep.

"*Bwana* Gabe, we will now take our rest. I have enjoyed your company. I look forward to talk more of our dreaming. I also must say you should continue to practice with the *Kidogo Kifu.* Talk is different than dreaming."

"I have enjoyed our conversation, too, *m'zee.* And thank you for your hospitality. I am ready for sleep now, but will be ready for my practice in dreaming tomorrow."

"*Salama* (Good night), *Bwana* Gabe."

"Salama, m'zee."

Gabe fluffed his sleeping bag and crawled into the nylon cocoon. He took off his pile sweater and poked it into the nylon stuff sack for the sleeping bag that served as a pillow. As his eyes closed, he could hear Sendeo's soft breathing. Gabe smiled in the dark and found a dreamless sleep.

17

MT. KENYA, 2005

GABE AWOKE IN THE DARK OF THE HUT, HIS MUSCLES TIGHT and knotty. He could hear Sendeo gently snoring in the corner of the *thanga* in his pile of woolen blankets and tanned skins. Feeling as though he were in a tomb, blind, his ears stuffed with cotton, Gabe wondered about the time. Bleary-eyed, he pushed the button on his Indiglo watch and saw it was five twenty-six a.m. He listened and heard shuffling outside the *thanga*. He smiled as he heard the crackling of kindling and the quiet sound made by twigs and small wood being arranged with care on a cook fire. The blowing on embers gave way to a snapping and popping as the kindling took to the flame. Gabe smelled the wood fire and next heard a gourd clunking in a wooden pail and water splashing into a billycan. The routine of early morning in the forest offered Gabe a peaceful and pleasing symphony.

The sound of his ringing cell phone offered a rude dichotomy to this sleepy and gentle world. Gabe wondered at the event, the phone continuing its incessant chiming. Sendeo rolled over, farted, and sat up rubbing his eyes.

"*Jambo, Bwana* Gabe. Did you feel it necessary to set an alarm? I was in the middle of a pleasant dream full of sweet honey and *bibis* with ample thighs."

Gabe was frantically searching for the source of the noise in the darkness of the *thanga*. He found the phone next to his ditty bag and felt for the correct button to push. He pushed the button and, in third-person voice, heard himself say, "Hello?"

"Drop your cocks and grab your socks, boyo. Weird fuckin' shit goin' down."

"Jimmy? What the hell—"

"Well, you remember I said I'd call you if I saw any spooks floatin' by? Well, saw a couple of for-real fuckin' spooks last night—and boy howdy, I gotta talk with somebody right now. My shit is shaky, boyo."

"Okay, all right, let me think. Jimmy, it's not even six o'-clock in the morning. What the fuck is going on?"

"Shit came down last night, puss nuts. There I was a makin' my move on these Euro-cunts and outta nowhere up pops this asshole who I've had dealin's with before. Then, outta the fuckin' blue, the big kahuna of juju himself shows up and tries to fuckin' off me."

Gabe calmly said, "Slow down Jimmy, I haven't even had my morning piss, and you're going a mile a minute. Slow down. Who did you see and what did they do and what did you do?"

Jimmy responded, "Okay, wish it were past ten o'clock so I could justify some stress medication. But anyway. There I was sittin' at the fuckin' bar with two Euro-babes and out of nowhere this old merc I've done business with shows up. Right outta fuckin' nowhere. In my business, Gabe, there are no coincidences. He was there for as many reasons as I was there. Anyway, this fucker exits stage left and the next thing I know, the big kahuna juju himself whispers in my ear—the same motherfuckin' wog that killed my team and tried to kill me fifty years ago. Why, he just appeared, right there in the Keekorok bar. Then he tried to do the tough talk with me—actually thought he was goin' to finish me off with this little fuckin' pig sticker. Well, I double-tapped the motherfucker and sent him to hyena hell. I notified my people and they clamped the whole, fuckin' place down tighter than a duck's butt."

Shaking his head in the gloom of the hut, Gabe said, "You mean Sendeo's brother Terrari tried to kill you again? And you killed him?"

"Okay, you didn't hear me say that, but I ain't takin' issue with it. The strange fuckin' thing is how they got here and how Bazaan got out."

"Bazaan? Jimmy, you said Bazaan. Who is this Bazaan?"

"Kinda ambitious motherfucker—done all right by himself, though. Kind of a spooky shit, too. In that world it was don't ask, don't tell. He was a good client. I figure him to be in the top-level circuit of mercs—maybe even a tapper."

"Tapper? What is a tapper?" asked Gabe.

"Sanction operator. You know, welcome to the hereafter, motherfucker."

"Assassin?" asked Gabe.

"A little more than that. Never mind, though. Anyway, you and him have things in common."

"What could we have in common?" asked Gabe.

"Both eaten up with this Dream Walker bullshit. A bunch of years ago, this *chingazo* shows up at an arms show in Bangkok. He thinks I'm more drunk than I am, and he's fakin' his shitface-ness and I-don't-give-a-shit attitude. Well, this fucker played the twenty questions with me on this Dream Walking during the Mau Mau. I could see the fuckhead was catalogin'."

"Jimmy, I didn't tell you this when we met at Keekorok, but a duo much like you describe paid me an early-morning visit with a gun pointed at my head. There was a Hispanic-looking guy with bristly black hair and an old man who looks like Sendeo on a bad day. I kicked the Hispanic guy in his eye and promptly got the hell out of there with the guidance of Sendeo. Is there any relationship?"

"Shit-fuck-fire, boyo, Ralph Chang Bazaan is more Hispanic than anything else other'n asshole. To boot, he was sportin' a pair of sunglasses even though it was darker than Coaly's ass. And his sidekick, Terrari, is an old wog with an attitude. Them sound like the couple that rousted you?"

Gabe pondered on the name, a memory bouncing in his head. *Ralph Chang Bazaan.* Gabe's memory flooded his being. Ralph Chang Bazaan—his adversary so many years ago. Could it be? Gabe remembered the circle fight and wondered about such . . . synchronicity. The last he had seen of Bazaan was on Twenty-second and Orchard, Bazaan lying still and no longer a threat. How was it that such a ghost was rising out of old graveyards?

"Jimmy, what do you think is going on? What can I do?"

"Don't know for sure, boyo. I gotta let ya in on some shit. Figure you know anyhoo. I work for our government, Mr. Gabe. The second most important person in America is comin' here soon to hook up with the first most important person here in Kenya. I gotta job to do. And I'm doin' it. But this Bazaan ringer is bothersome. Gabe, I had three birds sent aloft from Keekorok within five minutes of seeing this Bazaan. Nada. Zippo. The guy didn't get here by vehicular transport. No headlights within twenty klicks of the lodge. No, boyo, this asshole just showed up and exited—no hydrocarbons involved."

"Jimmy, what are you telling me? Are you Secret Service?"

"Gabe, I ain't sayin' shit. Just shag your juju-imbibin' ass down here, y'hear? Gotta have a spook to protect against a spook. I think this Bazaan is gonna try to pop the VP, and gonna do it usin' the juju shit. Since you're Indiana fuckin' Jones, shag your ass down here, boyo, and save the day."

The phone clicked off and Gabe stared into the darkness. Sendeo readjusted his frame on his bed and let out a deep sigh. The cook fire smell had shifted to that of chapatis and maize meal porridge. Gabe gently put a hand on the old man and called his name in a whisper.

"Sendeo, please—I need your help."

Sendeo farted and rolled over again, putting his back toward Gabe in the darkness of the *thanga*. However, the smell of fry bread and porridge aroused humming and mumbling noises from the old man. He sat up and rubbed the corners of his eyes, then blew a line of snot out his nostril into the darkness and adjusted his testicles before he drew his gaze down on Gabe, who felt it rather than saw it.

"You have no courtesy for sleep, *Bwana* Gabe. If you did, I would still be sleeping, dreaming of women with fat thighs and ample buttocks. My youngest *bibi* will fix us our morning meal. We need no meat or honey, so why do you wake me so early?"

Gabe answered delicately, "Your brother and his adept are, uh, posing problems."

"My brother? Terrari? What is he up to now?"

Gabe looked into the darkness of the hut and felt empty as he formed the words.

"Sendeo, your brother is no longer alive. He was killed last night as he was trying to take the life of another old man."

Sendeo offered no reaction to this news other than to exhale a long sigh. "He was lost anyway, *Bwana* Gabe. He had wandered deep into the forest—so deep that when he looked back to find his path out, it was gone—grown over. He had lost his way, *Bwana* Gabe, so many years ago."

The two sat together in the dark. The smell of fry bread chapatis and maize meal porridge mingled now with the smell of chai. The forest was without sound other than a quiet dripping, the wet sounds of dew drops falling on bamboo, camphor, and Saint-John's-wort.

"I must go to Keekorok Lodge, but have no time to drive," said Gabe.

"You will need at least a bit of the *Kidogo Kifu,* for you are too awake, *Bwana* Gabe. Do you wish for me to accompany you on this journey?"

"No, Sendeo. This may be a fool's errand, but I owe it to my new friend, Jimmy, to chase it down. Prepare a bit of the *Kidogo Kifu* for me, and I will dream myself to Keekorok."

"Let us have some food first, *Bwana* Gabe. My belly is tossing about to find some food right now. Can you not hear it yourself?"

Gabe smiled and, without saying a word, crawled out of the bachelor's hut into the gray of predawn. There, by the cook fire squatted Sendeo's youngest *bibi* turning over the chapatis with callused hands and a polished wooden stick. She smiled a silent good morning to Gabe and continued her work. Gabe could smell the moisture of the forest and absently gazed up in the direction of the main peaks. The snaggled teeth of Kerrinyaga were already cloaked in a thick layer of cloud and fog. *A summit attempt today would be a bitch,* thought Gabe as Sendeo's youngest wife handed him a chapati slathered with honey. Gabe accepted the offering as Sendeo, silently, took his leave behind a stand of bamboo and performed his morning ablutions.

Gabe and the old man sat in front of the cooking fire and attacked their morning meal. It was normal for many East African tribes to partake of only two meals in a day: the morning meal and another repast after nightfall. So it would be in this N'dorobo Brigadoon. Gabe enjoyed the porridge, which was doused with goat milk and coated with raw sugar. The chapatis were as abundant as was the honey. The two men ate in silence, hearing only the forest sounds and the crackling of kindling.

After the morning meal was completed, Sendeo called to his *bibi* and gave her curt instructions. Shortly thereafter, the baskets and containers appeared and Sendeo performed his dreaming alchemy. He held out a bit of the paste on a green leaf like a priest would place a wafer on the tongue of a penitent at communion. Gabe washed the Small Death down with a cup of chai. Gabe's conscious vision was again flooded by the rosy light of the dreaming of the N'dorobo. He dreamed of Keekorok.

Like a wisp of smoke, Gabe lazily floated over the pool of the Keekorok Lodge. A grounds worker was sweeping alongside the pool in slow, lazy strokes with a broom made of long grass bound with cord. Gabe could smell the morning breakfast table, its aromas wafting in the hazy morning light.

Gabe saw Jimmy in his wheelchair rolling slowly along the path toward the lodge's dining room.

Gabe silently came up behind Jimmy and began pushing the chair. The gun appeared out of nowhere. It was quickly shoved into Gabe's gut as Jimmy swiveled in the chair, barking out a guffaw when he realized who was behind him.

"Shit-fuck-fire, boyo, coulda' got a belly full of lead for pullin' that stunt. Been readin' up on that ninja shit, I see. Oh yeah, I forgot, you got the big mojo—the magic juju. Well, glad to have you here. Didn't expect you so soon."

Gabe smiled and responded, "You're the one who thinks this shit is so important as to wake my sorry ass up from my only sex dream since I've got ten in-country. I've already had one breakfast, but could pick on some fruit and down a glass or two of passion fruit juice. Feel the need for *kahawa.* The chai's gettin' a bit sugary for me."

"You drink that sissy shit? Didn't take you for no tea-drinkin,' chablis-sippin' no-load. Well, anyway, let's go tie into some grub. I'm so hungry I could eat a skunk's butt."

The two went into the dining room. Gabe sat himself down directly across from Jimmy. After they had ordered their breakfast, Gabe's stare seized Jimmy's eyes, and he said simply, "Jimmy, tell me what the fuck is going on here."

Jimmy shifted in his chair, but kept his eye contact with Gabe. "Gabe, the second most important man in the U.S. of A. is comin' here right shortly. We gotta make sure we keeps our veep—so they send the likes of me and my boys to make sure he comes to no harm. Now I got a fuckin' shit storm on my hands. When the likes of Bazaan shows up in a backwater joint in Kenya with a fuckin' wog who's killed our troops, plus a fuckin' brace of political friendlies shows up with him and the fuckin' vice president of the U.S. of A. is scheduled to show at the same fuckin' place, well, that, my friend, is a shit storm of trouble."

Gabe studied the old patriot. Mostly, he felt a strange compassion for this old warrior. Yet, at the same time, he knew this man who sat in front of him was genuine in his patriotism, and that was, for Gabe, infectious.

"What can I do to help, Jimmy? I want to help you."

"Okay, Gabe, I'm layin' this shit out straight up for you. I figure you got need-to-know status. Baker gets here on the afternoon of the twenty-ninth. Him and President Odinga have a doin's with Leakey and the Kenyan cabinet and Charlton Heston, too—some Safari International dedication of choppers for the war against poaching. Anyway, we have some pretty sound intelligence that a bunch of dipshit politicos with a bone to pick are goin' to have a go at President Odinga. This same bunch of Boy Scouts who want to pop a cap in Odinga's ass is supposedly in cahoots with some real nasty rat fuckers—ex–Al Qaeda shits who figure in for a penny, in for a pound. Anyway, we feel we have a clear and present danger leveled at Baker, too."

Gabe mulled over what Jimmy had told him. "You think there will be an assassination attempt on both Odinga and Baker?"

"You catch on right quick for a schoolboy," said Jimmy, letting loose another loud guffaw. "Anyway, last night I took one factor out of the equation. Old Terrari, that motherfuckin' asshole of a wog, is takin' his dirt nap."

"You think Bazaan will dream his way in and take a shot?" asked Gabe.

"Yep. Now yer catchin' my drift. Gabe, I'm tellin' you straight up, with this dreamin' shit, we've drawn a hand of threes and fives—mixed suits to boot. We need to fight fire with fire. We need to fight this fuckin' juju with the same fuckin' juju. You're the only game in town, the way I see it."

"So, I'm one of your operatives? I'm the critical factor in your turning around this assassination?"

"You're pickin' up on it pronto, Gabe. I can have the VP in total lockdown, but if somebody can play Casper the fuckin' Ghost and float in unseen, well, that's the shits. The VP won't stand for bedside guards, and I can't say that would do any good anyway—how do you guard against a spook? After all, he doesn't know 'bout this spooky dreamin' shit. Goes against everything that's real."

"Yeah, I know," replied Gabe. "I know about that all too well. So, Jimmy, what is it you would have me do? Shoot straight arrows with me."

Jimmy slurped in some coffee and dove into the English muffins covered with butter and marmalade. He fixed his eyes on Gabe, chewed his muffin, and swallowed, washing it down with the coffee and clearing the way for speaking.

"Gabe, I want your ass floatin' around here at Keekorok on the twenty-ninth. I want your sorry ass to be full of caffeine and propelled with that juju shit, floatin' around like a goddamned angel over Baker. If Bazaan shows, well, stall his ass or preempt his efforts. Anyway, we ain't got no shit to protect us from a goddamned spook. So give us the high sign and we'll pop a cap in his ass and then we'll all get some sleep."

Gabe sipped his coffee and poked a passion fruit around on his plate. He was concerned about such heavy responsibility being tied to something as esoteric as the dreaming of the N'dorobo.

Gabe quietly asked, "Jimmy, if I do come down here in the dreaming state, and if I do run into this Bazaan, do you really expect a college professor to take out an experienced assassin? What am I supposed to do? Say, 'Time out Bazaan, wait till Jimmy and his crew get here'?"

Jimmy smiled and looked directly into Gabe's eyes. "Don't be spreadin' that sheep dip on me, Mr. Gabe Karate Turpin. I figure with your martial arts experience you could even give a few of my bad boys some serious trouble."

"How did you know I train?"

"It's my goddamned job to know the assets of my team. Gabe, I know more about you than you can remember about your fuckin' self. Now cut the shit. You are highly capable. All the intelligence capabilities of the U.S. government have confirmed that for me."

Gabe shook his head and wondered if there was any privacy left in this day and age. It seemed as if it was impossible to keep even the deepest secret about oneself in the face of online access to the very profile of one's life.

"What martial art do I train in, Jimmy?"

"Okinawan Goju Ryu and Daitoryu Aikijujitsu. You hold dan rank in both. Your teacher is John Roseberry, retired

USMC gunnery sergeant—one of the meanest SOBs to have enlisted in the Corps, and also one of the nicest. Had a pleasant conversation with him a few days ago. Seems like a hell of a guy. Come to find out, we've met. He was training SEAL and recon boys we used in I Corps III MAF. Just before all hell broke loose in the Tet offensive, your teacher and I sent off some brave boys for an insert into Laos. 'Course, that shit didn't happen—officially."

Gabe smiled and looked down at his coffee cup. He looked up and saw Jimmy smiling broadly.

"Your teacher said to give you a message. Don't rightly know what it means, but he said, 'Remember the virtues of Bushido.' Does that mean anything to ya, Gabe?"

"Yes," said Gabe quietly, looking back at his coffee cup. "Yes, it does. Jimmy, I'll be here bright-eyed and bushy tailed on the twenty-ninth. I will do my best."

Jimmy smiled even more and barked out a guffaw that startled Gabe. He reached across the table and offered Gabe his hand. The two shook hands and stared into each other's eyes. Jimmy's handshake was amazingly strong for one who looked to be so infirm.

"Welcome aboard, Gabe. Welcome to the fuckin' monkey house."

"Glad to be here, sir."

Jimmy tossed the last bit of sausage into his mouth and wiped his fingers on a linen napkin. He started to nod his head, as if confirming something he had forgotten.

"Gabe, will you be wantin' a piece? Or, how does that shit work with this dreamin' hoodoo? If you carry a gun while you're spookin' around, will it float around too, scarin' the hell outta everybody like in an Abbot and Costello movie? Anyway, I can get you a piece, if you be needin' it."

"No," said Gabe, chuckling to himself. "Everything of your world is of your dream. It is not a breakfast conversation, Jimmy. But no, a gun would not be seen unless it were brought into play. Regardless, I will not be needing a firearm."

"Suit yourself, boyo. Hey, could you give me a little preview of this motherfuckin' juju? Like, can you disappear like a spook right now?"

"Are we done with our conversation, Jimmy?"

"As far as I'm concerned we are. I'll see you here on the twenty-ninth. Come early in the day. And confirm it with me once you're here. Want to know our spook is on the clock."

Gabe looked around and determined they were the only guests left in the dining room.

"Jimmy, take care of yourself," said Gabe.

The rosy world of dreaming asserted itself, and Gabe thought of the slopes of Mt. Kenya. He simply disappeared from the dining room of the Keekorok. Jimmy sat as still as death, staring at the empty chair across from him.

"Shit fire," was all Jimmy uttered.

18

MT. KENYA, 2005

Gabe walked along the Chogoria Track and patiently waited to be discovered. He did not trust he could find Sendeo's village, regardless of the advantage of dreaming. So he quietly chose to walk up the track—engaging the reality of his world—with the rosy world of dreaming still about him. It was early afternoon. Gabe could smell the bovine aroma of Cape buffalo. He proceeded up the track with caution, not wanting to surprise an old bull. He hoped Sendeo would find him soon. They had much yet to do. Gabe plodded up the track without burden of a pack and looked at the bowers of camphor trees, moss hanging like the beards of sages in the misty air of a foggy afternoon. He heard the bark of a bushbuck.

"*Jambo, Bwana* Gabe. I see you have fared well with your dreaming. You are still of your dreams, are you not?"

"*Jambo,* Sendeo. Yes, I am still dreaming, yet the dreaming seems more normal than the first time. I feel I am the one in control of the dreaming, not the *Kidogo Kifu.*"

"Yes, *Bwana* Gabe, that is the way of our dreaming. I must say, you are a rare student of dreaming. You command your dreams like an N'dorobo who has been dreaming for some years. That is good."

"Perhaps I am learning. At this point it feels quite natural. If I don't think about my old understanding of reality, it is quite natural."

"Is the emergency of your visit to the south solved? You seemed highly agitated then. Now you seem very calm. Have you seen to your responsibilities?"

"In a week I must again go south to Keekorok. Until that time, I must understand all I can of the dreaming. The dreams of the N'dorobo play an important role in this matter. I must truly master N'dorobo dreaming before the moon is three-fourths full."

The old N'dorobo smiled in the gray afternoon as they made their way to the village. Their pace was slow and methodical. They talked little as they delved deeper and deeper into the green maze of the forest. A colobus monkey floated in the air overhead. A vervet monkey sat, a silent witness to the two men, eating a green shoot. Unseen, a rare *bongo* with its striped skin melted into the background of the forest.

Gabe suddenly realized they need not walk back to the village, for he was still under the effects of the *Kidogo Kifu* and Sendeo needed no such aid in order to dream.

"*M'zee,* can I follow your dreaming? Need we tax our lungs and legs? If you dream of your village—can I follow your dreaming?"

"Focus your intent on me, *Bwana* Gabe. It should be of no difficulty as long as you keep your dreaming of mine."

They flew like Peter Pan above the forest's canopy—the rosy light of dreaming casting surreal shadows in the gathering gloom of another Mt. Kenya evening.

For both Gabe and Sendeo, immersion into the world of the N'dorobo dreaming became a comfortable routine over the days that followed. The regimen was one focused on facilitating the understanding of the dreaming in total. Gabe soon understood the order of cosmology of the N'dorobo, and how dreaming not only was not in conflict, but was the very cement that held together a culture—a theosophy.

Gabe and Sendeo, student and teacher, were blessed with unusually clear and pleasant weather during their time together. Usually, Mt. Kenya had only a few hours of hospitality each day. Then the weather could easily cull out those without proper intent.

Every morning, the two would talk about almost anything other than dreaming. Early on, occasionally, Gabe would cook breakfast for Sendeo, Sendeo's young wife more than happy to find more time on her hands as Gabe performed the culinary duties of camp. Then that, too, became a ritual. Every day, Gabe would cook breakfast in the gray light before dawn. He made the fry bread chapatis and the tea, and sometimes fixed rolled oats for his teacher.

They would spend the mid- to late morning just walking in the forest, voyeurs to the rhythm of life on the mountain. Gabe became wonderfully aware of the cycles of life that made up this great mountain. The forest quickly became Gabe's home—a bond not realized before in his numerous visits to this mountain. The forest of Kerrinyaga grew strangely familiar, wonderfully comfortable.

In the afternoons, Gabe and Sendeo would practice the dreaming of the N'dorobo. Sendeo smiled to himself as he noted it was taking less and less of the *Kidogo Kifu* to produce the dreaming state in Gabe. As he had learned the basic techniques of his martial arts at the knee of his sensei, Gabe learned the subtleties of dreaming from Sendeo.

Soon, the impossible became reality. Dreaming was now a part of Gabe's reality. Sitting around the cook fire in Sendeo's *thanga* one evening, Gabe reflected on the normalcy of dreaming.

"Sendeo, how is it the N'dorobo have dreaming and no other tribes, no other people, have found this thing?"

Sendeo sat in the yellow light of the *thanga* and smiled. Working the tobacco between his teeth and gums, he spat and let out a chuckle.

"I believe many people have the dreaming, but have misplaced it. Like you, they have just forgotten their dreams. Their dreaming built walls around their dreaming. The walls became the object, and the real object—dreaming—was then hidden within and long since forgotten. As I see it, that is not so peculiar."

Gabe reflected on this wisdom and smiled to himself in the dim light of the hut. In a few days, he would employ his dreaming down at Keekorok. He felt very much in command. Also, Gabe was itching for a change of scenery. He knew he either must leave the mountain and Sendeo very soon or commit to staying here for the rest of his life.

On the morning of the twenty-ninth, Gabe cooked a large breakfast for his teacher. He ladled the chai into an enamel cup and gave it to Sendeo as the old N'dorobo exited the tent, scratching his behind and rubbing the sleep out of his eyes.

Sendeo always looked to the home of his God the first thing every morning. Sendeo studied the main peaks, unusually clear and almost magnified by the thin air. Nelion and Batian stood as the very altar of God in the early-morning light. Not a cloud was to be seen around the ancient volcano.

Gabe realized there were no moist dripping sounds, as was usual. In fact, the air was relatively warm and without the perennial dampness so typical of the breath of N'gai on Kerrinyaga. Gabe presented the chapatis and porridge to Sendeo, who thankfully accepted the feast. Sendeo's *bibi* sat smiling out from the fire.

Gabe quietly said, "Today I must go to my chores in the south. I will take a bit of the *Kidogo Kifu* around noon and will keep a bit back in store, as well. If all goes well, I will be back for breakfast tomorrow. I would like to rely on your *bibi* to be responsible for your breakfast in the morning. I may wish to sleep late, for I will likely be late, going about my duties."

Both men sat around the cook fire, many words remaining unspoken.

Gabe, very reserved now, asked, "*M'zee,* what would become of my sleeping body if I were to be killed or seriously injured in my dreaming?"

"*Bwana* Gabe, it would disappear, for your dreaming would be either done or required elsewhere."

The silence remained palpable. The mood around the cook fire on this fine morning was growing grim.

"*Bwana* Gabe, I feel a very dark feeling about those duties you speak of. Please keep true to what you have learned over the past days. That will protect you. I feel you must be rooted like the giant fig tree—for a big wind will blow about you as you go about your duties."

"Thank you, *m'zee*. I will be as of the fig tree. I am ready for the blow."

The two spent the remainder of the morning walking, relaxed, about the forest. As if in a command performance, all of the forest's menagerie of wildlife did cameos. The brave brownish birds alighted on Gabe's shoulder and ate bits of cold chapati. The colobus monkeys and sunbirds filled the air.

Gabe pocketed a dollop of the *Kidogo Kifu* as a reserve and, without hesitation, popped a small bit into his mouth, as well. He shook Sendeo's hand, took his leave, and went into the darkness of the *thanga*. In the lazy afternoon on Mt. Kenya, Gabe dreamed of Keekorok.

⇎⇎⇎

Gabe took in the vast array of personnel assembled at the lodge. The security and assembly of people were incredible. There were roadblocks at every track that left the main road. The lodge was awash in a sea of men wearing suits and earphones. There was a large podium set up to the side of the parking lot, and there, on a platform, sat an Apache helicopter. A large red ribbon enclosed the cockpit of the chopper.

Just off from the stage upon which sat the copter, rows of folding chairs had been aligned. Many people were milling around, not yet content to take a seat. Gabe searched for Jimmy among the throng of guests—and operatives.

He saw his old friend Richard Leakey propped into an armchair on the dais, his frame looking uncomfortable in his sitting posture. Leakey had lost limbs in an airplane accident in 1993 and, though mended, was still visited by much pain. Leakey had had until recently the unenviable job of managing the Kenyan government through its bouts of graft, corruption, and the throes of being a debtor nation. Gabe knew he should err on the side of discretion, yet he could not resist greeting his old friend and fellow Explorers Club member.

"Richard Leakey, Gabe Turpin," Gabe introduced himself.

Leakey smiled broadly and sought Gabe's hand. They warmly shook hands, and Gabe gently patted his associate's right shoulder. The two men looked into each other's eyes.

"Studying the ways of the N'dorobo? Have you uncovered anything interesting?"

Gabe replied, still holding on to Leakey's hand, "More than we have time to go into. How are you faring?"

"Well, thank you for asking. I must say, I didn't expect to see you in this neck of the woods, as they say. This dedication is the type of thing I figured you'd avoid."

"Well, usually. However, I'm on a bit of an R and R and wondered about the crowd around one of my favorite Kenyan watering holes. What's the occasion?"

"Safari Club International has contributed to the Kenyan Department of Wildlife a state-of-the-art helicopter to be used for anti-poaching enforcement. We're making a big to-do about it. Why, even President Odinga and Vice President Baker are here to cut the ribbon. Quite a flap for Kenya, I must say. Even your Charlton Heston is here to help with the honors."

"Well I'll be," said Gabe, wondering about Heston's health. "Are they serving free drinks to commemorate the event? Must say, I'm dry as a popcorn fart."

"Howdy, Gabe." A southern drawl pulled Gabe's attention from Leakey. "Glad to see you," said Jimmy as he silently rolled up in his wheelchair beside them.

"I don't think we've had the opportunity to meet. I am Richard Leakey, an ex-MP with the Kenyan government. Do you know Gabe here, as well?"

"Howdy, doc. Glad to make your acquaintance. Yeah, I know Gabe here. In fact, we've got some talkin' to do right pronto, if you don't mind the intrusion. You know, grant stuff."

Jimmy gave Leakey an exaggerated wink.

"Go right ahead. Gabe, good to see you again. Hope to see you at next year's Club dinner. Perhaps we can catch up then. I'd be glad to know what progress you've made with the N'dorobo business."

Jimmy wheeled off toward the lodge. Gabe followed alongside, his hand resting on Jimmy's chair.

"Listen, puss nuts. I told you to check in with me first thing. Not to say I ain't glad to see you here. But don't be a-jawin' with the civilians before you clear your entry onto the grid. How in hell do you know Leakey?"

"We're both members of The Explorers Club. I've known him since 1986. He's a friend, for Christ's sake, Jimmy. Can't I even say hello to a friend?"

"Not without me knowin', please and thank you. Now, cut the shit, you gotta go to work. See any other spooks floatin' around out there in them vapors?"

"No, Jimmy. It's not like that. Anyway, where is the VP? If you want me to do my part, that's who I should be hoverin' over."

"Well, if you gotta know, he's havin' a beer with Charlton Heston in the bar. I recommend you go there covert posthaste. I don't want Bazaan or any other goat-fuckers seein' you and me. Most of all, I don't want any *bandidos* seein' you. Gabe, boyo—you're our secret weapon. You gots to be gone. You do your job, now. I'll do mine."

Gabe disappeared from beside Jimmy's wheelchair.

"Shit-fuck-fire, boyo. Give an old man a little warnin' before you go all spooky like that," said Jimmy into the air that, a moment before, was a human being. "Shit. Don't know how the fucker can put up with that shit himself."

Gabe, in the rosy world of dreaming, took station beside the vice president. Baker appeared to be enjoying himself in the company of Heston, an actor-cum-politician who seemed to have true passion—for his passions despite his acknowledgment of the advance of Alzheimer's. Gabe had first seen Heston as a child. The movie star was given the William F. Cody Award by the Nebraska Department of Tourism. Gabe remembered he had been quite surprised that this giant of the screen was rather small. Later, the two shared a first-class cabin on a United Airlines flight to LAX. Heston was truly a gentleman with a large presence, regardless of his deceptively small stature.

For the rest of the afternoon, Gabe shadowed Vice President Baker. The ribbon cutting went off without a hitch. Gabe was constantly seeking the intent of another also in the dreaming state. However, the afternoon ceremonies and the evening events were benign and without threat. Gabe patiently waited. He watched the moon climb over the escarpment. The moaning of hyenas could be heard out from the lodge, as could the grunting of lions. Despite the great intrusion of humanity on this land, the night was again claimed by an ancient trust. Another evening had come, another dance of death in the Great Rift.

19

MAASAI MARA, KENYA, 2005

Bazaan had slept in late, taking brunch on the patio of the Mara Serena overlooking the vast expanse of the Mara. He finished breakfast and began to go through his ritual of preparation, much as a Muay Thai boxer prepares to do battle in the ring. These were touchstones Bazaan developed over the years of a successful career.

The day of a job he concentrated first on his breathing—inhaling through the nose, belly breathing, and exhaling through the mouth. This yoga-like breathing calmed his mind and heightened his awareness and mental clarity.

He ate sparingly, a mixture of simple carbohydrates and protein, with no intake of alcohol or caffeine for the twenty-four hours prior to his job.

After his brunch was digested, Bazaan changed into swimming trunks, walked to the pool, and immediately dove into the deep end. Gliding deep, he cruised in the cool silence and did two lengths of the pool underwater. He surfaced, shook the water off his face, and looked at the deep, blue sky. A smile played across his lips as he shoved off the pool's side and proceeded to swim laps. He swam and rehearsed the sequences of his upcoming job, again and again—visualizing his Glock drawing down on the sleeping vice president's head.

He had planned to take out the more difficult of the two targets first. If he tried for Odinga first and something went astray, Baker's security would be the more sensitive and reactive—able to counter the entire operation without the element of surprise.

After forty minutes of lap swimming, Bazaan stepped out of the pool and laid down a towel over a lounge chair beside the pool. A waiter ambled over to Bazaan as he rested in the hot afternoon sun. Without opening his eyes, Bazaan ordered three bottles of water. He wanted to ensure his hydration and treated his body like a finely tuned machine. He always did this before a job. He entered a job completely pure and at one hundred percent of his incredible capacity.

The water came, and Bazaan sipped the cool liquid, continuing his yogic breathing. His mind was very calm—his spirit quite peaceful. Yet he was aware of everything around him. His training heightened his senses as he prepared for the very purpose of his life—the taking of a life against incredible odds. This heightened state of being was referred to by martial artists as *zanshin*. His mind at once was nowhere, yet everywhere.

Bazaan napped in the hot afternoon sun of the Great Rift. Slowly and methodically, he drained all three of the water bottles. At around four o'clock, the bite of the Kenyan sun was dulled by the breezes breathed down on the floor of the Rift from the escarpment. The shadows were longer and the tinkle of martini glasses could be heard coming from the *banda* bar. Gin and pinks were mixed, the glass stirrer against the pitchers sounding like wind chimes in the soft afternoon sun.

Bazaan smiled and knew he was again ready to ply his trade. He had spent the perfect day in preparation. His mind and body were ready to perform. His was a hard form of beauty, a dark magic. For the second oldest profession, his preparation for this job was most certainly complete.

Bazaan stretched and slowly arose from the lounge chair beside the pool. He stretched again and felt the muscles of his latissimus dorsi loosen in knotty clumps. He walked purposefully and slowly to his room.

Once in the room, Bazaan pulled on his light but warm Adidas sweat suit. His mind now repeated a relaxing mantra over and over—a mental chanting of sorts that kept everything about his mind and body calm. Self-talk, imagery, biofeedback, all were now brought to bear on his mission—his success in taking the lives of two men.

Bazaan walked loosely, slowly, down to the bar and purchased another bottle of water. It was now nearly six o'clock, and the expanse of the Rift was fuzzy in the gray shadows of dusk. Bazaan went back to his room, sipping on the water, the mantra of calm still playing in his mind.

In his room, Bazaan got out the Glock and thoroughly checked every mechanism three times. He screwed in the silencer and shoved it into a special shoulder holster that hung loosely under his left armpit. He placed five quick-draw clips in a special web belt he bound around his waist, fastening its Velcro tabs. He fished out the night-vision goggles from his duffel bag and smiled to himself, knowing even U.S. Special Forces technology was a year behind his. His NV goggles were developed by a kid who lived in Palo Alto and who had a meth habit matched only by his incessant need for playing violent video games. Regardless of the shortcomings of the lad, he was a technological genius.

Fully outfitted, Bazaan found the package of *Kidogo Kifu.* He took one of the dollops of the Small Death and studied it in the gathering gloom of his small room. Bazaan nonchalantly tossed the dreaming paste down his gullet and washed it down with one last swallow of water. The pinkish orange of the dreaming world overtook him and he found himself looking at his innate form lying on the bed. Bazaan thought of Keekorok.

Bazaan floated over the expanse of the lodge and methodically inventoried the security that was in place. He chuckled to himself as he studied all the tightly secured positions taken up on all roads and tracks in and out of Keekorok. His primary aim was to determine the sleeping quarters of both Vice President Baker and President Odinga.

It was past eight thirty p.m., and he knew that Baker was early to bed and early to rise. Bazaan hung like a ghost and studied the lodge and its cabins. The location of the two dignitaries quickly became apparent.

Bazaan saw the cabin farthest from the lodge had two actives on each of the four outside walls, one active on the roof, three out from the front, and another three out from the back, near the perimeter of the lodge's property. Each of the actives appeared to be in full field, covert gear, including the Heckler & Koch MP-5s used by the Navy SEAL teams. This was most certainly the abode of Vice President Baker.

At the opposite end of the Keekorok complex, Bazaan saw three actives with old AK-47s. One smoked a cigarette, and all three were bunched up outside the front of the cabin. Such was the security for President Odinga.

Bazaan waited for another half hour and saw there were no lights on in either of the two targeted cabins. As a raptor stoops for the kill, Bazaan silently swooped down to the cabin of Vice President Baker. He found himself in the darkness of the cabin and heard snoring from the bed. Clicking on his night-vision goggles, he saw the white head of Baker partially covered with a pillow. The number two man of the free world was deeply asleep, the cabin silent. Bazaan tasted the air and, his nerves alive with fire, took lightning-fast assessments of his security in the room. Within a second, he had cleared the room.

Then, as he had rehearsed so many times, Bazaan pulled the Glock from its holster and slowly drew down on the head of the sleeping vice president.

20

MAASAI MARA, KENYA, 2005

THE BLOW ON BAZAAN'S FOREARM FELT AS THOUGH A HEAVY, hot iron bar had hit his entire body. It was so devastatingly effective that Bazaan thought he had been shot. Miraculously, he still maintained a grip on his Glock. Thinking to avoid a second shot, Bazaan tucked and rolled away from the door. A sinewy arm suddenly snaked around his neck, attempting to crush his larynx, or at least choke him out. Bazaan violently butted his head back and heard a sickening crunching sound followed by a deep groan from his unknown adversary. As quick as a striking mamba, Bazaan sprang into a crouch, his gun firing into the dark. The quiet, spitting sound of the silenced Glock was making an arc of death in the darkness around Bazaan. Trying to assess his position in the room and the location of the vice president, Bazaan had to balance the need to protect himself from his invisible assailant with the need to remain focused on his job of killing Baker.

Bazaan felt the presence more than saw it. The tall form again struck for the nerve bundle in Bazaan's gun hand. The blow was slightly off target and had none of the effectiveness of the first strike. Suddenly, Bazaan was belly-to-belly with a very tall, strong enemy who was trying to disarm him as he shot hard knee kicks into Bazaan's groin. Grappling with the tall, seasoned fighter, Bazaan suddenly realized he was locked in a life-and-death struggle with his old nemesis, Gabe Turpin.

Gabe and Bazaan wrestled for possession of the pistol. Their sweat-and-ketone-filled breaths reeked with the unique aroma of death. Violently, they shifted their body weight, sought purchase and control—the gun a silent witness to who would control it, and the direction of death. The gun discharged once, and Gabe felt the blinding white of pain possess him. It discharged a second time and Bazaan groaned heavily. Both men crumpled in a heap on the rough, wooden floor of the cabin amid the smell of cordite.

Gabe felt a warm wetness against the skin of his belly and lower ribs. He lay on his left side, and his fluttering eyes focused on Bazaan, who lay beside him, unmoving. The left side of Bazaan's face was a bloody hollow, his right eye open, unfocused, and dead.

Then, a cacophony of panic—running feet, shouts from security and Secret Service agents. The door burst open, splintering the door frame. Gun-mounted lasers crisscrossed and painted red spiderwebs in the dim room, seemingly being invaded by an army. Strong hands searched Gabe's body. Unceremoniously, Gabe was rolled onto his stomach and his wrists were secured with heavy plastic binder strips. The movement sent shock waves of pain throughout Gabe's body. He was just trying to remain still and calm through a haze of pain and could not talk or even move of his own volition.

In the sudden stillness, Gabe heard the vice president briefing his agents, "I woke to that Hispanic man pointing a gun at my head. How he got in, I don't have a clue. Then, and I don't believe it myself, the tall guy appears out of thin air like Harry Houdini. He jumps the Hispanic guy and they started wrestling for control of the gun. Two shots went off. Both seem to have been hit. The Hispanic guy is dead—part of his brain is splattered on the ceiling over there." Baker pointed his chin across the room. "Looks like the tall fellow saved my sorry ass."

"That he did, sir," stated a voice from the broken doorway. Jimmy, perched in his wheelchair, calmly reflected on the scene in front of him. He looked down at Gabe and simply stated, "Get that boy some medical attention. If he punches out, I'm gonna have your asses in my briefcase."

Jimmy looked down at Gabe and smiled. "Hang in there, boyo. The cavalry are on the way and so is Florence Nightingale."

Gabe forced a smile to acknowledge his understanding. Then a wave of deep pain made him shudder as the metallic taste of his own blood flowed into his mouth. Gabe squeezed his eyes shut as the pain claimed him, and succumbed to a very quiet darkness.

Gabe floated in a dark world of fuzzy browns and blacks. Each breath weakened him. Each moment constricted the tunnel of his consciousness. The extreme cold assaulted the very marrow of Gabe's bones. He found his hands between his legs, his body gathered in a fetal position. The cold was omnipresent. Gabe slowly opened his eyes and saw the rime and icicles gathered about the hood of his anorak, annealed to his balaclava. The wind sighed in the late afternoon, creeping across the basalt buttresses, which were rimmed with ice and verglas. Gabe coughed deeply, bringing up a frothy spume of blood, and spat it onto the patch of snow against which his head rested.

Gabe's lungs labored to squeeze oxygen from the thin air. Drowning in a sea of his own blood, Gabe rolled onto his back and was taken by the nature of the clouds. Wonderful pinks and crimsons, Prussian blues and dark sienna cast against the dark silhouette of the main peaks, Nelion and Batian. Gabe smiled, knowing he could not have painted such a picture.

He lay below Firmin's Tower, succumbing to his life's end. The spindrift of snow played about the rope that lay beside his body. His arms and legs were beyond movement in the mountain cold. Gabe's boots were lying exposed to the elements, and a layer of hoarfrost coated his feet. His breathing was now an afterthought. Gabe was clearly dying on this mountain. So, his dream of life had come to an end. Gone was the dream of decades, wives, grown children, and old students. The reality of his death on Mt. Kenya was like the tide, lapping over, drowning his long dream of life. Gabe's life, at long last, floated away on giant manta wings. Gone. Gabe heard, as though from a great distance, his own laughter.

EPILOGUE

HE SQUINTED AT THE FUZZY IMAGE BEFORE HIM—JIMMY, his gaze intent on Gabe. When Jimmy saw Gabe's eyes flutter open, the old warrior actually lunged forward to hug him from his wheelchair. The IV tubes got in the way.

Confused and beyond navigation in these parameters of the here-and-now, Gabe just clung to the goodness of feeling. The smell of disinfectant and antiseptics could not defuse the smell of charcoal fires and diesel. The window of his hospital room lay open as he fixed on his current reality. Each time he closed his eyes, he felt the transience of this reality.

The vice president stood at Gabe's hospital bedside. Jimmy wheeled his chair into the corner closest to the door, out of the way. Vice President Baker reached out and offered his hand to Gabe.

"I owe you a serious debt, sir, as do President Odinga and the people of Kenya. Someday you'll have to tell us how you got into my room, but for now, just rest and heal up. If there is anything you need, Jimmy here will see to it. I have to take your leave now, but perhaps next month sometime you'll stop by and have lunch with me—my treat."

The vice president of the United States smiled broadly and warmly shook Gabe's hand good-bye, clasping it and its tubes softly between both of his own hands.

Baker nodded at Jimmy and quietly said, "Good-bye sir. Take care of this friend of yours."

The vice president smoothly walked out the door of the hospital room and down the hall in the wake of security agents.

The Indian doctor came into the room and appeared mildly irritated. He took note of who was in the room and, in a soft yet insistent voice, said to Jimmy, "Mr. Turpin must have complete bedrest. You must leave him now to sleep. I must assume you have secured your own accommodations, so kindly say your good-byes."

With much disdain, Jimmy said, "Go to hell, you puss-nutted push-start. I leave this room when my boss tells me to and not until then."

The doctor impatiently asked, "Who is your boss, sir? Perhaps I could have a word with him."

Jimmy chuckled and responded, "He doesn't listen to anybody, me included. He just talks *to*—me included. See this here?" Jimmy pointed at his small earpiece. "There's my boss, and his conversations are always one-way."

Jimmy flashed a small, golden badge in a leather case pinned across from a photo ID. The doctor studied the credentials and sighed deeply.

"You see, it's my job, doc. Don't want to git fired. Why, hell, these kind of jobs are hard to find."

The doctor shook his head in exasperation, turned, exited the room, and walked quickly down the hall, his shoes tapping a quick, percussive beat that sounded hollow in the darkening shadows of the hospital.

Jimmy sat in his chair and studied Gabe, also assessing the monitors above Gabe's head. Gabe lay silently in bed, smiling thinly at Jimmy.

Jimmy let out a sharp guffaw and said in his acquired South Florida accent, "You figured that dreamin' shit out, dintcha boyo?

Popped a cap in Bazaan's ass instead of him doin' the dreamin' and a-poppin'. I'd say you did a fair bit of work back there at Keekorok. A real fuckin' hero, boyo. Whatcha gonna do for an encore? Rid the world of all lawyers and the ACLU?"

Jimmy chuckled and yawned widely.

"Now I'm gonna catch a little shuteye, Gabe—you should as well. Sweet dreams, boyo."

The old frogman's head nodded forward and, soon thereafter, Gabe could hear Jimmy's soft snoring.

The rock doves cooed in the jacaranda trees outside the hospital. Gabe peered into the early-evening shadows outside his open window. He could see cleaning women laying the washing of the ward onto the hedges to dry in the cool air of Kenya.

The tinny music of a radio floated on the air, and Gabe heard the quiet, singsong voices of the women.

Gabe saw an open bottle of orange Fanta beside his bed and slowly and painfully reached for it. He gratefully poured the sweet liquid down his throat, past his parched and crusted lips. Swallowing was difficult.

"Jambo, Bwana Gabe."

The familiar, friendly voice came from the shadows of the room. Gabe peered into the darkening gloom and saw the old N'dorobo.

"Jambo, m'zee," replied Gabe. The first words he had spoken in some time sounded hollow and without substance.

"Habari?" (How are you?)

"M'zuri. (Good.) *Hapanna, m'baya rafiki."* (No, bad, my friend.)

Sendeo responded with a soft "Mmmmmmm? Your heart seems very thin, *Bwana* Gabe. Is the wind blowing through you?"

"Yes, Sendeo, I feel just—empty. It is like I'm watching myself go through motions."

"*Bwana,* you have struggled greatly. You have suffered bad wounds. You must take time and take care to just rest. Perhaps you should sleep now. Dream of Ngai's *Thanga.* Heal yourself, *Bwana* Gabe."

"I'm going back stateside as soon as possible, Sendeo. I will likely not be seeing you for some time. I am like a shy schoolgirl—not knowing what to say, Sendeo. I will miss you."

Sendeo smiled at the floor. He fished in his toga-like wrap, found a plug of tobacco, and bit off a goodly load of chew.

"*Bwana* Gabe, you will not miss me, for you can have the dreams of the N'dorobo. Oceans are no barrier when one can dream. Go now to sleep and let us talk no more. We know what we each feel and that is enough. Sleep now, *Bwana* Gabe, and dream of N'gai's *Thanga,* for that is a healing place for you. *Salama, rafiki. Salama.*"

The rosy alpine glow made the main peaks of Nelion and Batian glow like charcoal embers. Purple-and-gray sheets of cloud scudded the sky behind the peaks. The iridescent green of the sunbird shone like fireworks against the crackled white of the Northey Glacier. The sun was setting in the late afternoon. Gabe heard the small cascade, its sound drowning out the click and hum of the hospital monitors. He saw the ribbons of water plunge quickly into a bubbly froth that lapped against the black basalt boulders. Tussocks of elephant grass framed the scene with tawny yellows and contrasted against the dark green leaves of lobelia. Now, in the gathering dusk, the twin peaks of Nelion and Batian loomed like dark sentinels, hanging back in a darkness that was not of this place of alpine glow. The feldspar crystals reflected the rosy light and were like wonderful brooches offered up by this witch of a mountain. Deep in his dream . . . within a dream . . . Gabe smiled.

ABOUT THE AUTHOR

Gary Gabelhouse has led climbing expeditions in Africa, South America, Europe, Asia, and throughout North America and has lived for long periods in Kenya, trekking game reserves and the bush. Gabelhouse is a member of The Explorers Club and he has been a leader of five expeditions to Mt. Kenya. A graduate of the University of Nebraska, with a masters from the University of Minnesota at Mankato, he lives in his hometown of Lincoln, Nebraska, where he is the CEO of an international media research firm.